D0916626

Saudade

Miriam Winthrop

CaliPress

2014 CaliPress Paperback Edition

Front cover art *Saudade* by José Ferraz de Almeida Junior, 1899
All other illustrations are the property of the author.
Published in the United States by CaliPress,

ISBN-13: 9780615982731

ISBN-10: 0615982735

Printed in the United States of America
CaliPress@comcast.net

To Amelia

Saudade—

—a deep and persistent longing for something that is missing in the present, and will most likely remain forever in the past or the future—

1

Like the lone survivor of a clutch of sea turtles, misfortune had cut me off from all that had gathered to create me. I was left stumbling toward an uncertain future, until I found Pico.

The prevailing winds carried moisture-laden air from the Pacific Ocean over the coastal mountains and into California's immense Central Valley. Thirty thousand feet below me, software engineers at tech companies and migrant workers in artichoke fields were ending the day in a rare shower. Meeting the Sierra Nevada, snow-capped even in summer, the winds were driven higher into the atmosphere where more water condensed and fell, swelling hundreds of streams beside which vacationing families were setting up camp for the night and newly graduated seniors were celebrating. On the other side of the high mountains, the dried air wicked water from the land and formed deserts, where small groups of Ute gathered to perform the Bear Dance of their ancestors, casting off feathers to symbolize leaving behind struggles to begin a new life.

I traveled ahead in time. Minutes passed slowly, and hours compressed into moments. The sky darkened, and I left behind unseen grasslands, rivers, and mountains. Clustered pinpricks of light sent skyward from a thousand-mile swath marked the eastern coastal plain. Mothers gave birth and comforted little ones waking from nightmares. School plays ended and proms began. Friendships were forged, plans were made, and dreams were dreamed. People loved, fought, rejoiced, and clung to one another in hope and despair.

Lives like those were no longer possible for me.

My first conscious act was trying to fill out the customs and immigration cards. Twice I had to ask the flight attendant for a replacement. Occupation? Married? Children? The answers were too complex to fit into the small boxes. In the end, I left them blank. The pen hovered above the line for my signature. I wanted to write my real name, but I knew what was printed on my passport. I finally scrawled something that looked like both.

My dark hair melted into the blackness outside, leaving a pale, oval face in the plane window. Large, mournful eyes and the tiny scar that made one corner of my mouth turn down gave me a sorrowful look, and I wanted to reach out and comfort the soul floating in the night sky.

The eastward progression of the plane and the spinning of Earth erased time. It was the dawn of a new day when the airplane wings stroked the velvet tops of clouds, cut into the milky screen, and revealed the Azores archipelago. The tips of towering volcanoes rooted on the floor of the Atlantic Ocean, the nine islands lay surrounded by thousands of miles of open water. Pico, the *Black Island*, was my destination. Its perimeter of volcanic cliffs was laced with foaming white waves, and at its center Ponta do Pico rose steeply to a snow-powdered summit. As the plane descended, dark mountain lakes appeared in the foothills, the land pixelated into fields of gold and green, whitewashed houses with terra cotta roofs resolved, and boats became visible in the straits. What I saw through the small, hazy window seemed no more real than what I had seen on my laptop.

When a runway problem forced the plane to bypass Pico and land on a nearby island, my only thought was an emotionless confirmation of my destiny to experience the many ways in which desire could be denied, and when the passengers applauded the pilot at touchdown, something I had forgotten was ever done, it sounded like they were mocking the future that was my fate. Setting foot on Azorean soil did not resurrect me. I may have lived the moment for many years but I was only playing a passive role in the progression of events, blankly walking into a life so familiar and so unknown.

It was not until I looked across the strait and saw Ponta do Pico rising at the center of a misty landscape that I felt something, a shimmer so fleeting and insubstantial that it might not have been at all, like a change in light that catches your peripheral vision and could have been the ephemeral quiver of a leaf or just the watering of your eyes.

As the ferry slowly chugged toward Pico, I kept my eyes on the volcano. Topped by thickening clouds, it fell steeply to the ocean, leaving only narrow coastal plains that scalloped the island. Approaching Madalena harbor, I could make out tightly-packed white buildings clustered around the waterfront and a church that dominated the town square, a layout repeated in villages along the coast in both directions.

I was surrounded by a melodious dialect of Portuguese, made distinctive by the island's isolation, but the native population was not otherwise distinguished by any one physical appearance. Some showed Mediterranean heritage in smaller builds and darker hair, skin, and eyes; some showed their descent from the early Flemish settlers in their height, reddish hair, and fair skin; and many showed a blend of traits that reflected the islands' history as a maritime crossroads. All moved at a more leisurely pace than I was used to, and—in both words and gestures—had a relaxed, expansive way of communicating.

It was easy to spot the visitors. They wore bright tee-shirts, and carried net bags filled with water bottles and energy bars in glossy wrappers. Two young Swedes exchanged a passionate kiss, while several women averted their eyes and a man looked on amused, sucking his pipe and puffing leathery smoke into the air. I wanted to will away the backpacking students on vacation, the camera toting day-trippers, and even the few locals who had succumbed to a culture I wanted to leave behind.

I felt a greater affinity for those who would not have been out of place a fifty years ago: women in plain dark dresses that reached below their knees, men smoking cigarettes beneath their battered straw hats, older couples returning from the occasion of shopping off the island in worn but neatly pressed clothes, and day workers clutching heavy tools and newspaper-wrapped bundles of raw fish in their weather-beaten hands. They neither called attention to themselves nor paid attention to me.

I tasted salt spray when the ferry slapped whitecaps as it rounded two islets, the remnants of a submerged crater, to approach the seawall. There were motorized dinghies crossing the water in front of colorful rowboats, and battered fishing boats mooring to unload the day's catch. A squat lighthouse at the end of the jetty blinked a dim warning in sets of three, mesmerizing me until a jolt against the dock let me know I had arrived.

The church bells sounded. A low sun lent the small cathedral's flat, white façade a golden glow and softened the black basalt trim of its rounded arch windows to velvet. The plain conical towers and unadorned architecture were typical of Portuguese churches around the world. I knew its interior well. Curtains of dust suspended in dim light. The deadened creak of wood pews. Mingling scents of beeswax and incense. Supplicant votives flickering for cures or salvation. The statues of beseeching Saint Isabelle, suffering Jesus, virginal Mary, grief-stricken Mary, triumphant Mary.

Tourists raced off the ferry and headed toward the square, stopping briefly to take pictures as they went. The other passengers stood aside respectfully for two nuns wearing full habits, and the captain made a point of lifting his cap to them. I was surprised by the trembling in my legs, a visceral response that betrayed emotions I did not acknowledge, and I waited for it to subside until everyone else had disembarked. Then I walked down the swaying gangplank and onto Pico.

There was no rush for the three taxis parked on the small plaza between the dock and the front of the church. Most people were met by others or walked directly up the narrow streets that fanned out from the main square. I approached the drivers, who stood talking and smoking together by their cars. Plastic cards pinned to their shirts identified them. Noticing me, Jack flicked a butt to the ground.

"Hello, Miss. Do you need a car?" I knew English was widely spoken on the islands but hadn't expected to hear such a broad New England accent, the R disappearing from the end of his question.

"Porto Velho. I need a ride to Porto Velho." I showed him a sweat-softened piece of paper on which I had neatly printed the directions to my rental house in both English and Portuguese.

"A ride to Porto Velho for the young lady, it is," he announced loudly, opening the door of a 1980s era Ford sedan for me. Below a generous cap of curly dark hair, Jack had light olive skin, a strong nose, and eyes that were at the same time steady and energetic.

He started talking the moment we cleared the center of town and continued almost without stopping as he drove on a two-lane road running parallel to the shore. I wasn't listening but knew when a pause indicated that some sort of response was expected. A slow nod to the rearview mirror and a few distracted *mm-hmms* were the best I could manage. I had no thoughts other than reaching Porto Velho and closing the door behind me.

I wasn't surprised when he explained the origin of his name and his perfect English. "I left Capel when I was eight and Capelinhos began erupting. The ocean out there," he swept his arm to the west, "boiled." He was silent for a moment, "I remember the smell most, the terrible smell. The tremors went on for months. Tiles kept falling off roofs, and all our windows were shattered. Day and night, we lived with the sound of lava hissing into the ocean and the loud explosions."

His hands gripped the steering wheel. "Fifty percent of the population went to America and, after a year of fighting the volcano, my parents decided to move the whole family to Massachusetts. Before we left, everyone went to look at our farm one last time. Black ash had covered the land. Everything around us was gone."

I had seen the lunar landscapes of gritty sand, dotted with the roof peaks of a few buried houses and the crosses of church bell towers. They were the only clues that people had once lived there.

He chuckled suddenly. "Now I'm back, enjoying island life!" Emigrating and returning had been a pattern of life in the Azores for generations.

Two thoroughfares, called simply Longitudinal and Transverse, formed a cross on the island; we travelled on the third, Perimeter. With the island's maritime history, the road passed through nearly every village. As we entered each one, pavement narrowed to a stretch of cobblestones that cut through the town center, separating the coast from terraced hillsides set with small houses and farms. On scraps of land between the serrated shoreline and the base of Ponta do Pico were hundreds of tiny vineyards laced with networks of low basalt walls, against which papery leaves shivered in the breeze.

The few narrow cobbled sidewalks were inlaid with white stones to depict the ships, whales, lighthouses, and anchors that were central to life when the villages were laid out five hundred years earlier. In most places, however, houses were built right up to the edge of the road, and I could see the backdrop of lives as we slowly bumped along.

Between wild heather as tall as trees, I glimpsed the remnants of once-grand estates, built in the glory days of winemaking and abandoned after disease claimed all but a few grapevines in the 1880s. The crumbling stonework of the vacant wineries was laced with climbing passionflowers and overhung with thick tangles of bougainvillea.

"My grandfather picked *verdelho* grapes in Criação Velha when he was a boy," Jack said. "They make a sweet dessert wine. On the other side of Madalena, south of the city, we are starting to grow the grapes and make the wine in the traditional way again, but with the help of modern fungicides."

He had lit a cigarette, so I put down a window. The air was misted with saltwater, and reflexively I inhaled deeply, the smell transporting me to the peace I had found on another island.

"The vines aren't in soil," Jack went on. "They're in the cracks between the rocks. Look. Look," he stabbed here and there at a landscape that was passing by too quickly for me to see. I understood his pride, though. I had once felt it. Ahead, where the road reached into a low valley, cows blocked our passage. Jack stopped, put the car in reverse, and swerved to the side of the road. He got out, still talking, and held my door open. I didn't have the strength of mind not to get out.

He laid a hand on the top of a wall. "These are the *curraletas*," He spoke each syllable slowly, giving me a Portuguese lesson I did not need. "They were built to protect *currais*, the vineyards, from wind and saltwater. Some are as old as 1580, when the grapes were first brought to the island." He glanced back at the procession of cows still slowly crossing the road and started walking to the crest of the hill, motioning for me to follow him. When I caught up with him, he was standing tall beside a large boulder, his chest puffed out and his hands on either side of the bronze plaque set in its front. "Here. Read this," he beamed.

I stepped to the edge of the road and read:

UNESCO World Heritage Site

> *The Pico Island landscape reflects a unique response to viticulture on a small volcanic island. The extraordinarily beautiful man-made landscape of small, stone walled fields is testimony to generations who, in a hostile environment, created a sustainable living and much-prized wine.*

"Yes," I said flatly. Shame at my lack of enthusiasm forced its way to my attention, and I tried to generate a more appreciative response. I nodded and said, "Yes. It's remarkable. It is special."

"Of course. Of course," he said, his Yankee accent carrying in the wind to sound like a crow's call.

When we returned to the car, he continued his tour, chattering on about vineyards, tobacco plantations, orange orchards, and wheat fields, and how one after another, each had been dealt a death blow by disease. He spoke sadly about the toll emigration and, more recently, tourism had taken on the culture. "Even now, men who in generations past would have been bringing in the catch or milking the cows are tending bar or hiring out on foreign fishing boats," he paused and, almost to himself, added, "or driving taxis."

We covered the thirty-mile length of the island quickly on the well-kept road, terrain and weather changing from minute to minute, until Jack directed the car away from Porto Velho, a small village nestled in a cove. He left me off at a point almost directly above the town center, on a secondary road lined with arbutus trees that had decorated the ground with large red berries.

"I guess I talked a lot. I hope you liked it, anyways," he said.

I thanked him, although I knew I could have given the tour myself.

"What have you come for?" he asked through the open window as he pulled away.

I didn't hesitate. "I am meeting my family."

We had left the sunshine behind, and it was drizzling when I climbed shallow stone steps cut into the hillside to reach a path running alongside several houses. I stopped twice to catch my breath, but I didn't need to look at the directions I had brought.

> *From Porto Velho, take R. Ribeiras to the steps. Walk up the steps to the milk path. Casinha Goulart is across from the top of the steps on the hill directly above the town. It is white and has a round terrace in front.*

The whitewash on the exterior may have faded and the huge stones weathered to smooth gray, but the roof and chimney that capped the smudge of greenery in front of me were so familiar that I couldn't have known them better if I had lived my life beneath them.

I stepped through the narrow doorway and let my eyes accustom to the dim light. Other than dust motes dancing in a blade of sun and the faint sour smell of woodsmoke in the air, it was exactly as I had expected. An age-darkened table and two simple chairs, all smooth from decades of use, were tucked into the far corner. A rocking chair by the fireplace and a small painted table set in a nook by the front door completed the furnishings in the front room. There weren't even pictures on the wall. It was as plain and forlorn as I had expected, and I had no need for anything else.

I had thought about this moment for so long without ever moving from vision to reality; in the end it had happened quickly, a leap over a cliff that was crumbling beneath my feet.

I turned back to look at Porto Velho, a gray crescent in the waning light. "I'm back. I'm back," I said softly, before I fastened the latch and fell to the floor.

The crowing of roosters ended my sleep. I found myself in exactly the same position I had been when I closed my eyes, in a bed made up with scratchy cotton sheets and a thin blanket that I had barely disturbed during the night. I lay there a long time blankly staring through the small window at leathery white-marbled leaves ticking against each other in a breeze.

"I don't care," I said aloud in response to a barely formed challenge in my mind. I was stifling a confrontation with myself over choices I had made, and confirming that they no longer mattered to me. I had been defeated.

I pulled myself out of bed and left the house. Against a radiant blue sky, Ponta do Pico followed me as I retraced my steps down to the graveled road that wound its way to the town. There were no signs to guide me and no need for them. I was walking on the only visible connection between myself and the town below. The road switchbacked down the hill, past whitewashed cottages with clay roofs and brightly painted trim. Most were small, and the larger ones had been extended over the decades, the size of the house growing with the family's prosperity. I could see reflections of the self-sufficiency that, out of necessity, had become a way of life: vegetable gardens used every bit of space between the road and the front door, chickens clucked in pens, and wash hung from clotheslines in nearly every backyard on the hot, sunny morning.

Where the ground leveled off, I slowed my pace and took several deep breaths to calm myself. I was entering Porto Velho. Alone with birdsongs and the rustling of leaves, I had felt safe. Closer to people, my heart beat faster, shallow breaths dried my mouth, and it became harder to lift my feet.

I reached the first street that fed into the center of town. A round-faced woman wearing an apron peered through the low window of a house as she adjusted the curtains. We exchanged smiles, mine tight and reflexive, and I kept walking. It wasn't as quiet as I had thought it would be. Boats pulled up to the dock off the main square and then pushed off quickly, carrying fishermen, tradesmen, and women out for a day of shopping. People shouted greetings and jostled each other as small groups gathered in front of shops and outdoor cafés, their noise amplifying inside me and sapping my small reserve of strength. I moved more and more slowly, finding it hard to shift my focus from one place to another.

Reluctant to ask for directions, I followed a Scottish family across the square and into a store on the corner of a narrow street, where they quickly stocked up on batteries and bottles of Fanta before leaving. At the back, I picked up the first few cans of soup I saw, peeking over the shelves at a petite woman cleaning the front window, her short, loose curls swinging from side to side and her metal bracelets jingling as she swiped a feather duster across the panes. Beside the register, an electric kettle whistled sharply. I looked in its direction, unable to break my stare until the clerk unplugged it and started to pour the steaming water into a large teapot. After putting the cans of soup on the front counter, I returned three times to add peanut butter, tea, bags of beans and rice, steak, cheese, jams, and produce, mindlessly preparing for a long siege.

Without reading the labels, I reached for some cans stacked on the counter and for the first time, my eyes met the clerk's eyes. I gasped, my hands went cold, and fear of losing control over my body drove me further from consciousness. Sweat broke out across my forehead, and my field of vision started to collapse. I could hear distant voices while someone held me under the arms and a stool was pushed against the back of my legs. A hand was placed firmly on the back of my neck, pressing my face against the counter where I helplessly gazed at hallucinatory colors shifting on i-tunes gift cards and boxes of candy bars.

I lifted my head and stood, steadying myself on the counter, but my legs were still rubbery and I fell back to the stool. Headlines in the *International Herald Tribune* danced in front of my eyes: Political Unrest in Egypt, Food Riots in Sri Lanka, Wildfires in Colorado; and, in *Diário dos Açores*, a headline about the falling euro wavered and left me stupidly grinning as I congratulated myself on being able to read Portuguese. The woman stood quietly by my side. I took a deep breath and looked at her. The nametag on her flowered apron, full enough to be a modest dress in any American city, read *Manda*. She was older than I had thought at a distance, at least in her fifties, with graying hair at her temples and a network of fine lines on her forehead.

It wasn't until after I had composed myself that I noticed the net bags hanging on a hook. It hadn't occurred to me that I could not carry even half of what I had piled on the counter. I looked between my things and the bags several times, stood slowly, and started to gather up some of the heavier items to return to the shelves. I tried to speak. "I ... *Eu* ..." I couldn't capture the words I wanted.

"*Fredo pode trazê-los levar para você.*" She pointed to a thin boy putting a box on a high shelf and mimed lifting bags.

More Portuguese came to me as she was speaking. "*Não.*" I shook my head. "*Eu vivo no morro.*" I pointed up the mountainside to where my house was. "*Eu andei.*" I used my fingers to show that I had walked the distance.

"*Fredo pode trazê-los levar para você,*" she repeated firmly. "Fredo will carry them for you," she said again in English. She spoke as if to a child, quietly and slowly.

"I'm staying up on the hill."

"Yes. I know. You live in the Goulart house. I lived near Dairy Road when I was a girl." I made the connection: Dairy Road ... the milk path. She had gone to the back of the counter again and was pouring tea from the pot. She placed two cups on the counter between us. "Drink some. It will make you feel better."

"I'm fine. I'm fine," I said. I didn't want the attention, but I had no strength to resist. I picked up the cup with shaking hands.

"Just drink while I put your things in boxes and add the prices." She took a sturdy cardboard box from under the counter and started to fill it with my food. "I knew the Goularts. The old mother lived in your house, the children on São Miguel."

I was barely listening but was powerless to stop her monolog.

"Mother Goulart died a long time ago. Then the son, Oscar, died. His wife still lives on São Miguel. The grandsons rent the house to visitors." Every word she said hammered me. I wanted to be left alone. "Usually students—two, three, more—stay a week, and then they go." She waved her arm to suggest good riddance to them.

Manda filled the first box and started a second, and I waited for the moment when I could pay my bill and flee. I held my cup in both hands and sipped the hot tea, keeping my face close to the rising steam, steadying myself by focusing on how the surface rippled with every beat of my heart.

Manda was still talking. "You will also want wood. Nights can be cold, and there is only a fireplace and the old stove. Fredo will bring that to you, and he will come again next Tuesday with more for you."

My thank you was just a conditioned response.

The last item on the counter was a box of Typhoo tea. Manda took a long look at it, then asked, "Did you like the tea?" For a moment, I thought she was commenting on my failure to thank her for the cup she had offered me.

"I have better tea, special tea from the plantations on São Miguel, the only plantations in all of Europe." My heart sank as she started another topic of conversation. "The first plants were brought to the islands three hundred years ago, along with advisors from China to explain the way they made tea for drinking."

She reached up to the top shelf on the wall in back of her and took down two large square tins with domed lids, wrapped with a paper band that labeled them as *Chá Açoriana,* Azorean Tea. Painted with tiny flowers, the tins looked enameled like cloisonné. "The jobs picking and drying the tiny leaves are only for five months a year, so…" I didn't have to hear the rest of her thought. That was another traditional trade in danger of being lost.

She pried the lid off a light green tin and put it under my nose. The loose leaves were pale pistachio in color, softly-fuzzed, and smelled of the deep woods. Then she pulled the lid off a red container, filled with dark, fruity leaves, and offered that to me before capping it. "Would you like one?"

I was desperate to retreat to the stone house above the village. I finished my tea in one long gulp. "I'll take both," I said to end the conversation.

I pushed open the door to Casinha Goulart. No key had been provided; it latched from the inside with a mechanism so simple, it only offered protection against gusts of wind, not intruders. With the sun at my back, the bands of limestone mortar between the black stones were startlingly white, and it looked like I was walking into a giant cobweb. Logs were already stacked beside the fireplace, and my two boxes of groceries sat on the broad sill of the large front window.

Across from the doorway was an area allocated to food preparation, with a tin sink and an incongruously large cast iron stove. Open shelves held a few mismatched cups and dishes, and a box with two spoons and one knife. Again and again, I crossed the room slowly, each time carrying just a single item from the boxes to the shelves. There was no need to finish the task efficiently. Finally, I placed the two tins of tea side by side on the table.

I put my wallet, earrings, and notebook in the drawer of the painted table across the room. Above it, a small window looked out across a broad buttercup-spattered pasture, and up to the forest-darkened hills and the blue sky above. Distortions in the thick glass made the scene look like a watercolor about to dissolve, just as time had done to the cover of my notebook. Once, there had been two notebooks, each covered in the same pattern of interlocking scallops and swirls, one in a spectrum from foggy gray to glossy turquoise that reminded me of ocean waves under changing skies, the other in shades of green. I had filled page after page of both notebooks with my small, neat print, the first one a key to Pico and the second a record of hope and failure that ended with blank pages when there was nothing more I could write.

I was set to disappear from my life.

For a week, I did nothing and saw no one except at a distance. I stayed in the house or within feet of the front door, unable to think of the past or into the future. Governed by an unfamiliar mind, one below the level of sentience and incapable of higher thought, I became absorbed in the details of what was around me. Day turned to night as I listened to rain on the windowpane. Fires burned to ash and extinguished themselves while I sat in the rocking chair. I spent hours looking through the window at the meadow, its flowers turning from yellow and pink in the morning to orange and dusky purple late in the afternoon. I lined up the tiny stones I found on the floor in order from smallest to largest, and then scattered them to begin again. Cosmos petals flip-flopped in the breeze, cows switched their tails at flies, and ants made their way across the ground, all as I sat unthinking.

For the first time in eight years, I did not open the notebook that I had shut away in the drawer of the painted table under the window or think about the other one, the green one I had shredded as my last act before locking the door and escaping to Pico.

Through the window, I saw Fredo carrying firewood and a box of groceries up Dairy Road.

Most of what I had bought the week before lay untouched. I had eaten only when the sight of food reminded me that I should. It was beyond me to cook. I drank the milk directly from the bottle, emptying it at once on the first day. I tore off hunks of bread, chewing them slowly, either alone or with spoonsful of jam and cheese that I bit directly off large wedges. Without hunger or desire, the meat and produce spoiled, and I dug a small hole at the side of the house to bury them when they started to smell.

The only thing I looked forward to was the tea. I opened the green tin first. Even though it was large, and I had another in reserve, I used the tea sparingly, anxious on some level about being left without. I made it by heating water in a small iron pot and pouring it over a couple of pinches of the light green leaves. I let it steep a long time, and then poured it from one large cup into another, holding most of the leaves back with the side of a knife. Those that did remain in the cup, I usually drank—and sometimes fished out and chewed.

I hid behind the door, anticipating Fredo's knock. When it came, I held my breath. I was frozen, unsure if I wanted to come out of hiding and unsure why I felt that way. I opened the door slowly. "*Sim?*" In Portuguese class, I had learned that saying "yes," when a question hadn't been asked sounded curt. Perhaps that was my original intent, but when I looked up and saw the boy's uneasiness, I added, "What is it?"

"This is from Manda," he said, leaning into the room without stepping over the threshold. He was young, probably no older than fourteen, and still had a child's voice.

I moved aside. "You can put the groceries on the table." My voice still sounded angry.

He put the wood by the fireplace and carried the box across the room. He hesitated and said, "I have to take the box back," as he pulled a bill out of his shirt pocket and handed it to me by stretching his arm out as far as it would go. We unloaded the box together. It had more of what I had gotten the first time, most of which still filled one of the shelves.

I got cash from my wallet and paid him what was on the bill, adding some as a tip. "You could also take the ones from last time," I said, pointing to the two cardboard boxes under the table.

"Manda said to ask if you want anything else." He swallowed hard and waited for my answer.

I looked over what was laid out on the table. With so much still left from the first order, I already had enough for several weeks. Still, I watched myself reach for a pencil on the shelf, turn over the bill, and start to write. As items filled the paper, I wondered why I was asking for more, and I wondered what more I could ask for. I handed the list to Fredo, thanked him, and saw him to the door.

Then I walked.

In the past, walking had been either a way to get from one place to another or a task performed on a treadmill. On Pico, walking filled other needs, most of which I was not aware of when I started, and it became as vital a part of my day as sleeping or eating. The focus needed to find my way over unfamiliar terrain brought me short respites of peace when I was not tempted to think about what had brought me so far from a life I was glad to forget, and the thumping of my footfalls and the rhythmic beating of my heart soothed me. Step after step, breath after breath, new vistas and sounds pulled me away from what had been and what had not been.

At first, I went only short distances—back and forth along a path on the hill to the south—keeping my house in view at all times, so I could make a quick retreat. I avoided the other houses on Dairy Road altogether and travelled in the direction that promised the least chance of meeting someone. On the rare occasions when I did see other people, they were almost always at work chopping wood, filling baskets with fruits, or leading cows downhill, and we exchanged brief waves. To my relief, they carried on without any attempt at conversation.

When I tore away from my need to keep the house within view, I surprised myself with an aptitude for navigating the island with an instinctual part of my brain, one I hadn't been aware of in a life with road signs and GPS. I became familiar with the crooked branch that pointed toward a stream, the cracked boulder beyond which the land dropped off steeply, the patch of buttercups that led to a high meadow with a view of a distant island. I was freed from the need to fix directions in my mind, memorizing them as right turns or quarter miles; instead, my subconscious guided me where I went and brought me home again.

Ponta do Pico, rising high above the island, was the most prominent reference point. Toward the volcanic cone was inland; away from it always led to the shore. The mountain changed daily, sometimes wearing a dome of thick clouds like a cap, sometimes encircled by a ring of fog, its sharp peak poking through the center of a misty white wreath. I could watch a blanket of haze roll back before my eyes to unveil a palette of greens in the pastures and forests of its foothills, and then suddenly shift direction and tightly wrap up the landscape again.

Even on well-traveled tracks, walking the island was physically demanding for an urban dweller used to flat, paved streets, but my stamina increased quickly. Within days, I was climbing over the low curraletas, cutting across farmland, and wading through creeks to climb higher toward the peak or further along the coast. The ground underfoot changed from hardened path to soft soil, from grass to leaf litter, from scree to flat expanses of rock. I surprised myself with how fast I traveled, often setting my sights on a point in the distance, only to have time compress and, an instant later, find that point behind me.

I ventured further and further each day. I found deep chasms and landslides left by earthquakes, abandoned quarries and boatyards, and tiny villages hugging the coast. I could make out thin lines that branched off the roads running parallel to the Perimeter Road, and ended in patches of trees or in hollows between hills. They led to farms, orchards, and vineyards with human lives that were in some way connected to my own.

The history of the Azores was recorded on its land. The archipelago had formed as melted rock forced its way from Earth's molten interior at an extraordinary *triple junction* of three tectonic plates on the floor of the Atlantic Ocean. Over millions of years, rock strata were laid down, thrust up, and folded over on themselves. Submarine volcanoes had broken the surface of the water to form Pico in the recent geologic past of 270,000 years ago; it was the youngest—and most active—of the islands. Ruptures left in the crust continued to vent hot ash and to deposit more lava through active volcanoes. Waves smashed into the rims of partially submerged craters just offshore, sending out sprays of foam as reminders of past eruptions, and the cavernous pit at the summit of the volcano left a faint sulfurous smell in the air, warning that destruction could come again.

Man, too, had left records. The mantle of dark volcanic soil, formed when cooled magma eroded and the land lay fallow over millennia, had brought farmers and ranchers, and the wheels of the oxcarts that had carried their milk, meat, and produce to market had left ruts in the rock. Pico was dotted with Dutch windmills, once used to grind wheat that no longer grew, and along the coast were low stone buildings, scattered with disarticulated skeletons, where whales were once processed. Houses abandoned in the diaspora were hidden in vegetation, some still holding the half-rotted belongings of emigrants who intended—or perhaps just futilely hoped—to return.

The geography had shaped the people as much as the people had shaped the land. The landscape had asked much of the first settlers who had to clear rocks and the tangled growth of hundreds of thousands of years. Self-sufficiency, an intimate relationship with nature, and cohesiveness were born of isolation in the harsh environment. When the first settlers arrived in the 1420s, the new land—like the Americas—was open to all, and they came together to survive. Portuguese, Italians, English, French, and Germans were joined by exiles from other societies: Sephardic Jews, Moorish prisoners, and so many Flemings that the islands were once known as the Isles of Flanders. Seasoned soldiers, educated merchants, and hardworking farmers came and stayed. Since the topography did not lend itself to the large scale agriculture of lucrative crops, the one group not represented was African slaves. Located about halfway along the route between the Old World and the New World, the islands quickly became a convenient provisioning stop, and the population grew for four hundred years.

From the start, it had been a struggle between nature and man. Nature had been more powerful, but man had been more resilient.

2

"Where were you born, Nana?"

"On an island."

"Can we visit the island?"

"There is no one left to visit."

"Where did they all go?"

"I don't know."

A popular notion is that everyone is born with certain gifts, hardwired to excel at communication or organization, sports or art. To the extent that is true, I had been aware of my gift since the day I applied for my first passport at the age of seventeen; I know when something is not true. It tickles my mind in a certain way, and I clearly see its faults.

I knew most of what my mother told me about my family history was either a refraction of reality, distorted by how it was presented, or a distillation that fashioned truth from something inconsequential, while letting the essential element escape. But I could never be certain which of the two a particular story was. Among the stingy truths hidden in the stories I had been told, a key had slipped out: the Azores.

"Let's start with what you know." Rosemarie welcomed me when I signed in at the genealogy library, and from the start, my search became hers. "What was your grandmother's name?"

"Amelia Howe. Amelia *Cabral* Howe." I winced remembering that I knew her maiden name only from papers I had taken from my mother's apartment. The discomfort was short-lived. Simply saying her name aloud comforted me.

"And where was she born?"

"I think on the Azores Islands."

"And her parents' names?"

I was on uncertain ground. My mother had once told me their names were Matthew and Mary, but that didn't mean it was true. "It might have been Matthew and Mary," I said.

"You had to choose two of the most common names in the Azores," she said shaking her head. "In many of the families, half the men were named Matthew, and most of the women were baptized Maria."

"But what about Cabral?"

"Portuguese names are different. One child may be given his mother's second name, another may take his father's, and a third may have a second name that's never been in the family before, so they're not really surnames as we know them. A single family could have a Manuel José, a Manuel Henrique, and a Manuel Vieira. Even today, a child can be baptized with the second name of an ancestor, even if his parents never had it. To make it more difficult, nicknames are common, and those don't appear in official records."

I followed as Rosemarie led me into another room, relieved not to be in charge of at least one part of my life. She looked like a leader; tall and ramrod straight, and moved through the library as doyenne of her realm, speaking with confidence in a brisk, husky voice. In the many times I was to see her over the following years, she always wore crisply pressed khakis, a solid color knit shirt, and unmarred white sneakers. On warm days her black cardigan hung on the back of her chair; on cold days it was buttoned over her shirt from neckline to waistline. Although it grayed in the time I knew her, her hairstyle never varied from the short cap that I walked behind on that first day.

"To add to the problems, the spelling of the names could be changed when people immigrated to America," Rosemarie continued, "and it could be changed in different ways by different people. Cabral might have become Cable or Carrell." She pulled out two chairs, sat in one and indicated that the other was for me. "We're starting with the 1910 Census," she informed me as she signed into a computer. With that, she became my ally and my friend. She, like me, would not give up simply because the odds of success were slim.

She settled me in with instructions on how to navigate the information. I found my grandmother easily enough, living in the house that had once been my refuge. I took out my new notebook, covered in shades of ocean blue and gray, and I made my first entry. By 1910, she had already married and was known as Emma Howe, so with that I gained nothing other than confirming that she had been born on January 2, 1889. I followed her into the 1920 Census and found her children, my mother not yet among them, and neighbors who were still in the same homes, although sometimes with their last names spelled differently.

I jumped when Rosemarie tapped me on the shoulder. "We're closing in five minutes."

"I had no idea it was this late," I said.

"I hear that a lot." She smiled. "See you next week?"

"Actually, are you open tomorrow?"

"Mondays, Wednesdays, and Thursdays only."

"I'll see you on Monday. Thank you so much."

It was nine when I stepped out into the dusk of a warm summer night. I looked out over the parking lot to the rosy sky and silhouetted trees, and sighed deeply. For the first time in four years, I had replaced failure and loss with something more compelling.

I returned to the dim and quiet research rooms countless times, trying to find the threads of my grandmother's life with census records, property deeds, marriage certificates and death certificates, draft registrations, and naturalization petitions. She first appeared in 1900, an eleven-year-old living in the Boston home of William and Mary Garland. At twenty-three, she married—or as Rosemarie put it, "was likely married off to"— an American of English descent living in Gloucester, a small city near Boston. This was curious, according to Rosemarie. Recent immigrants, particularly those from the Azores, almost always married within their ethnic group.

I filled in the gaps of her sixty-five years in America. In census records, she had been recorded variously as Emma, Emily, or Amelia—the name I had always heard her called. Under occupation, she was listed first as 'at home' and later as 'tailoress'. Her household grew as children were born, shrank as they married and left home, and grew again with lodgers or when my uncles sometimes returned home. Three of her four sons joined the Navy during World War II; two died when their ship went down off the coast of Morocco, and the third returned home to father her only other grandchild. The son who was repeatedly rejected for military service because of his diabetes ultimately died of the disease in his fifties. My one aunt, who I remembered meeting only twice when she returned home for family funerals, became a Benedictine nun.

As a child, it had never occurred to me that my maternal grandfather was never seen, never mentioned. He was simply a blind spot in family stories and pictures. I saw him vanish from the family home early in the 1920s, appearing afterwards in city directories as the lodger of a widow living just a mile away from my grandmother. On a visit to the Catholic cemetery in Gloucester, I found him buried beside that woman. I thought I had confirmed my suspicion that he had left to share his life with the woman he loved, at a time when divorce would not have been considered.

On that same trip, I also found something unexpected, several court records charging my grandfather with assault and battery. Grasping for some inoffensive explanation, I brought copies to Rosemarie, who—as she always did—added to the facts with her astonishing ability to extract far more from a document than what was printed. "Let's see what other such records from the time looked like," she said.

My ears filled with the click of the mouse and the whirr of the printer, as she pulled over thirty conviction records from the database. She put the pages side by side on a polished conference table. "Look—," she pointed to one and then another, "—here and here."

I was looking at the same records she was, filed in various Massachusetts towns in the 1910s and 1920s. "They are convictions for assault and battery," I said slowly, while searching for something unusual. She started to sort the records into two piles, tapping the name and the fine for each one: John Hennessey, $20, Matthew Goodman, $20, and Marco Carnazzo, $25 went to the left; Leon Machado, $5, Frank Beecham, $3, and Jack Kennedy, $3 went to the right.

"There's a big difference in the fines," I said hesitantly. I wasn't sure where Rosemarie was going, but I knew from experience that she was slowly building a case. "Some are smaller," I added.

"Exactly. Much smaller. And look what else is written." She pointed to a single word on each of the reports with a small fine.

"Those have 'wife' in the margin," I said, a terrible idea forming in my mind.

"Wife-beating was not seen as a serious issue," she said with tight lips.

"My grandmother filed the charges? And they didn't believe her?"

"Oh, they believed her. These show *convictions*, remember. Look how the fines for Philip Howe increase from $2 to $10—," she said, ordering the papers by date, "—and here …"

"… they fined him $25." I finished for her.

"They knew she was telling the truth. He was beating her, and she either had witnesses or the physical proof."

I swallowed hard. Anger twitched my muscles and prickled my skin. A hundred years later, I wanted to exact revenge.

"Now look at the associated court summaries," Rosemarie continued. "What is the outcome?" This time, she laid out just the eight reports on my grandfather, ran her finger under the handwritten notes, and waited for me to talk.

I shuffled through the sheets and read. "On these two, it says, 'Convicted. Discharged upon payment of fine.'"

"And?"

I saw the notations change over a period of three years, with additional information under the charge of assault and battery.

Convicted. Mr. Howe advised to restrict himself.
Convicted. One night confinement for public intoxication.
Convicted. Two days confinement for disorderly conduct.
Convicted. Final reprimand.

"It was rare enough for a wife to bring charges against her husband, rarer still for her to do so many times, and that was calling attention to the fact that he was a threat to the peace of the community."

The last report, dated February 22, 1923, had a black line drawn through *Convicted*. *Remanded to Essex County jail for two months incarceration*. There was an addendum at the top: *2-23-23:*

Mr. Howe removed from 18 State Street. Mrs. Adelaide Howe gives assurances. Charges withdrawn.

"Your grandfather wasn't just sowing some wild oats. He drank, he beat his wife," she turned to a nearby computer and tapped a few keys, "and he was a problem long before he married your grandmother." It took me several minutes to scroll through a history of public intoxication, disorderly conduct, vandalism, assault, and two counts of solicitation. Again and again, fines were paid and charges were dropped.

Rosemarie's voice startled me. "Do you want to print those before we go on?" I shook my head slowly. It had become too ugly.

"This also explains something that had puzzled me." Her face told me she was sorry to tell me something. "An immigrant girl—regardless of how educated she had become or what she looked like, or even how much money her family had—was not usually seen as a suitable wife by a family such as your grandfather's." She lowered her eyes and said quietly, "On the other hand, if his faults were well known, your grandmother may have been his only choice."

She gave me a few moments of silence, then asked, "Who was Adelaide Howe?"

"My great-grandmother." I had found that she lived less than a quarter of a mile from my grandmother's house; yet, I had never seen her or even heard her mentioned. I opened my file, removed the bundle of papers related to Adelaide Howe, and handed them to Rosemarie.

After several minutes, Rosemarie laid out the papers on the conference table. "Your great-grandmother was a wealthy woman," she said as she made a stack of the bank records. "She seems to have been behind all her sons' businesses." She showed me the deeds to the factories run by one son and the fish processing plant run by another, and added those to the bank records. "She probably inherited her husband's entire estate when her children were quite young, and she kept power by putting them in positions where their success was tied to her good will. Very clever."

I imagined what it must have been like for my grandmother to marry into such a family. If her mother-in-law had controlled her own grown sons in that way, what would she have done to a young, sheltered girl?

My eyes wandered over the papers spread in front of me and picked out a detail that didn't jibe with Rosemarie's theory. "But my grandfather worked in a bank."

She picked up a large piece of yellowed cardstock pinned to the deed to my grandmother's house, and looked it over. It was among the papers I had taken. "He mortgaged and remortgaged his house, until it was finally owned by—"she drew a line with her finger under my great-grandmother's name, "—his own mother."

"My grandmother owned that house," I protested.

"Exactly, Ann." Rosemarie topped off the pile of papers with the deed to the house issued to my grandmother on February 23, 1923, and waited for me to put everything together.

"My grandfather had been arrested again on the same charges." I paused. "The fines and the jail time had been increasing and would have been even more after the final reprimand." The next piece fell into place. "It would have been an embarrassment to the family in a small town ... but the charges were withdrawn ... because ... because ..." I looked at Rosemarie with a furrowed brow. "His mother offered my grandmother the house in exchange for withdrawing the charges?"

"She got the house," Rosemarie said, refolding the mortgage record, "but—," she reached for the 1930 Census, "—her occupation changed from 'at home' to 'tailoress' and three unrelated people joined the household as lodgers."

"That's all she got," I said slowly. It hadn't crossed my mind until then that, as the wife of a wealthy man, it was unusual for my grandmother to take in sewing or rent out rooms. She had the courage to do what women of her time almost never did: she left a marriage and supported her children on her own. And it had cost her.

When I told my mother about what I had discovered, she lectured me on not spreading salacious gossip.

I could move forward in time but never backward. I could follow my grandmother to the end of her lineage, but I could not find a single trace of the beginning.

Rosemarie ordered baptism records that had been filmed in the Azores by volunteers from the Mormon Church. Twice a week, I sat in the dark microfiche room, silent but for the drone of the viewer and the sound of my own breath, threading spools of film onto sprockets and slowly spinning them to show what priests had written over a century before. Acid deposits from skin had left fingerprints, and I wondered if any of them belonged to relatives who had put their signatures on the records, accepting responsibility to raise the newly baptized infant in the Catholic Church.

Turning the crank disturbed the still air, and frenzied motes animated the illuminated images of script. Some pages were blurred or faded, some fragmented by rips and patches, and the ink from cramped addenda in the margins had run together. My biggest impediments, though, were the ornate cursive script and the unfamiliar Portuguese language that sent me out to the reception area many times to ask Rosemarie for help deciphering what I saw.

She brought and then took away films of the 1889 baptism records on every one of the nine islands in the archipelago, starting with my grandmother's January 2nd birthdate and continuing through to the end of the year, since baptisms could be delayed by weeks or even months, with fathers at sea and mothers busy with many young children. I could find no record of Amelia Cabral, the daughter of Matias and Maria. I looked at every Amelia and Emelia born, regardless of the names of her parents. I looked at every girl with the second name of Amelia, and then any girl born that year. I wound and rewound, ordered and reordered every film.

I began to see the bigger picture of family relationships on the islands. The three brothers of one family married the three sisters of another. An aunt married into a family, and years later her nieces and nephews cemented the connection by doing the same. A young widow or widower married the dead spouse's younger sibling. Everyone seemed related to everyone else in one way or another.

For some parishes, at least half of those baptized had no *obituário*, or death record, and many families vanished from the documents entirely after marriages and the births of children were recorded. I understood the reason when I found notations some priests had made in the margins of some baptism registers. *Died in New Bedford. Died in Providence. Died in Gloucester.*

In bed, I fell asleep with the hum of the microfiche reader and afterimages of old parish records in my head. I tried to imagine the reasons I had found nothing about my grandmother. Perhaps she had not been born in the Azores—and either my mother had lied or had been lied to. Perhaps the record of her baptism was among those hidden by priests who mistrusted the motives of the Mormon missionaries. The most discouraging possibility was that the start of her life might never have been recorded. That left no hope.

Even after I had reached the dead end of every lead, I continued to go to the genealogy library, losing myself in a world of people I was not descended from, always hoping that someone's distant relation or even a neighbor could lead me to what I sought. I became privy to the minutiae of their lives in a way they could not have imagined, and vicariously suffering and rejoicing in their world helped me endure in my own world.

I lived the lives of the immigrants. At a time when even a trip to a nearby island was an adventure, leaving the boundaries of their world was a test of courage. Without the ability to reach back, they were cut off from the people, places, language, and culture that had defined their world. They could not board a plane to return to a dying mother. They could not telephone to hear the voice of a loved one when they were overwhelmed by cities and trains, or by crossing unfamiliar dry prairies and frozen lakes. They could not turn to the priest who had baptized them or the grandmother who had cradled them or the cousin they had shared secrets with. Many carried no pictures with them, and the faces of those they left behind would surely fade over time. It was absolute separation from everything.

On docks, desperate, excited, frightened, happy, anxious, bewildered people gathered. Their number typically exceeded the entire population of the emigrant's home village. Piles of possessions pebbled the boards, and young children held on to rope tethers, the corners of shawl-wrapped bundles, and the leather straps of suitcases. Anything left behind would be lost forever.

Men from the steamship company called out, "This way to America. This way." The emigrants joined long lines and stood before a shipping company representative who examined their passports and filled out the manifest, which would be signed over to American officials on arrival, so the human and cargo contents of the ship could be checked off against them. Some must have hoped that they would be refused passage before the ship left their world behind.

There were twenty-nine questions on the manifest. *How much money do you have?* Few arrived with more than $5. *Do you read and write?* Most did not, and by 1917, a literacy test for those under seventeen would keep many out. *Are you a radical, a polygamist, an anarchist?* Everyone said no. *Who is your nearest relative where you come from? Who are you going to?* I searched those answers carefully, always hoping to find a lead to my grandmother's family.

Then they made their way up the gangplank and competed for a place along the ship's rail, from where they could watch as the faces of loved ones grew smaller and smaller. I felt the anguish of mothers who waved goodbye to their children, knowing they would never see them again, and I cried the tears of those children, some as young as eight, alone, dazed, and terrified.

I watched as ships carrying immigrants from Northern and Western Europe started to share the waters with those from other parts of Europe, and as manifests added Palestinian, Dalmatian, and Gypsy to Irish, German, and Italian. I saw the six weeks that sailing ships took to cross the Atlantic shorten to two weeks when steamships replaced them in the 1880s. Passage became easier but never easy. Better hygiene reduced cholera and typhus outbreaks, but diarrhea and skin infections remained widespread. Shipping lines did away with dangerous on-deck passage, but steerage below deck became even more crowded with people and all the possessions they could carry. Laws reduced starvation after many died from lack of food and water, but hunger and dehydration continued to be the norm. With narrow, dirty bunks, crying babies, constant seasickness, and the lack of privacy in close quarters, it was difficult to sleep. As the days went by, the stale human smell became fetid and wastes spilled over from buckets when they hit the inevitably strong winds of the North Atlantic. And through it all, they were haunted by the ships that had gone down to a watery grave and never made it to the Promised Land. I hoped that the immigrants were able to draw a curtain between themselves and their new reality.

At the end of those long weeks at sea, I stood with others on deck and saw the wondrous New York skyline after a lifetime in a small village, and I heard the chanting of "America. America." around me. Even then, it was not over for the weary. While the first and second class passengers—who were not seen as a risk to society—were greeted on board by inspectors and transported to the dock to be cleared through customs in a matter of minutes, those in steerage faced hours, even days, before they were free to walk into their new lives. Every hurdle cleared was followed by another obstacle, and every obstacle was a torment of uncertainty.

Officials turned away some, labeling them imbeciles or senile; I wondered how much of what they saw was exhaustion, malnutrition, or disorientation. In what was known as *the six-second physical*, health inspectors weeded out more who were diagnosed with trachoma, tuberculosis, and other illnesses. I felt hope vanish for the 250,000 who were turned away at Ellis Island, sent back across the ocean alone, their loved ones never to be seen again.

I rejoiced for those who had relatives waiting for them, and were greeted with welcoming hugs and bags of food. I was troubled by those who walked out into a world of swindlers and hecklers, cheap boarding houses, constant hunger, and the struggle to find a job in a country where, as one newspaper article of the time put it, "immigrants worked more cheaply than machines."

I imagined the tension of acculturation. Mothers, the bearers of traditions, would have been torn. The cost of the opportunities they wanted for their children would be the loss of their culture. The process of Americanization was held in such high esteem that companies offered classes in it, newspaper editorials lauded it, and preachers extolled its virtues in Sunday morning sermons. Mothers would want their children to be part of their new world, to play the same games, sing the same songs, speak the same language, and eat the same foods as those who had come before, but they would also want to pass on what they had been given by their own mothers. What would they hold tightly to? What would they let go?

I followed fourteen-year-old brides and women who had fourteen children. I cried when one mother lost five of her six children to diphtheria, and smiled when the thirty-year-old spinster finally married. I read names no longer heard and saw occupations I hadn't known existed: Wilmur, the lector who read aloud to workers toiling in factories; Horace, the ice man whose job carrying huge chunks of ice into homes disappeared with the advent of refrigerators; Ezra, the lamplighter who lit the gas streetlights every night; Gertrude, the cigarette maker who could not be seen in public using the product she made.

I met extended families of twenty living in one small house, and watched as one generation grew old and died, while the next moved into homes of their own and raised families. The number of children born in America grew with every census, as did the number who could read and write. The size of families decreased, net worth increased, houses became less crowded, and more people owned their homes rather than renting. People moved westward out of larger cities and into smaller ones, which themselves grew from decade to decade.

Early pictures captured the immigrants wearing shawls woven in the style of their home villages, peasant blouses embroidered with ethnic designs, the rough pants of the Portuguese fisherman, and the straw hats of the Dutch farmer. In later tintypes, they wore formal dress that crossed cultural origins: bustier jackets and frock coats, ascots and ties, top hats, bowlers, fedoras, and extravagantly-feathered picture hats. Most of what identified a person's origin had been erased, and the ordeal of the immigrant had faded—but not for me. I used their persistence to inspire my own.

I laid claim to the Azorean people I had not known that I shared kinship with. I learned their history and took pride in their achievements as masters of the oceans during the great age of nautical exploration. I filled folders with what I had learned, and when I looked at them, I wished I could show them to my mother. I wanted her to know that I was proud of my heritage.

Weighing poverty against the opportunities of the New World, many Azoreans found sufficient reason to leave. Between 1860 and 1970, the per capita number of immigrants from the islands was second only to those from Ireland, and by 1910, there were 100,000 Azoreans in the United States and only 300,000 left on the islands themselves. By 1960, there were more people of Azorean descent in America than there were in the Azores themselves.

One by one, their ghosts rose out of computer screens and the pages of dusty books to populate their world again, this time sharing it with me. The indistinct shapes of tables and chairs in the nearly dark room where I scanned films stood as guards and witnesses while I visited people who knew my secrets, listened patiently to my sorrows, and asked nothing of me.

I immersed myself in their culture, played their music, baked their bread, and learned their language, re-creating for myself parts of their world. I felt like the keeper of their stories and, at times, the only one who understood their lives and held sacred what they had sacrificed and accomplished.

Alone in the still rooms, I had a sense of belonging I no longer had in the other parts of my life. My time in the past crossed into the realm of the personal and private. The drive to trace my roots became—even I admitted—an obsession I began to hide, first from casual acquaintances, then from close friends and my husband, and finally from seasoned genealogists who understood an avocation that could become a consuming passion.

But still I went to the library. I had not been able to keep the promise I made to my grandmother.

Miriam Winthrop

3

The round stone terrace, or *eira*, was as large as the house itself. Centuries earlier, it had been an outdoor threshing floor or a place to dry fruits and nuts in the sun. For me, it was a place where I could sit hidden by the dense hydrangea bushes that grew just outside its low wall. Through the thicket, I could see the four other houses on Dairy Road. I named them Big Meadow, The Vineyard, Bodgerville, and Two Trees.

To the west, Big Meadow was separated from me by a rich green pasture that sprawled in back of both our houses and blanketed the hillside behind us. It was occupied by a large family with children of various ages, all of whom appeared just after dawn and again late in the afternoon. Watched by siblings, the older girls did the milking, sitting on stools usually left stacked by the front door. Sometimes they all climbed the hill to bring in cows that had roamed away, a parade of wobbly toddlers, playful children, and giggling teens following like ducklings behind their mother. On a terrace much like my own eira, two men collected the pails and emptied the milk into tall metal cans, so heavy when full that they both struggled to load them onto a cart, which was eventually pulled past my house and into town. The rest of the adults continued working all day: caring for the donkeys, chickens, and pigs; tending a patchwork of gardens; and washing the milk buckets before upending them to dry on the grass. They must have known I was watching them, but they wouldn't have realized how detached I was, watching without interest, like a television show left on just for company.

On the other side of me, The Vineyard housed an elderly couple who smiled so broadly and waved with such animation whenever they spotted me, it looked like they were welcoming a long-lost relative. They often walked arm in arm along Dairy Road, and I never saw one without the other, the woman wrapped in a shawl even on the warmest days and the man wearing a hat that he raised whenever he caught my eye. They must have been short in their youth, and in old age, shrunken and stooped, they could not have been taller than four and a half feet. In that way I had seen before, their genders had blurred and, without the clues of hair and clothing, it would have been hard to identify them as male or female.

Behind their house was a currais with well-tended vines, heavy with grapes. A few of the larger stones of the curraletas had fallen, but the couple worked together, using their slight weight to nudge smaller ones back into position. An assortment of pots by the walls that delineated their vineyard held flowering plants. Sheltered from the scraping winds off the ocean, they thrived and made splotches of red and orange against the grass.

Bodgerville, tucked into a small cove where the hill dropped into the pasture behind me, was named for a quartet of nearly identical dogs whose short golden fur and muscled bodies reminded me of Bodger from *The Incredible Journey*. They raced up and down the hill all day, happily leaping over each other and dashing under the cows. In the heat of the day, they sometimes lay on the shaded stones of my eira. I thought long and hard before doing it, but eventually I left out two large bowls of water for them, and they were always drained by evening. When the dogs did come up to me, my response was as conditioned as theirs; I reached out and patted a head, or offered them pieces of cheese from my dinner. Then we ignored each other.

I could see just the roof of Two Trees, set almost directly across from me on the downslope of the hill, so the only signs of life were wisps of smoke that rose from its chimney on chilly nights and the occasional sound of a television that carried on the wind. The laurels in front of it were so large that their broad branches and the large, leathery leaves of their canopies screened nearly everything else from view. So strong was the symbolism of the laurel tree for me that when I realized I faced two of them, I alternately resisted and looked to them as portent of my future.

Late in the evening, exhausted from hiking and relaxed by dinner, I stretched out in bed and daydreamed about a life in one of those houses. In Bodgerville, I could live out my days in solitude, walking the island with my dogs. At Big Meadow, I could be part of a large family, my life woven with others so I would always be part of a whole. If I were the old woman who lived at The Vineyard, I would have a lifetime of memories with a loving man. Two Trees was a mystery, so my fantasy about life there touched tenderly on what I knew I could never have.

I fell asleep to those musings and in the morning, they mocked me with their absurdity.

What would come to occupy hours of my day started during my first week on Pico, even before my first tentative forays away from the house. I had paced the eira with my eyes down, each step short and deliberate as I focused on the mechanics of walking like practicing a skill I had just acquired, not trusting the memory in my muscles to keep me from the pain of a fall. I made my way slowly along the perimeter, watching my feet plant firmly on the stones one after another. Heel to toe, my bare soles pressed into the warm stone and my toes gripped their ridges. I'd always found it hard to do something that had no defined purpose, to sit without reading, look without analyzing, walk without weeding, so when the familiar with the pattern and color of those stones was interrupted by a newly emerged weed, I stooped to pull it out, sometimes occupying my hands by picking it apart and throwing the shredded leaves and stems over the wall and onto Dairy Road. I had an urge to do more.

I managed to open the warped door to a tin-roofed shed leaning against the back wall of the house. Inside, I found an accumulation of items saved because they might find a use on an isolated island where supplies were hard to come by. Metal buckets held coils of rope and copper wire, and a large enamel washtub was filled with jars of fishhooks, screws, and nails. Ceramic pots were suspended in midslide off a shelf that had given way, one end caught by an empty barrel and the other resting on a workbench. They seemed to be in good condition, and I made several trips to the cistern to wash them under the faucet. Cleaned of decades of cobwebs and dirt, they looked gently timeworn, painted with misty pink peonies or with Moorish patterns in softened reds and blues.

I also found a few garden tools, all in varying stages of decay and corrosion. The handle of one spade crumbled when I picked it up, and the rusted metal gave up a cloud of particles when it hit the packed dirt floor. I took a pair of clippers and spent hours scraping the rust against stones that seemed right for the job, relying on common sense rather than any knowledge of how to sharpen blades. I finished the job by rubbing a drop of olive oil over the shiny metal.

One afternoon, I took my salvaged tools to a fringe of vegetation along Dairy Road to pull out tangled vines that were strangling the hydrangeas at the front of the eira, and I quickly built up a sweat, wrestling the plants with an aggression that may have been meant for parts of my life that were beyond my reach. Looking down at my gloveless hands, I took the welts I saw as signs of both my struggle with and my connection to the land of Pico.

I stopped to stretch my back and looked down the valley, following the scalloped coastline east to where it disappeared, a thin line of white foam against the sharp black cliffs. When I looked back, I saw the elderly couple from The Vineyard, walking so slowly in my direction that I would not have noticed any progress if I had kept my eyes on them. I continued to pull the weeds and cut away dead flowers, while they disappeared from view behind rangy shrubs and reappeared in sharper focus as they came closer and closer. My mind did battle with itself over which was the lesser of two evils: leaving the gardening unfinished or leaving myself open to conversation.

The old man called to me as I was wrapping my arms around a pile of vines to carry it to the back of the house. "Hello," he said, raising his hat to me. "You did a good job." He swept his arm along the bottom of the wall where I had cleared away all traces of vegetation. He and his wife nodded in synchrony. They had almost identical milky brown eyes, thick white hair, and dark olive skin, carved in mazes of deep creases, but his outgoing nature contrasted with her shyness.

"Thank you," I replied without making eye contact.

"You are American?"

"Yes."

"Where in America do you live?"

"California."

"Ah," he said, as though that explained something. "I am Umberto. My wife is Celina." Celina looked at me, smiled slightly and bobbed her head. "We live just there." He waved his hat in the direction of The Vineyard. "My grandfather built our house, and his brother built your house at the same time." He looked up at my house and shook his head sadly. "Yours has been empty much of its life."

A whispering inside my head warned me of intrusion; still, I let go of the vines and brushed the loose dirt from my hands. Umberto and I exchanged observations on the terrain and the weather. Then Celina spoke in a voice so soft that I would have had to strain to understand what she was saying even if the words were in English. "If you put plants at the bottom, the weeds will not grow there." She added hesitantly, "I could bring you some."

"Ah." My guard was up. I could imagine what might come of accepting the offer, and I didn't want any obligation, not to planting and certainly not to a relationship with the couple.

She named a plant, but I had no idea what *hortĕnsia* was until she said she was from Fayal. "We are called the Blue Island, because so many grow there. It is beautiful to see our island from the sea." *Hortĕnsia* was hydrangea. Emblematic of the Azores, the plant had nicknamed several of the islands: Fayal was the Blue Island; Terceira was the Lilac Island; and São Miguel, with its many colors of flowers, was the Green Island.

"They are easy to plant, and they take care of themselves," Celina said quietly.

I began to hear Celina's encouragement as pleas. "I won't be here long enough." I stooped to pick up my bundle of weeds again, hoping to end the conversation, and simultaneously both regretted my lack of civility and was upset with myself for caring about the feelings of two strangers.

"Put them in Pico soil, and they will grow fast and beautiful," she said.

"Maybe. I will think about it. Thank you."

Umberto had picked up on the changes in my voice and body language. I wasn't interested in talking any longer. He bowed slightly at the waist, put his hat on, and started walking away, tugging a bit on Celina's arm as he went. I dumped the weeds on the growing pile in back of the cistern and cleaned the clippers, returning to the eira just in time to see Umberto and Celina go through the door to The Vineyard, still arm in arm.

The next day, I found a package by the front door. I unrolled the burlap wrapping and found hydrangea stems stripped of flowers, wet soil around the roots. It took a moment to realize who they were from. I didn't want to be responsible for their care, but I couldn't bring myself to let them die. One by one, I stabbed them into a pot half-filled with rocky soil and turned away. A fleeting moment of shame for handling them so roughly gave way to anger with myself for feeling any remorse at all.

I had searched the house on my first morning at Casinha Goulart. My suitcase was not there. I had no memory of claiming it at the airport, no memory of carrying it off the ferry or out of the taxi. At one time, I would have mourned the loss of the beautifully patterned scarves, perfect jeans, and silky pajamas. I was beyond caring about such things; they no longer brought me pleasure. There was nothing other than the flannel shirt I had worn on the plane, the notebook under my pillow, and the ring on my finger that would sadden me to lose. I had enough cash in my wallet to replace anything I needed, and the only files I still cared about were backed up, not that it mattered; I had long since committed it all to memory.

I approached the first place I found in Porto Velho that sold clothes—an old house with a bright blue door— determined to be in and out quickly. In front, two young women sat in webbed lawn chairs on the narrow sidewalk, sewing and chatting. They looked very much alike, with the same small build, Cupid's bow mouths, and large eyes lined in shiny black. Only their hair was different, the one in green shorts had a thick brown pony tail, and the one in yellow shorts had a blond page boy with dark roots.

They smiled at each other, revealing identical dimples, and the one in green shorts got up and pushed her chair aside. Her upturned mouth straightened quickly. "The clothes are inside. Go in," she said in English. "The prices are on the tags." The seated woman kept smiling, without making eye contact with me, as if she knew a secret I was excluded from.

Inside, I quickly made a pile of several cotton shirts, a few pairs of pants, a pale pink silk shift, a broad-brimmed straw hat, and other necessities. I was drawn across the room by a vintage cape, black and full-length, that was displayed on a mannequin. The wool was faded at the shoulders and the top of the hood, and the lining was frayed where hands had poked through the arm slits at the front. I swung it around my shoulders and felt the weight. It was hardly a practical choice for summer days, but I added it to the other clothes I had gathered.

I was startled by a voice directly behind me. "Do you see what you want?" It was the woman who had remained seated. "This is our store, my sister's and mine. She is Sofia. I am Natália. We call our store SoNa. See?" She pointed to a hand-painted sign hanging on the inside of the door. I said nothing. "This was our grandmother's house. My father said Sofia and I can use it until he sells it, but that was two years ago," she snickered. "Sometimes we collect old clothes and sew them up to make more money. We are going to move to America next year."

I had a fleeting image of the island, deserted and returning to the way the original settlers had found it.

As I walked back up Dairy Road, I could see two children leaving Big Meadow carrying what looked like a heavy basket between them. I went up the steps to Casinha Goulart and watched them from behind the bushes. They covered the distance between Big Meadow and my house slowly, stopping along the way to pick dead hydrangeas and wave them in the air, sending dusky blue petals swirling as I used to do with dandelion seeds.

When they were near the bottom of the path to the eira, where I sat still and low—the observer who did not want to be observed—they put the basket down and looked at me, the boy through lowered lids and the girl fixing me in her sight without moving a muscle on her face. She shifted her weight from one leg to the other, and waited silently.

I waited a moment, expecting them to move on. When they didn't, I said a curt hello, hoping one of them would explain why they stood there. The older girl pulled on her brother's sleeve, and he moved closer to the eira.

With wide-set, honey eyes, they continued to stare at me in silence. I looked at the basket and said slowly in Portuguese, "That looks heavy." Varnished a shiny brown and covered with a pressed, snow-white napkin, it had the same well-tended look as the children, with their neat clothes and carefully combed hair. The girl had focused on me for so long that my voice startled her. Using both her hands, she lifted the basket a few inches off the ground and bent backward, resting its weight against her body. She carried it a few steps, shuffling one foot in front of the other and bumping it against her legs, before she dropped it again. The little boy hid in back of his sister.

"Can I help you?" I walked slowly across the eira. "Can I help you carry the basket?" I repeated loudly.

"It is for you," she said in English. "It is from my mother."

"Are you sure?"

"You are the American woman who lives alone in the Goulart house." She sounded like a student who was confident of the answer to a math question her teacher had asked. "Look in the basket," she prompted me with the eagerness of a child who wanted a present unwrapped on Christmas morning.

If she had been an adult, I probably would have said a determined, "No, thank you." Instead, without thinking, I went down the path and lifted the napkin. She followed my movements and nodded.

One half of the basket was filled with ruffled leaves of young kale and chubby carrots, moist and warm from the garden; the other half held a small round of white cheese and an unfamiliar fruit with a yellow rind. "What is this?" I asked, and I tried to swallow my words as they came out.

"Guava," she replied, stretching out each syllable clearly as if to teach me a new word.

She watched me closely as I picked up the cheese and said, "My mama gets that from the lady who makes it."

As I looked through the basket, I discussed the situation with myself. I could dismissively say, "Please take them back. I don't need anything," and turn my back. There were a number of reasons to do that. I didn't want to open the door to people. I could picture children followed by parents, parents followed by neighbors, and my peaceful world filled with crowds of happy people who expected me to feel as they did.

Instead, I asked, "Would you like some cookies?" It was as much a reflex as the scratches I gave the Bodgerville dogs when they came around. The boy came out from behind his sister slowly, and she grinned. "I have some inside." My voice sounded businesslike at best, and probably verged on angry. I quickly carried my new clothes and the basket inside, came back to the door, and beckoned.

They stopped short of the front door, looking into the shadowy room with apprehension, and for a moment I felt like the witch enticing Hansel and Gretel into her cottage in the woods. "Perhaps we could eat on the eira," I said without enthusiasm. They bobbed their heads in approval. I opened a tin of assorted cookies, made drinks with Ribena syrup and cool water, and carried everything to the low eira wall.

The girl sat next to the cookies and said, "His name is Beto."

"Beto, would you like a cookie?"

He nodded, looked at his sister, and then took one.

"My name is Carolina." She, too, took a cookie.

"I think you live at Big ... in the house over there," I said.

Carolina quickly finished chewing, swallowed, and took a deep breath. "Yes. We live with my Mama and Papa, my grandmother and my grandfather, my aunt and uncle, and Bárbara, Anton, Emanuel, Maria Manuela, Ana—," she counted on her fingers as she named the crowd that made up her family, "—and four dogs, two cats, two goats, and lots and lots and lots of cows." With everything she named, her delight grew, and she kicked her legs against the eira wall faster and faster. She stopped suddenly and said, almost to herself, "Yes. That is who I live with."

Beto cupped his hand around her ear and whispered. After swatting his arm away, she added, "And Uncle Toni and my cousins come to help with the milking."

After taking a bite of a second cookie, Carolina stared at the half full water bowls I had set out for the dogs. She looked puzzled and asked, "Do you have dogs?"

"No. The water is for the dogs over there." I pointed to Bodgerville.

She nodded her understanding. "Do you have dogs at your house in America?"

"No. No dogs."

She nodded. "Who do you live with?"

"It's late. I need to get the basket back to your mother." I got up and walked quickly toward the house. Coming in from the sunny patio blinded me, and I stood blinking into the darkness for a few moments before heading to the table and taking everything out of the basket. I carefully folded the white napkin in quarters and laid it at the bottom of an empty basket, relieved to have staked a claim to my seclusion.

As the sun reached the tops of the hills beyond Dairy Road, I sat on the eira wall and slowly ate the sweet, lemony guava. Trees made silhouettes against clouds that burned red before dimming light slowly drained color from flowers, leaves, sky, and my skin. Smoke rose from the chimney of Two Trees, the door of The Vineyard house closed, the Big Meadow family returned the milk cans to the shed, and someone whistled for the dogs of Bodgerville.

I thought about how I hovered just outside the little neighborhood, existing physically at its heart but without the ties of shared history and kinship.

Then it struck me as strange that with such tight ties in the islands' communities, my grandmother would have said there was no one left to visit, that she didn't even know where everyone had gone.

I awoke suddenly, my mind struggling to make sense of a surreal world. The sky swirled with luminous patches of blue, and clouds flashed outside the windows, shimmering from within. Through the doorway to the main room, I could see the softened shapes of furniture bathed in hazy white light. It wasn't a dream; the Earth's crust was changing shape and discharging piezoelectricity.

A bump against the outside wall had jolted me from sleep. The rumbling that followed had made me wonder why I had never noticed train tracks so close to the house. As the sound grew came the realization that there were no trains on Pico, and I thought a fierce storm was bearing down on the island. Then the entire house shook. My brain tried to process unpredictable movements as—along with everything around me—I was carried back and forth, right and left, up and down, moving in several planes at once.

My fear was primal, an inability to control or even understand my world. One jolt followed another, each one more intense than the one before, each one lasting longer than the one before. The entire house juddered, the curtain between the two rooms swung wildly, and the windows vibrated so violently I thought they would shatter. I could hear china breaking as dishes were thrown from shelves. A pot thudded loudly to the floor, making my already trembling body jump.

I rolled over on my stomach and buried my head in the pillow, hoping the earthquake would end before I was thrown from the bed or pierced with shards of glass. Outside, the barks, yowls, and squeals of animals carried in the night air.

The window shivered for a minute after the rumbling faded. Then the darkness and the silence became so profound, I thought I had lost my senses.

Dawn came but I remained motionless, still clutching the covers with both hands. My head cut off circulation to one arm, and still I didn't move. When my neck cramped, I gently stretched it without leaving the bed. When my full bladder became more insistent than my fear, I crept to the edge of the bed and put one foot on the floor and then the other, bending low over the bed, so I wouldn't break contact with its surface. With one hand touching the foot of the bed, I reached out to the wall and stood.

I spent the day gauging the distance from where I was to the nearest safe place, warily looking around as though I could see another earthquake coming, and walking restlessly around the house. I checked to make sure my notebook was safe and whole, although how it could have been otherwise when shut away in its drawer never came to mind. I felt the loss of some pieces. My favorite plate, with faded rosebuds strewn on a pale yellow field, was shattered. I told myself bitterly that I should have known that would happen. I had started to take pleasure in it, so the universe had taken it from me. The handle of my teacup was broken into three pieces. I wondered if I could save it; then I asked myself why I should care. I hurled it into the metal wastebasket with such force that a shard flew out and cut my palm.

What started as wiping up a single drop of blood escalated to something that felt beyond my control. With no mop in sight, I filled a bucket with water and used a towel to wash the floor, moving methodically from tile to tile. I backed into the bathroom and cleaned that. I heated water on the stove, put it in the tub, and washed towels and sheets, rubbing them with soap and carrying them outside to dry on the rosemary bushes at the side of the house. I carried clean water from the cistern and dirty water to the plants so many times that the muscles of my arm trembled uncontrollably when I reached up to clear a cobweb from the window. All I knew was that the frenzied cleaning soothed me.

I put my new clothes in the wardrobe, a piece so large it had to have been built there in the bedroom. On the top shelf I found two quilts. The squares of one were made from scratchy wool and lined with faded flour sacks that had come loose in places to show lines of tiny, black stitches, and I imagined the woman who had made them, sitting by the fireplace on windblown nights. It had a faint musty smell but no more than that, so I laid it on the wooden floor of the living room as a rug and placed the rocking chair on top of it. The flowered cotton on the second quilt was velvety with age. I folded that in quarters and draped it over the rocking chair as a cushion.

Sipping my tea at the end of the day, I questioned the rationality of my actions; certainly, there was no need to make a home of a place that was at best a temporary refuge. I tried to tell myself that all the activity was to occupy my mind. But another voice whispered a deeper truth: the earthquake had cracked the shield behind which I had locked my emotions. The day's distractions had kept me from feeling.

I didn't know if I had been sleeping or not. I opened my eyes to a sun high in the sky, and only knew that the last time I had looked through the window, the evening song of thrushes was filling the air.

After the earthquake, I hadn't wanted to leave the security of being near the house, but the walking that my mind and body had come to depend on was pressing me. I anxiously went through several scenarios, from short strolls up and down Dairy Road to circuits around Big Meadow—an image of clinging to a cow came to mind. I even considered, and quickly dismissed, asking my neighbors if anyone wanted to walk with me. I knew none of those would satisfy my needs.

From the eira, everything I saw was as it had always been. Under a cloudless sky, trees were firmly rooted, dogs roamed, cows grazed, and young children played. After tentative steps close to the house, always with the nearest handhold in sight, I headed across the pasture. That was when the first aftershock hit. Without warning, a violent jolt threw me to my knees, and a low rumbling spread through the ground into my bones. Fear followed the thumping of my heart, as awareness of what was happening caught up with the adrenaline surge. I froze in place even after the ground settled, not trusting that it was over.

In California, stringent building codes meant that the best place to be during an earthquake was inside your house, a notion contrary to what was considered essential in most other parts of the world, where everyone fled for open spaces to avoid being trapped under less sound structures. The house at Big Meadow emptied, children screaming as they streamed out with the adults. One of the women extended her arm and pointed at me, sending a teenage boy running in my direction. Stopping only to hear my reply, he asked if I was all right. As he headed back, I wished I had thought of a reason for needing help.

It hit me hard. I was completely alone. I was even known as *the American woman who lives alone.* Disconnected from the rest of humanity. Tears started to flush out thoughts about the people who had come into my life, and gone. I remained the sea turtle separated from all others.

I turned my back to Dairy Road and took a sharp turn away from the paths I had explored before, and I climbed almost directly up the side of the steepest foothill, taking fierce delight in the relief that came from the focus and exertion needed to make every step.

The meadows, yellow-green in the sun, turned deep emerald in the shadow of the mountain. Ponta do Pico wore a wreath of frilly clouds, the strait glowed a solid blue, and crater lakes sparkled through the trees. I had seen sights like these since arriving on Pico and did not deny their beauty, but mine was a detached appraisal. I had only the memory of that gasp of delight in shapes and colors and sounds that suspended all else. I had been blinded to joy.

I wondered how much of that was my choice. Certainly, if asked, I would have gladly sacrificed joy to lock out sorrow. Had I preemptively made that choice? Was that why I chose to live in the most basic of houses, without heating or electricity? Was it the reason I had brought so few things with me and had made no attempt to recover them when they were lost? I may have told myself I was experiencing how my ancestors had lived, but was the greater truth that I was avoiding pleasure?

Delighting in what was around me had once been so easy, but years of failure and loss had left me struggling to find joy. At the end of my darkest days, I could only find it just before escaping to sleep, when I held tight to the hope it would return. For a long time, that was enough. On Pico I'd freed myself by accepting that happiness was not to be.

I was breathless when I reached the stark lava fields of the Black Island, a place where greenery is replaced by lifeless vistas of charcoal rocks. Heat radiated through my soles, and when I picked up one of the black rocks, the scorching pain took me by surprise. I had left without the water bottle I usually carried, and without my hat. My sunburned skin throbbed, and I was getting lightheaded. A dark green cleft between two knolls below me looked cool and inviting, but the entrance was obstructed by a pool of milky yellow water, above it a sulfurous miasma.

Rather than backtrack, I half slid down a steep slope to try to reach the copse that capped the hill in back of Dairy Road. The land ended at a precipitously deep ravine. I slowed my steps as I neared the drop and, a few feet from the edge, I got down on my belly and crawled closer, using long blades of grass as handholds. At the rim of the crevice, sod held to the underlying rock only loosely, and I could push clumps away and listen to them fall. Looking down, I saw a rotting Flemish oxcart caught in the branches of a long dead tree that had grown sideways into the gap from the opposite side. The image of a skeleton at the bottom of the cart came to my mind, and I wondered if its owner had fallen with it.

I pictured myself tumbling as the ground beneath me broke away. I felt myself pulling away from reality, like flotsam—the wreckage of my former self—being sucked out by the tide. In front of my face, a rock gave way and ricocheted against the face of the cliff. I listened as the sound faded. I couldn't make myself release the straps of grass wound around my hands, and I lay still for a long time, unable to think of what to do next.

The person I was and the life I had lived had been disassembled. I had no interest in rebuilding and wouldn't have been able to if I had wanted. Too many parts were gone. I had cried for each piece as it broke away and was relegated to the ashes of memory, and then I had quickly wiped away those tears to conserve strength for the pieces that remained. When I left for Pico, I knew there was nothing left to save my strength for.

I imagined stepping over the edge, gravity pulling me into free fall, and it struck me as odd that it wasn't a terrifying sensation; I was surprised by how calm I was as I died. It would be over quickly. I would not feel anything again.

Heat radiated from the black soil and enveloped me in a cocoon of warmth. I closed my eyes. As I drifted in and out of consciousness, I wondered if I wanted to surrender or to stake a claim to life. A pinprick of light in me was searching for a reason to carry on. It was not without mercy; it felt so sorry for me, the way a mother would feel for the child she was going to put through a painful medical procedure with only a slim chance of survival.

Dense fog was sinking into the valleys, smothering sounds and animating shapes into phantoms that floated past. My clothes dampened with the rising mist, which carried the smell of the ocean, the smell I had once thought could bring me back from any dark, sad place.

I called to mind the people I had known and lost. The only part of them that remained was in me, as were the stories of those unknown and forgotten souls of the past, whose real families had no interest in their lives. I told myself I had not yet finished what I came to Pico to do, but the irrationality of that mocked me. It made no difference to any other living person.

Lying flat on the soft ground, I felt my Nana's hand on my shoulder, my head on her chest. "You're just tired, Annie," she said.

Yes, Nana. I'm so tired.

"Go home, my child."

I knew she meant home on Pico. *I'm all alone there.*

"You are never alone. I'm always here for you."

I opened my eyes. Above me, spectral trees swam through my tears.

"You will be fine, dear one." I did not respond. I didn't think I would be fine, but my grasp on the blades of grass loosened, and my hands slipped free.

My inescapable resilience was condemning me to a ghost of life—because the alternative, an actual life filled with memories and feelings, would be so much worse. I pushed away from the edge, inching backward until I could no longer see the precipice.

As I got to my feet, my grandmother's voice flamed, "There is more on Pico than you know now."

4

"I didn't know you have a sister, Nana."

"I have five sisters."

"Where are they?"

"I do not know."

"Don't worry, Nana. I'll find all of them. I promise."

I called the small coastal city of Gloucester, Massachusetts my hometown, although I wasn't born there and usually visited family just two summer months each year, when I wasn't attending a private girls' school in Manhattan or accompanying my mother to one of the rich assortment of activities she had planned for me. My parents usually brought me to Gloucester, staying just a couple of days before traveling on to other places, but once my father alone came, and he spent a full week with me. He was as excited as I was, waiting for the drawbridge to come down so we could cross the river to reach the island.

My father was from an old European family, displaced by World War II and living in New York on the considerable wealth brought with them when they escaped the Nazi occupiers. As a young man, he had been left an only child and then an orphan, and later he was disconnected from any extended family he might have had by the Iron Curtain of the Cold War. What little I remembered about him had led me to believe that he had felt more at home in the working class city of Gloucester than on Park Avenue.

I sat next to his suitcase on the bed in the small room across the hall from mine and watched him unpack. "No need for suits here, Annie!" He smiled as he hung up the tailor-made jacket that my mother had insisted he wear while traveling. "It's going to be shorts, T-shirts, and sneakers for the next week," he said, and he triumphantly held up a pile of wrinkled cotton shorts and poured them in a drawer.

I loved listening to the melody of my father's voice, deep and slow. Years later, I found the recording of an interview he had given for a radio program on Eastern Europe before Communism, and I was surprised by an accent I had never been aware of when he spoke to me.

"Can we go to the beach tomorrow?" My own swimsuit was already laid out on the top of the bureau in my room.

"That we have to ask your grandmother about. In this house, she is the boss."

"Nana won't mind."

"Your Nana would do anything to make you happy, my Annie, but you must remember to try to make her happy, too." He looked into my eyes. "Family is most important."

I never knew who would be there for dinner at my grandmother's house or, in retrospect, how there was always enough food for anyone who showed up. Most evenings, we would just hear the front door open, and those already eating would shift positions to accommodate the newcomers. My two uncles and their wives came frequently, as did my cousin, Bobby. The aroma of my grandmother's food must have carried through the open kitchen windows because whenever dinner was ready, relatives from my aunts' families, neighbors, and even the priest who lived around the corner could show up unannounced. We ate at the large maple table that also provided a place to prepare food in a kitchen without counters that, with the exception of a stove and a refrigerator my uncles had bought, had not been updated since the 1920s.

One night, my uncle Russell appeared at the kitchen door. "Smells good, Ma. What's for dinner?"

My grandmother was already on her feet, headed toward the stove. "*Couves*, Russell."

"Lots of the broth, please, Ma." Whether it was because they were raised at a time with different expectations or because my grandmother had taken pains with their manners, my uncles were unfailingly polite, a counterpoint to their gruff voices and rough appearances.

My father stood. He was a small man and looked even smaller next to my uncle, who was several inches over six feet in height and had the muscles of a man who spent his days doing physical labor. My father's pale skin and green eyes were also in contrast to my uncle's creased, deeply tanned skin and almost black eyes. Physically, they shared only the same reddish hair.

They hugged warmly, and spoke like old and dear friends.

"So, what brings you here, Will?" my uncle asked.

"Time with family," my father's eyes twinkled, "especially Annie!" He reached across the table and patted my arm.

"What's going on in high society?"

"They still haven't realized they're not so high." They shared a laugh. "Soon, they will have to get on without my wit and charm."

"Are you leaving New York?"

My father was more serious. "Not now," he said slowly, "but when my Annie goes to college, I can leave. Clare…" he paused. "Clare and I both want her to continue her education in the city." He came down heavily on the word "both" as if to convince himself. I knew it was not true; I had heard the discussions.

While my grandmother and I cleared the table, the two men talked about plants, my uncle with the expertise of the head gardener at one of the big estates on the shore, and my father with tales of exotic flowers and fruits he had seen on his world travels. I saw my father look up as my grandmother headed to the door with a bag of garbage. He quickly pushed back his chair and stood, reaching for the bag.

"No. William, I will do that," she said. "You are a visitor."

"Am I family or not, Nana?" He looked over the top of his heavy, tortoiseshell eyeglasses at her and smiled.

"Here, Will," my uncle said, unbuttoning the flannel shirt he was wearing over his tee-shirt, "take this. It's cold out there tonight." After my father left to take the garbage to the covered metal bucket buried in the backyard, my uncle said, "That man is a prince." Whenever I heard others talk about my father, it was with great respect.

In my memory, I always picture him as part of the Gloucester landscape, adopted into my mother's family, making its vernacular and mannerisms his own. He enjoyed using the appropriate colloquialism to show he was proud of being as American as he was—but he delivered it with a hint of reticence that said he knew he was still knocking on the door of being a true American. Whenever we gathered at one of my uncles' houses for a barbeque, he followed formal kisses on the ladies' hands with a turn in front of the grill, happily calling out when the hotdogs were ready to load with relish and mustard. He never gave up trying to hit the baseballs my uncles gently tossed for him at family gatherings, he liked ice cream cones and Boston baked beans, he sang *Yankee Doodle* loudly, and he faultlessly recited the Pledge of Allegiance. He was the proud immigrant.

Later that same summer, long after my father had left to join my mother, I heard my uncle open the front door and call out from the bottom of the stairs, "Ma! Where are you?"

"Come up, Russell. I am in Annie's room." She always spoke slowly and clearly, her measured diction a reflection of the care she took with her adopted language.

She was dabbing Calamine lotion on my mosquito bites with a cotton ball, a summer ritual so tied to feeling loved that decades after her death I bought a bottle and made bright pink splotches on my unblemished skin, just to watch them sink into my pores and dry to the familiar chalky crust.

My uncle's work boots were heavy on the stairs. "Ma, you got the time to fix this for me, please?" He held out a woolen jacket with one pocket flapping down. I looked up at him from the bed. He was handsome in a way I would later learn was called rugged. He loved nature and, in a town where being a blue collar worker—especially a Portuguese one—meant working on a boat or at one of the two fish processing plants, he had followed his heart and chosen to be a gardener. While my other uncle and almost everyone else around us carried a slight odor of fish with them, he always smelled like freshly cut grass and pine needles.

"It's our big city girl," he said thumping me on the top of my head. "You must have sweet blood for those mosquitoes to come after you like that." His blood was truly sweet. A diabetic since childhood, he was considered a living miracle by the doctors he saw in Boston. More than once, I heard him say that he was supposed to be dead by the age of ten but had a guardian angel who didn't listen to doctors. I scratched a bite on my elbow and smiled at him.

"I will go down in a moment, Russell. I am helping my Annie with her itchy bites."

My uncle nodded solemnly and rubbed a hand over his five o'clock shadow. "Ma," he stopped and cleared his throat. "There's a guy I met who says his wife knows your sister."

Nana lowered her hand to put the cap on the Calamine lotion, missed, and tipped the bottle over.

"Oh," she exhaled without taking her eyes off my uncle. "I will get a towel."

When she returned, her face was pale and her eyebrows had pulled together to make two deep, vertical creases in the middle of her forehead. I saw her hands trembling as she mopped up the spilled lotion. "My sister?" she said very quietly.

Uncle Russell was looking through the Sears catalogues stacked on an old sailor's chest under the dormer. "Yah." He scratched his head, searching for words to break bad news. "It might not be, Ma."

"No. It probably is not."

"I dunno if it's true, Ma. Call her. It's Gil Parisi's wife, down on Orchard. I gotta get going. I'll leave my jacket in the Little Room."

We all knew it as the Little Room, the only space in that vast house that was my grandmother's alone, barely large enough to hold a single bed with a small table beside it. A shelf ran the length of the room at a height that, as a nine-year-old, I could reach by standing on the bed. On it were all the treasures a girl would want to explore: boxes of flowered notepaper, tins of unusual buttons, tiny velvet rolls with necklaces and bracelets.

That evening, I sat in the Little Room, holding a doll I'd found in a box under the bed. When I moved her, she made a sound somewhere between *Mama* and the noise my old plastic trumpet had made, and I clamped my hand over her mouth, lifting my ears to hear the sounds coming through the wall, as my grandmother made a phone call.

I only remember that it was a brief conversation, an exchange of questions and pauses during which my grandmother's hope faded.

After the call, I waited for the silence to end and when it didn't, I slowly made my way to the sitting room and climbed onto my grandmother's lap.

"I didn't know you have a sister, Nana." I saw the faraway look in her eyes and heard the catch in her voice when she told me she had five sisters and didn't know where any of them were. I put my head on her chest and whispered the promise that I tucked away until another summer evening thirty years later. "Don't worry, Nana. I'll find all of them. I promise."

In the two years we had spent trying to find my grandmother's family, Rosemarie had become my closest friend. She was my partner in trying to solve my genealogy puzzle, celebrating when we found something and sharing my disappointment on the far more frequent occasions when we did not.

One evening, she met me at the front door of the library. "You're going to love this, Ann. A university in Portugal has put together a searchable online database with baptism records from—," she smiled, and I held my breath, "—*all* the parishes on the island of Pico."

In my head, I heard the promise I had made to my grandmother and knew I had another chance to keep it. I reached for the notepad Rosemarie held out, the URL printed clearly across the top. "I'll try," was all I manage to say. I had lived through too many cycles of hope and disappointment to abandon myself to optimism lightly.

We sat together. Each small parish had its own records, and there was a different link for each one. My grandmother's name was a very common first name and often appeared as a second name. I had to read each baptism record to find an Amelia or Emelia whose parents were Maria and Matias; even then, I would have to trust that the names Mary and Matthew that my mother had given me were correct.

Night after night I sat in bed, my laptop propped on a pillow in front of me. As Lee slept beside me, I searched for Amelia. Weeks passed as I went through all the Amelia Cabrals, and then all the Amelias with no second names, marking them off one by one on sheets of paper. Maybe this one, I told myself. Maybe this one. But I kept finding Amelias who were born too late or had died on Pico or had only brothers.

One Amelia, born January 2nd, 1888, was baptized Emelia Simas. Her parents were Maria Umbelina and Matias Cabral. It took a moment to realize that the birthday was my grandmother's. Then I saw the list of siblings: five sisters. My hands went icy, and the sound of Lee's snoring faded to a rushing in my ears.

I couldn't wait for our usual Monday evening together; I called Rosemarie at home.

"You found her," she said, before I could wipe away my tears and speak. I could picture her smile and the crinkles around her blue eyes.

"I found her." I sobbed. "She was there, the youngest in a family of six girls."

"We looked at those records on microfiche. Why wasn't it in the original records?"

It was only then that I realized: the birth year of 1889 that was on everything from my grandmother's marriage certificate to her death certificate was based on a single document, the emigrant visa signed by her cousin, Luis Machado, and it was wrong. Since my search had moved forward in time but not backward, I had never had any hope of finding her.

The names of my grandmother's sisters and their birthdates led me to immigration records, and from those to the places they had lived and the families they had. At first the threads were tangled, too many and too few. I found tantalizing clues in census records and city directories, names that were very close, birthdates that matched. I sent letters, followed up with calls, filled in applications for birth certificates, death certificates, and cemetery records. Slowly, I peeled away the years between me and my grandmother's sisters to meet my family. And with every discovery I whispered, "I found them, Nana. I found them."

The diaspora had begun with an uncle, Francisco Simas. His parish record showed the same telling detail of all those who emigrated, a blank space where the obituário was usually noted. Following him were three brothers, their spouses and children, and in many cases their extended families, all of whom settled in the tiny town of San Diego. At the time, its population was recorded as 731 but—despite a decade that saw a magnitude 6.0 earthquake, a smallpox epidemic, floods, and the Great Drought that all but destroyed California's cattle ranches—that number tripled by 1870.

Those first immigrants from Pico swelled the population further and, in the following twenty years, the city transitioned from a place plagued by gunfights and devastating fires to a modern urban setting, adding a public library, telephone service, electric streetlights, schools, an opera house and theater, the first public park west of the Mississippi, and a stop on the transcontinental railroad. Most of the Azorean immigrants lived close to the coast, gravitating to familiar landscapes and to each other. They helped to cement their community's central role in the tuna industry, moving the fish from its place as fertilizer to one of the food staples of the twentieth century.

Predictably, the names of my grandmother's sisters varied little. Francisca Simas was followed by Maria Rita, Maria Vitória, Maria Rosella, and Francisca Rosa. Francisca Simas remained on Pico, married, and had five children, but the trail ended there. Where other baptisms were entered in the database with both first names, *Joao Henrique* or *Maria Cecilia,* or at least one of the two names and a question mark for the second, *Estela ?* or *Manuel ?*, Francisca's children were each listed with just two question marks. After having spent her life in the village where she was born, she died at the age of thirty-three, about the time my grandmother married and moved to Gloucester.

Life was very different for her sisters.

The first few weeks of the sisters' experiences after leaving Pico must have been much the same. Each would have crossed the channel to Fayal in a family boat, probably accompanied by her mother and the sisters who remained on Pico. I could picture some weeping openly. *I want to stay with you Mama.* Others might have put on a brave face. *This will be an adventure, Mama.* Their mother would have said words to reassure them, and to comfort herself. *You will have a good life, my child. You are going to family who will love and care for you as I do.* And what everyone knew was almost certainly not true: *We will see each other again.*

The transatlantic steamships docked a couple of miles north of where the boats came in from Pico, so they had to carry the only material connections to their birthplace along the coast, following a rough gravel road that almost immediately took a sharp turn and presented an immense black steamship rising higher out of the sea than anything they had seen before. With each step, it grew larger, until it towered over them. Most of the emigrants from the Azores converged on that spot; on that day, there would have been more people than in all of Porto Velho.

When the sisters were asked the name of their nearest relation for the ship's manifest, all said their sister, Francisca Simas of the Western Islands, a synonym for the Azores. When asked who they were going to, all gave the name of the same cousin, Luis Machado of San Diego, California.

Already halfway across the Atlantic Ocean, the sisters were among the more fortunate immigrants. Their journey took only ten days. There would have been some lightheadedness and disorientation during the crossing, as dehydration from scarce drinking water and diarrhea set it, but the food they carried from home kept starvation at bay. At some point, they ate the last bite of their mother's bread they would ever taste.

The disparity between the lives they were born into and the ones they were to live in America, during a period when fixtures of modern life, such as telephones, radios, refrigerators and airplanes, transitioned from concept to reality to common usage, must have been even greater than for immigrants at other times in human history.

Maria Rita and Maria Vitória entered Ellis Island on April 4, 1899. Within a year, Maria Rosella and Francisca Rosa made the same journey together to join their sisters.

It took longer for the sisters to cross America than to cross the ocean, much of the distance covered on rails that split and came together, again and again, running over trestle bridges, past cities, across plains, and through mountain passes, cars disconnecting and re-connecting as they were passed from one rail line to another. There were ten-minute rest stops, during which they raced across platforms jammed with people and their belongings, and crowded into the stations that had sprung up along the new railroad lines to get food and relieve themselves. Day after day, they handed the same ticket to conductors, who punched holes to mark their progress. To young girls, who could travel slowly from one end of their world to the other in a day, it must have seemed endless. At least, those four sisters had someone to cling to at night for comfort and warmth, and someone to share memories and milestones with. My grandmother had crossed the ocean alone and lived apart.

The collective birth, marriage, and death certificates, census records, deeds, wills, and newspapers told the story. Three of the sisters married within the transplanted Picoense community, all to fishermen and all to distant relatives, but their immigrant experiences differed.

Maria Rita, the oldest of the sisters who came to America, founded a dynasty. At the age of sixteen, she was married to a thirty-nine-year-old man, the brother-in-law of the cousin who had met her at Ellis Island. She had eight children before his death in 1915, lost three of them to whooping cough and institutionalized a fourth, listed in hospital records as an imbecile. Her name changed from Maria Rita to Mary Rita, and finally to Mary, and the Portuguese names of her older children were Americanized over the years, Joao becoming John, and Matias becoming Matthew. As newlyweds, she and her husband rented a room in a cousin's house and lived there, saving their money, for five years. That room was replaced by a small cottage next door, which grew over the years into a large and rambling house by the shore of La Jolla, California—a home that stayed in the family until it was sold in 1985 to make room for a sprawling complex of ersatz Spanish Colonial condominiums.

Following her husband's death in 1916, Maria Rita remarried, only to lose her young Navy lieutenant six months later in the Spanish flu epidemic. After giving birth to twins soon afterward, she turned her attention to the tuna fishing boat she had inherited and grew the profits from it into a lucrative fleet of three boats. Records of boat sales and purchases, payrolls, and investments show a firm, clear hand and a sharp business sense. When her children were grown, she bought and managed three orchards and shipped truckloads of apricots and cherries to twenty states. Two newspaper articles mentioned her among the volunteers who helped the San Diego immigrant populations that grew exponentially between 1920 and the Second World War. She died at the age of one hundred and two. The wealth she had accumulated was squandered by her descendants.

Few records included Maria Vitória, the second oldest sister. She started her life in America on the same spit of California coastline as her older sister, and also married a fisherman. Her family grew to include four children, each baptized with a traditional name. She, herself, never Americanized her name, and she was the only one of the five sisters who immigrated who did not become a citizen. A plaque in the hall of the Catholic Church commemorated her work making soup for festivals honoring the Holy Spirit, baking sweet bread for Easter breakfast, and teaching Portuguese to children. A picture of her as an old woman was included in a church newsletter. She wore an embroidered white blouse and her thick hair was pulled into a bun at the back. I examined it through a magnifying glass many times; family pictures were crowded together on a deeply-carved credenza behind her, and a statue of the Virgin Mary sat on a tabletop altar, surrounded by flowers.

Maria Rosella was the middle of the five sisters, and her life was devastated by immigrating to a culture she did not know. In 1910, she lived near her sisters with her four young children and husband, who—not unexpectedly—was a fisherman. Then, all six vanished from the records. Working backward from California death certificates, I found a woman with the same first name as one of the children. Her parent's names matched, and her birthdate was within the right timeframe, but she had grown up as an only child on a farm in northern California. A 1923 school record listed her as a *half-orphan*. I assumed the entry referred to a child who had lost one parent, until I happened on one of the only seven admissions records that had survived a fire in the archives of a San Diego orphanage. One page told the story of a thrifty, hardworking woman who had had the courage to take her abusive husband to court in 1911. She was granted one of the first divorces of the time but, forced to work outside the home, she had to place her four young children as half-orphans, paying $20 a month for their care. As it turned out, that woman was Maria Rosella.

Within two years, the children had all been sent to different families around the state. One court record noted "the mother claimed not to be aware that placement was permissible," and ended, "Judge Reed denies the mother's request for return of the children." Between 1912 and her death in 1927, she went to court thirty-two times in futile attempts to learn the whereabouts of her children.

Francisca Rosa, a young woman in what had become a leading family in a community where men outnumbered women two-to-one, somehow remained unmarried. In the 1920s and 30s, Rose Cabral was found in yearbooks as a teacher and a principal, and later her name appeared in newspapers as the assistant superintendent of a school district, overseeing 200 people and a million dollar budget. She sold war bonds, piloted after-school care for mothers working in factories during World War II, and raised money to give breakfast to the children of migrant workers in the 1950s, before retiring to Palm Springs in 1955.

Grainy black-and-white photographs gave me clues to how the sisters looked as they grew into mature women. From other records, I knew some were tall and some quite short, and that two were redheads. As older women, the contrast of luminous ivory skin with a halo of extraordinarily thick hair, usually parted in the middle and drawn back, was striking. I stared at large, generous mouths and gentle eyes for long minutes, trying to imagine them alive with smiles and songs, and it pleased me when I saw I had inherited some of their features.

The sisters were young when they had their children, as were their descendants. Five and six generations had passed in the time that my grandmother and my mother, both the youngest in their families, had given birth, my mother at the almost unheard of age of thirty-seven. After far too many searches ended with deaths from diseases that were eventually made preventable by vaccines and antibiotics, with casualties in World Wars I and II, and with couples who had no children, I was able to trace only two living descendants.

I tried to contact Wallace, Maria Rita's great-great-grandson, three times, but I never received an answer. I visited Maria Vitória's granddaughter, Mame, in a San Diego nursing home. She was generous with what she knew, filling in some gaps and adding color to dry facts with a couple of anecdotes, but she could not answer my remaining questions. There had been too many years.

I grieved the end of every line—and the losses of my world inside the library doors synergistically intensified the losses of my life outside those doors.

In finding my grandmother's sisters, I had kept my promise but uncovered a greater mystery. *Why had everyone in the family come together in California, leaving a young child on her own in Massachusetts without knowing how to contact them?*

5

Unless it rained heavily, my routine was the same. I left the house soon after dawn and walked as the sun rose in the sky, adjusting the broad brim of my straw hat to shield my face as I went. Every day I pushed further away from Dairy Road, deeper into the woods, higher toward Ponta do Pico, eastward along the coast. I would set my sights on the crest of a hill or a lone tree in a distant meadow, and make my own footpath switching back and forth around massive outcrops or scrambling down rocky grades.

The land became an entity with a dimension beyond what I could quantify as a scientist. Hills lifted me up and set me down. Towering cliffs dared me. Sweet grass invited me to stretch out and offered oblivion. The island played music in the tinkling melodies of brooks and breeze-driven leaves.

Pico absorbed my thoughts and cleansed my mind.

I devised a backpack from a canvas bag and two lengths of rope I found in the shed, and in the morning I filled it with my water bottle, fruit, and a sandwich. When I felt hungry, I found a shady spot on a fallen tree trunk or a crumbling stone wall warmed by the sun, and I sat in silence, watching an ever-changing panorama.

Soothed by nature and drained of the restless energy I had when I awoke, I retraced my steps to Dairy Road more relaxed than I had been in the morning. I spent the rest of the day close to the house, on a comfortable seat against the side of the house that I had made by draping a quilt over the flat top of the eira wall. The broad sill of the window to my right was a convenient place for my cup of tea. I also put my notebook there. Inside were lives, described as pivotal events: birth, marriage, children, and death. Although the texture of those lives—the blend of emotions a single moment had held, the dreams that had been cherished, the curiosity that had never been satisfied—was missing, the traces left behind brought me some comfort. I could be alone without feeling alone.

I watched my neighborhood. One afternoon, branches were removed from the laurels in front of Two Trees. From my seat, I could now see a cottage that looked like an illustration in a child's book, set in a garden with orderly rows of carrot tops, round heads of lettuce, and newly emerged kale. The shutters were freshly painted in the same bright blue as the front door, and the one small window I could see at the front of the house sparkled. Behind the house, a small grove of olive trees was laid out on a stretch of flat land.

Perhaps because I saw them so much as they went about their daily lives, the crowd at Big Meadow felt as close to being neighbors as anyone. On weekends, shortly after sunrise, a contingent of adults and older children came up from the village to join the family who lived on the farm. Everyone was at work when I started my hike, and long after I returned, they were still tending the gardens and washing milk pails. I looked up whenever they passed by and returned their enthusiastic waves and greetings with a smile I gauged to be friendly but not welcoming.

Occasionally, I saw Celina and Umberto on their walks to and from The Vineyard, and tending their grape vines. I tried to deny that I wanted to talk to them again, but was confronted with a truth that made me uncomfortable: I missed them. It still made sense to have severed ties to the life I left behind, but I couldn't think through why it was important to keep such a distance from the people around me on Pico.

My evening meal was whatever struck my fancy, sometimes a pot of mashed potatoes with heavy Pico cream, other times rice and melted cheese or a bowl of vegetables doused with olive oil and herbs. I relished every bite without once thinking about how what I ate might affect me in other ways. I stopped feeling the urge to occupy even the time I relaxed with something more. I didn't miss the stack of books and magazines that had always been close by to educate me or the television shows that had played in the background to take me away from a disappointing day.

As the day drew to a close, I poured hot water over a pinch of tea leaves. What was left in the large painted tin became a sad reminder of the finite number of days I had on Pico. If it was raining or if the winds carried especially cold and damp air from the ocean, I sat in the rocking chair in front of a warm fire. Otherwise, I spent my evenings on the eira, listening to the chirps of bush crickets and to distant voices that carried on the night air.

From my hill above Porto Velho, I watched what became a familiar pattern. From all around, boats converged on the shore and lights began twinkling on the hillsides. I heard whistles, and the dogs went racing back to Bodgerville from around our little neighborhood. The Big Meadow family went in for the night, and as the sky dimmed and night fell, the bright spots of color from Two Trees faded. Wavering light turned neighborhood windowpanes into metallic gold. I lifted a silhouetted finger and held it in front of each of those lit squares behind which people were gathered, and I touched them from a distance.

When I closed the door to a dark and empty house, and silence deepened to a hum in my ears, I sometimes wondered what it would be like to live with the people in the houses around me.

With tourist season at an end, the town settled into a less hurried life. I saw no day trippers, and only working boats loaded with nets and crates crossed the strait I faced. In the town square, locals went about their business at a leisurely pace, stopping to socialize, sitting on the sea wall to enjoy a rest, and taking their time with errands. They lived in a way I had not thought still existed but found I was comfortable with. Some children played tag, weaving in and out around pushcarts and people, while others wandered freely around town. An elderly man leaned on his cane as he hobbled from shop to shop greeting people, and shopkeepers came out to talk to people, or called and waved from a distance.

It crossed my mind that I liked having a place—however marginal—as one of them, not a visitor but someone who lived in Porto Velho. That thought unsettled me; I had reached the conclusion it was best to keep social ties to a minimum.

I spent much of the afternoon strolling around the town, pleased that—despite an accent that clearly clued my nationality—my new language was coming to me easily. I spotted a poster that protested the Azores membership in the EU. Officially an *Autonomous Region*, its decision to join the EU had not been straightforward, and some still argued in favor of political association with its American neighbor to the west, a sentiment that went back decades. Throughout the twentieth century, newspaper editorials had argued that, positioned almost as close to North America as to Europe, the Azores should become part of the United States.

A narrow shop, with a front door that took up most of the width of the building, sold religious objects. An old woman dressed in black sat just inside the open doorway, her chair nearly filling the floor space. On one wall, silver rosaries and wood crucifixes hung; on another, shelves held a few Bibles and more small statues than I had seen in my lifetime. Most I recognized as Saint Isabelle or the Virgin Mary, her benevolent face looking out from under a veil. Several were of Jesus, his heart exposed and dripping bright red blood.

The third wall was papered with pictures of saints, Jesus, and the Virgin Mary, as well as black-and-white photographs of a middle-aged man in clerical robes. His face was a gentle male version of my grandmother's. The woman noticed me looking and offered, "That is Father Xavier." She stopped to bless herself. "He is one of our own, born here in Porto Velho."

To me, the rituals and trappings of religion seemed as bizarre as chants to a sun god or magical incantations. Although raised Catholic, my mother had selected her own church using criteria other than family tradition or conviction, and—once affiliated—never showed much devotion that I could see to her new religion. As a Jew, my father's beliefs were usually hidden from public view, and I never knew whether Judaism was anything more to him than an acknowledgement of his origins.

At a second-hand store that carried a hodge-podge of curiosities, I bought a pair of heavy binoculars and the first volume of *A Natural History of Europe*, dated 1948, that showed line drawings of birds and butterflies. The leather case for the binoculars was worn thin and stamped in faded gold with the initials AGW. Since the Portuguese alphabet has no W, I imagined they were left by a traveler long ago.

I got a cup of coffee, drawn from an urn outside a café, and watched the local scene. A large family was re-uniting on the dock. Returning Americans in jeans and tee-shirts dragged themselves down the gangplank, carrying bags of gifts in addition to their suitcases. More than one traveler stripped off a watch or ring and placed it on the hand of a relative. No wonder nineteenth-century America had been seen as the land of plenty, I thought, a land where relatives had left poor, sent emigrant remittances, and returned with lavish gifts—

grandfather clocks, sewing machines, and brass bedsteads had not been unusual.

Parents, siblings, aunts, uncles, and cousins embraced in a frenzy of kisses, bear hugs, and shouts. Tears were wiped away and flowed freely again. Adults bent to pinch the cheeks of dazed children. And the entire group slowly made its way out of the square and up a side street.

Wandering from the center of town, I followed the smell of paraffin to the back of a small house with a sign in the window, *Candles for Sale.* In the backyard, twig lattices suspended from the branches of a tree held dozens of candle twins hanging by a shared wick. They looked like shiny, white carrots growing wild. When no one appeared, I turned to go, but a hand tapped at the window overlooking the yard and beckoned to me. I couldn't see past the light reflecting off the glass to the person inside, so I made my way back to the front of the house and knocked on the door.

Someone called out from inside, "Come in. Come in."

I opened the door to an area that served as living room, dining room, and bedroom, and walked through to a back room where light streamed in from a large window overlooking the yard. There, a woman was cutting wicks with a knife and packing candles into a wood crate. The skin on her rectangular face was relatively unlined, but her hands, knobby and roped with veins, showed their age. She must have been extremely tall in her youth; even compressed by the years, she looked down at me.

"You want to buy candles?" she asked, and she told me the price.

I reached into my pocket and counted out enough to buy ten candles. "I think that's right."

"You are not from Pico." She looked directly at me and waited for a response of some sort.

"No. I am from—," I wondered whether to just say America or give a more specific location, "—California in America."

She nodded. "I know California. I have family in San Diego." She stooped to pull a sheet of newspaper from a shelf under the window and started to wrap the candles. "I am from Santa Maria. I told my father I wanted to live at the convent in Vila where my mama cleaned, but he didn't have the money, so I married a Pico man." I reached out for the package, but she held it tight in her hand and asked, "You know Santa Maria?" It sounded like a challenge to tell what I did know.

"I do."

"Santa Maria is more beautiful than Pico." She grimaced. "All the beaches here are black. The whole coast is black rock, then black sand, then more black rock and more black sand." She smiled again with her memory of Santa Maria. "Our beaches are white, the only white beaches in all the islands."

She turned to the front of the house and walked away, motioning with her ancient hand. "Come." She struggled to pry the top of a small round tin on a table by the bed. "These are *melindres* from Santa Maria. Taste." She raised them to my face. It was more than good manners that made me take one and thank her. I felt comfortable around her; she had told about being disconnected from her heritage, and we shared the same feelings of pride and loss.

The small cookies were intensely perfumed with honey. Crumbs tumbled out of the corners of my mouth, and I stuffed them back in with sticky fingertips that I licked clean. "These are delicious."

Praise for her native island continued to the moment I thanked her and turned to leave. Just as when my neighbor, Celina, had talked about Fayal, it struck me that the woman had probably lived on Pico for sixty years or more, yet she still spoke of her native island as home.

"Where is the cemetery?" I asked as she was opening the door for me. In other villages, bodies rested in their graves for only seven years, before being disinterred to make room for others. Arable land was too valuable to be used for the dead. Porto Velho was different. With a thick layer of soft soil deposited by its network of streams, it had been able to allot a small area as a cemetery in the mid-1800s. "I'm looking for my family." I wanted to let her know that my interest was not that of a tourist.

I followed her outside, and she pointed to a patch of green at the foot of one of the hills, very close to the town. "The older graves are there." Once she had pointed it out, I could see the jumble of markers speckling a grassy field bordered by trees and a single wall of black stones frosted with limestone. "You have many relatives there?"

I didn't know. "Almost all of my grandmother's sisters, aunts, and uncles went to America. Only her mother and one sister stayed." I knew I was reaching out for sympathy when I added, "I don't know about her father."

In volumes of detailed records from Pico and America, there had been no trace of my great-grandfather after the birth of his children. There was no obituário for him in the Azores and no death certificate in the United States. Rosemarie had told me that many men left the islands illegally to avoid military service, but he was far too old by the time his youngest daughter was born for that to have been an issue. I had searched for some trace of him in the households of his daughters, but there was none. Someone suggested that he might have stowed away, not to get out of Pico but to get into America, an idea that both Rosemarie and I dismissed as implausible when we considered the timeline; quotas were not established until 1924, long after he had vanished from all records.

She gave me the candles and put a hand on my shoulder. "Maybe he went to America. Maybe he died there."

"I looked. He isn't buried in any of the cemeteries where his children are buried. There is no record of him."

"Records," she harrumphed. "Records can be wrong."

I knew that. It had taken me months, even years, to accept what Rosemarie had told me. People ended up places you never expected and for reasons you could not imagine. "I know. I just can't believe that of everyone in the family, only he would leave no records at all. He just disappeared."

"Men do things like that," she said.

The entrance to the cemetery high above Porto Velho was defined by a wall of irregular basalt stones that rose in jagged steps to a cross at the top. I clambered up and stood with one hand shading my eyes, a ship's captain looking to the horizon.

From the top of the wall, I could see the quadrants of the cemetery formed by two perpendicular paths paved with mosaics of Crusaders' crosses. Headstones of many shapes and colors were scattered randomly in the green grass. Settling, or more cataclysmic geologic events, had made almost all lean to one side or another, some precariously.

I was hoping to find a clue to what had separated my grandmother from all her sisters, leaving her without family, and presumably without a way to contact them. I threaded my way between markers, but without orderly rows, I kept losing track of which ones I had already seen. Some gravestones were kissing the ground, and I had to work my hand underneath to read the name by touch. Some had several names on one side, and many had names on both sides. Half a day passed.

I almost didn't know it was my great-grandmother's headstone when I saw it.

Maria Umbelina
1858—1913

She was buried next to her daughter, Francisca Simas, the only one of the sisters who stayed on Pico. Neither of their husbands was beside them.

When I knelt to clear leaves near my great-grandmother's grave, my fingers brushed the sharp edge of a stone between the two graves. Buried deep, a corner had been lifted up by the root of a tree. Looking over my shoulder, I followed the stone into the ground with my fingers. I scraped away the soil and grass that had accumulated around it, and stashed it behind the headstones. The stone was a polished three-inch square with a cross incised in the center, unlike anything I was familiar with.

I was considering whether to right it or lay it flat, when I spotted the edge of another stone. By the time I finished digging, I had unearthed three more flat squares, each with the same cross cut into one side. Along with the one that had been slowly nudged to the surface as a nearby tree grew, they had been placed side by side in neat order, equidistant between the two graves.

I carried one over to a rain barrel at the back of the cemetery, immersed it, and rubbed it gently with my thumbs. Silt lifted and swirled before sinking. Slanting the stone against the rays of the sun, I saw scratches under the cross that looked like handwriting. I cleaned off the remaining stones and found the same thin lines. I patted the stones dry with my shirt and ran a fingernail across the surface of each stone. There seemed to be numbers and letters on each, but I didn't have Rosemarie's talent for making sense of disjointed marks.

I returned to the two family graves, replacing the stones and soil, and I used my cape to carry dried leaves and twigs to a pile just outside the cemetery wall.

As the sun began its descent, I sat by the graves and spoke to the souls of my departed family. "Can you help me, Francisca?" I asked aloud. "Can you tell me what happened?"

Tears spilled down my face. "Why, Maria Umbelina? Why did you send your children away? My Nana never even knew where her sisters were. You left her all alone in the world. Why?"

Wide awake in the pre-dawn hours, I thought about the words of the candlemaker from Santa Maria: records can be wrong.

I had found what little I knew about my great-grandfather in databases, in heavy volumes filled with tiny print, on photocopies, films, and scans. I had taken it all as fact. When I made room in my mind for the possibility of error, fresh ideas came to me. The original baptismal records might have had a different name or a different birth date. The transcriber's eye could have wandered, mismatching my great-grandfather's first name with the second name of someone else. Ink had smudged, and *1853* was read as *1858*. Two pages of church records were stuck together and turned as one. Electrons moving on silicon chips had done something unanticipated by programmers.

By the time I reached the town center, the sun had risen, and I was convinced that something like that must have happened, and that I could find my great-grandfather and solve the mystery of why my grandmother had been set adrift in the world at such a young age. I slowed my pace and practiced what I had to say, trying out approaches from crisp and businesslike to pitiable and pleading.

Porto Velho's church was small, and typical of churches on the islands, its facade flat and white, and its trim painted bright cobalt blue. The plain wood door was ajar. I smelled the incense and candle wax before I could see anything. Then, scant light from two stained glass windows and a stand of lit candles showed pews on either side of the nave and a deep china stoup with holy water that quivered when I stepped on the wood floor.

I knocked on the door of the rectory at the back of the church with no result. I knocked again and waited nervously as sounds inside grew louder. In my brief childhood interactions with clergy, there had been only recitations of memorized words, murmured responses to questions that seemed designed to trip me up, and challenges to common sense, none of which prepared me for what I wanted to do.

A voice called out, "Wait. Wait. I'm coming." He was still chewing when he opened the door, a self-important look on his face. He lifted fleshy eyelids and fixed his eyes on me. "What do you want?" His impatience ran the words together so quickly, I could barely follow what he was saying.

I hesitated and fell back on what was natural to me, a straightforward request. "I'd like to see the baptism records from the nineteenth century." I could tell he was about to say no. The lie came easily. "I talked to someone at the diocese office in Horta. He said you would arrange it."

For a long moment, the look on his face told me he had caught me in a lie, but then he opened the door a bit wider, turned his back on me, and walked down a short hall. Without looking back, he grumbled, "This way." He led me past a sitting room, a half-eaten bowl of soup and crust of bread on a small table by a wingback chair.

"*Padre?*" A woman of at least seventy came into the hall, anxious when she faced the priest and suspicious when she faced me.

"She wants to see baptism records," he flipped his head in my direction. The woman looked me over and shook her head.

The priest stopped abruptly at a door, took a brass ring with keys from a hook on the wall, and unlocked it. "Down there," he said, as he pulled the door open and pointed down steep steps that disappeared into darkness. He walked away without glancing back, leaving me to search for a light switch. After fruitlessly running my hands along either side of the barely lit stairwell walls, a string hanging from the ceiling brushed the tip of my nose, and I pulled it to turn on a dim bulb in a porcelain fixture inelegantly attached to the ceiling by a nail.

Cool, musty air rose from the cellar. Holding onto the plank railing, I made my way down a solid staircase. By the time I reached the next light fixture, my eyes had become accustomed to the darkness, and it felt comfortable and welcoming. The huge space was divided into sections only by the nature of the objects each area held. There were shelves of preserved food, boxes with candles and string, glass jars holding nails, and a large wood crate addressed to *P. de Andrade; Porto Velho; Azores,* with a return address of New Bedford, Massachusetts.

Behind a hill of steamer trunks was a short hallway that led to a room with glass-fronted bookcases. I felt the same sensation, a blend of calm and anticipation, as I had when entered my library. The shelves held a disorganized collection of records: ledgers with parish expenditures noted in narrow columns of tiny numbers; bundles of correspondence with the *matrix*, or diocese, written on heavy linen paper in flowery script; folders with receipts for the purchase of candles, wine, ink, shoe polish, and one pair of wire rimmed glasses.

I could have happily spent days looking through them, but what I wanted was stacked on top of one bookcase—the records of baptisms, marriages, and deaths in the parish. These were not the projection of invisible electrons blinking patterns on a screen; they held tangible substantiation of my family.

The mismatched volumes were slim; the population of Porto Velho had never exceeded a few thousand. The earliest was dated 1596. I took the records for 1883 to 1899 to the table.

Nana, I'm here.

The paper was in surprisingly good condition, barely yellowed and filled with cramped handwriting in black ink. Each entry was signed *Padre Diogo Luis Bartolomeu Borga.* I read the first page.

> *This book serves as the record of baptisms, marriages, and deaths for the church of Nossa Senhora da Boa Viagem, in the town of Porto Velho, in the parish of São Roque do Pico, diocese of Horta, from April 2, 1887 to October 12, 1894.*

In September of 1887, Maria do Conceição and Maria dos Anjos were born. There were no births in October. In

December, Manuel and another Maria were born. I turned the page.

> *On the second day of the month of January, in the year one thousand eight hundred and eighty-eight, in the church of Nossa Senhora da Boa Viagem, in the parish of São Roque do Pico, on the island of Pico of the diocese of Horta, I solemnly baptized a girl with the name of Emelia Simas.*

I held my hand over the page. *I love you.*

The account filled an entire page, but I stopped reading when I reached the name of her father, *Matias Cabral.* One door closed. The name I had was correct. The only other mistake I could think of was that his birthdate had been entered incorrectly.

I brought an earlier volume to the table. In that one, I found more family and others whose names I recognized from ship manifests and census records. Working back in time, the years passed too quickly. I reached the 1850s, dreading and looking forward to the sight of my great-grandfather's name next to an 1858 date. He was there, born May 2, 1858, the son of Ana Rosa and José Manuel, exactly as in the online database. There was no mistake; he had simply vanished after 1888.

I returned the books to the shelf, telling myself it was time to let go. I knew I would not.

6

"I care for those who came after me, but I cannot care for those who came before me, as a person should."

"Don't be sad, Nana, I'll take care of them."

My mother had taken me to see the early fall foliage and experience country life in Vermont. She and her friends delighted in air that was scented with woodsmoke and apples being pressed into cider, the charming Cape Cod houses, and locals dressed in colorful flannel shirts. We stopped at a general store cobbled together from small houses connected by short hallways, where I was left to wander while the adults shopped for maple syrup, polished wood salad bowls, and chipped pottery that was labeled as antique.

In a back room I found a rack with packets of seeds. I studied the pictures of beautiful flowers and perfect vegetables for a long time, eventually choosing to grow what was promised to be the sweetest white corn I would ever eat.

Under the watchful eye of the doorman back in the city, I used one of my mother's sterling silver spoons to scoop dry soil from a tree well on the sidewalk, and I carried it upstairs in an ice bucket to distribute into ten paper cups. I watered them every day, and was so excited when I saw the first bright green shoots that had emerged while I was at school. I gently dug up the seeds again and again, examining the growing roots and patting them back into place, and every day I measured the height of the shoots against the print on my bedroom drapes, marveling at the mysterious process that made them grow. Fifty-eight floors above the streets of Manhattan, their struggle to survive was in vain. Yet despite failure, growing them became the earliest indication of the love of science that would become a driving force in my life.

I came home one afternoon to find my mother in my room, directing the maid to clear away my corn seedlings, which had begun to shrivel and yellow. She turned to tell me that a car was waiting to take us to Gloucester.

It was my cousin's funeral. I wore a dark brown dress delivered from Bergdorf Goodman, and held the crystal rosary I had been given tightly wrapped around my fingers. In the church, I tried very hard not to look at the open casket, focusing on my hands when I knelt and blurring my vision when I stood. I leaned lightly against my grandmother, taking in the smell of the starch in her dress and her lavender cologne.

My mother moved in a cloud of Chanel No. 5 when she parted the crowd of mourners to stand with the rest of the family around the plot next to my Uncle Lloyd's headstone. I overheard the words of admiration and saw high regard in other people's eyes when they looked at her. She was noted for her elegance and commended for the dignity she showed to the world, raising me after my father's death at the age of forty-two.

There was never a need to exaggerate about her to my friends, and meeting her would bear out any praise. She was welcoming, giving of her time, and generous with compliments. Overnight guests were touched by the personalized cards she left in their rooms and the scrambled eggs she herself made them in the morning. She always seemed to know the right words to say, the correct way to act, and the most appropriate clothes to wear. Once I got a call from a school friend who wanted me to ask my mother what she should talk to her boyfriend's parents about when they had dinner together, and I made sure everyone we knew heard about the conversation.

My mother always had time for me. She made me a healthy breakfast every morning and brushed my hair every night. We spent most evenings side by side, me doing homework and she writing letters or reading books. When she did go out at night, she checked in with me every couple of hours, asking what I had done and what I was planning to do in the time before we were together again. My weekends were usually filled with shopping expeditions along Fifth Avenue, visits to museums, young people's concerts, and the time-honored tradition of Sunday brunch in the elegant Palm Court at the Plaza Hotel, a vast space domed with an ironwork and frosted glass ceiling that let in light for the potted palm trees. I sat at a table laid with pink linen, sterling silver, and china for over an hour, listening to lessons in etiquette, thoughts about fashion, and opinions on politics. It was only during the summer months when I was in Gloucester that my mother was not a constant presence in my life.

We were so dissimilar in looks, in the timbre of our voices, in our tastes. She was petite in every way; by the time I was twelve, I was taller than she was and had wider hips. In her presence, I was self-conscious about my too-broad forehead, too-thin nose, and too-curly hair. Her caramel-colored hair, which she dyed lighter and lighter as the gray hairs grew in, was mine but only in childhood, after which it darkened to the brunette I kept. If not dazzling, her beauty had a slightly European air of elegance, every hair in its perfectly-coiffed place, her face discretely made-up with ivory powder, rose lipstick, a hint of blush on her cheeks, but nothing more. She wore suits with low-heeled pumps and a matching handbag, and adhered to her own advice of wearing one less piece of jewelry than seemed appropriate.

No one would have suspected she did not come from a moneyed background. Her manners were aristocratic, and her diction was faultless. She never spoke with the Boston accent my uncles had, and her vocabulary was far larger than theirs. From grade school through high school, I had heard visiting friends say, "I wish I could talk like your mother. She sounds like the Queen."

My mind ignored the question of why, coming from a small city in Massachusetts, that was true.

On the day of my cousin's funeral, it was unusually warm and humid for fall, and mosquitoes swarmed around my legs at the cemetery. My grandmother stooped to swat them away. I kept holding on to her sleeve even when she bent over. She looked very elegant to me that day, dressed in black silk with a white lace collar she had probably made herself. She wore the only piece of jewelry I had ever seen her wear, a simple onyx ring that she said would be mine "one day."

My only aunt, Sister Mary Barnard, stood on the other side of my grandmother, dressed in a full habit and fingering a rosary. As everyone else prayed aloud, I looked sideways at her face, sweating freely in the heat, and thought about her life of devotion to God, as described in the little books by the church door. Giving someone else control over everything you did seemed to be making a decision to remain a child. I concluded that hers was a squandered existence.

My only cousin was buried close to others in my grandmother's family. During the graveside service, I kept thinking of how my father, who had died a few months earlier, was lying separated from everyone who had known him, in a large plot in New Jersey that to the best of my knowledge was never visited.

Alone in his study years later, I found medical records showing he had carried with him from Hungary a parasite that over the years had slowly destroyed his liver. I also found the soft flannel shirt that my uncle had given him the summer my grandmother told me she didn't know where any of her sisters were. I had taken that shirt out of my bag at the last minute to wear on my flight to the islands, and I wore it most nights on Pico as I sipped my tea.

After my cousin's funeral, I followed my grandmother to the two plots on either side of the newly-scarred ground. The markers bore the same last name, her last name: Howe. "We will leave Bobby next to your Uncle Lloyd," she said, a rare moment of emotion breaking her usually strong voice, "and next to your Uncle Pete."

As the last mourners disappeared around a turn in the cemetery path, my grandmother bent to pull stray weeds and said to herself, "I care for those who came after me, but I cannot care for those who came before me, as a person should."

"Don't be sad, Nana, I'll take care of them."

I remained as her only grandchild.

When I was fourteen, a school friend asked if I would like to go to her grandmother's house in upstate New York for a few days in the week before Christmas. We talked about tramping through real snow to cut down a tree and making the star-shaped cookies that were a tradition in her grandmother's family. That night, the phone rang. "This is Clare Parker," my mother answered in the part-British, part-American accent that had been labeled *mid-Atlantic* by reporters describing how film stars like Katherine Hepburn spoke.

The phone hummed with a distant voice.

"Yes. The Milford School," she confirmed. "How are you?"

I strained to hear what was being said on the other end.

"I'm well, thank you."

There was a long silence as my mother listened, nodded, and raised her eyebrows.

"Yes. I see. Well, I am so sorry to say that Ann will be with her own family during the holiday season."

A few more words were said on the other end.

"Yes. Possibly another time. Thank you so much. Goodbye." My mother hung up and sadly shook her head from side to side. "Can you imagine thinking that a mother would not want her child at home with her at such a special time of year?"

The following summer, another school friend invited me to spend a week with her family on Cape Cod. My mother quietly listened to me, nodding her head as I told her about it. She took a few moments before answering, a few moments during which she appeared to be carefully considering the invitation. "Well, Ann," she took a slow breath, "who are these people?"

I explained that the Burkes were Molly's parents.

"No," she said. "I mean what do I know about them?"

I repeated what I had already said.

"That tells me nothing, Ann, nothing important," she said gently.

I pointed out that Molly had been to our apartment many times.

"When you are here, I know you are safe."

I protested.

"I'm not the sort of mother who just lets her daughter take off with people she doesn't know," she said in a voice that told me she was trying hard to be patient with me. "Goodness knows it would be easier to do otherwise, Ann, but I've always done my best for you."

I knew there was no point in arguing. After all, she had my best interests at heart.

Babysitting was out of the question because of the danger it posed. "You don't know how dangerous it can be out there in the city."

A weekend celebrating my friend's fifteenth birthday was cancelled because I was coming down with a cold. "I'll prop you up in front of the television and spoil you!"

A spring vacation trip with my class was not possible. "I was going to take you to the Cyclades." She looked so disappointed. I just nodded and went to my room.

The silent auction was my school's big annual fundraiser. Although an evening for the parents, juniors were asked to pour drinks, record bids, and offer brochures for various programs the school was associated with. I chose my table carefully and planned what I would say.

I saw my mother arrive and work her way around the library floor, cleared of carrels and chairs for the occasion and decorated by one of the groups of mothers who occupied their days volunteering for such good causes. She greeted other parents and stopped to make a couple of bids. As she walked to my table, I bent over the clipboard I had been given and started writing.

"Victoria Webster," I said under my breath, as I wrote a name she was very familiar with.

She squinted at me, waiting. "What is this, Ann?" she asked brightly.

"Just a summer program in Italy." I held my breath.

She picked up one of the brochures and glanced at it.

"I've already told my friends I'm spending the whole summer with my grandmother in Gloucester. I'll ask Nana if one of them can visit me there!"

My mother opened her mouth to speak, then shut it quickly. She looked at the list of surnames on the clipboard, all belonging to one of society's leading families, all printed by me. "What is the program?"

"It's not what I'm into. Art and culture—that sort of stuff."

"Don't say stuff."

"Anyway, it's only a small, select group that is going."

"Hmm," she exhaled.

"Besides, it costs a fortune."

"We are not exactly destitute, Ann."

She walked away and made the rounds, chatting with one group after another for the next two hours, as winning bids were announced and polite applause accompanied people to the front of the room to claim a winter week at an Aspen ski lodge or a summer week at a Maine resort. At the end of the evening, she walked to my table and entered my name at the bottom of the list. "I think exposure to Italian culture will do you a world of good, Ann."

I had to wait until she had disappeared into the darkness outside before I slipped the top sheet from the clipboard, crumpled it up, and put my name on the second sheet under those of my two best friends.

I was going to Italy without her.

Although I dated my passion for science to watching the corn seeds I had gotten in Vermont sprout and grow, I dated my commitment to the dispassionate process of science to a single day when I was seventeen. Until then, I had shared a passport with my mother—our pictures side by side on a single page, as was done then—but I needed my own to go on the school trip to Italy.

She took me to her bank, a magnificent turn-of-the-century edifice that ran from Fifth Avenue to Madison Avenue. The uniformed doorman tipped his cap as he swung open the heavy brass-framed door to a hushed lobby, lit with crystal chandeliers hanging from a gilded ceiling. To the left, small Art Deco lamps were lined up on a long mahogany counter, behind which a row of tellers in starched white shirts, dark suits, and subdued ties worked in silence. She walked directly to the first of several polished wood desks on the right and said she wanted to be escorted to the vault. I followed her, impressed with the grandeur.

Behind closed doors, my mother extracted a sealed envelope from her safe deposit box. She placed it on the high table between us and covered it with her open hand. "This is your birth certificate," she said, "and a legal document changing your last name."

I tried to process what she had said. "What do you mean?" I searched her face for an answer. The one that came to me was stunning. "Am I adopted?"

"Don't be ridiculous, Ann. I did not *adopt* you." Her tone made it clear that adoption was not something she would resort to.

"Then why would I need to show that my name was changed?" I reached out for the envelope, still under her hand.

She drew a breath of exasperation. "It is something that is done all the time. It made your father's last name easier to pronounce."

"What was my real last name?" I asked tugging at the envelope.

Between her teeth, she said, "Pavka." It made her uncomfortable.

Pavka. I said it first to myself and then aloud. "My last name is Pavka."

"*Was* Pavka!" She tightened her red lips. "You have been a *Parker* since you were six years old." She had only ever referred to my father as William Parker; any other name I might have heard had been bleached from my memory. Then, like secret writing appearing under the right circumstances, I remembered. I *had* seen that name on papers from time to time, and I had heard some of my father's friends call out to him, "Pavka!" Yet, it had never once raised any questions in my mind.

"Why? Why change it?"

"You are an American. You are entitled to an American name." She was becoming angry.

"But my father—"

"*I* am an American! I was born here." She paused slightly between each word.

"I—"

"Enough! I don't have all day. Just take this," she said as she handed me the envelope, "and do not lose it." She pursed her lips and glared at me. The conversation had ended.

"I won't lose it." My faint words were all but absorbed in the still air of the vault.

"I know you. Keeping track of things the way you should is not something you do well. We will work on that, Ann."

I held the envelope securely, already planning where I could stop and read the papers before showing them at the passport office in Rockefeller Center.

"Stop wrinkling it, Ann." She was speaking in the kind voice that good mothers used with young children. She smoothed my hair. "Mother has to run now. I'm very late."

I lagged behind as we returned to the bank lobby. After my mother exited through the Fifth Avenue door, I walked toward the Madison Avenue one. My feet sank into the plush carpeting, heavy and hard to lift. I was short of breath when I reached an armchair. I sat for a while and looked around the bank lobby, looking for my mother to return, and tell me she was sorry and everything was fine.

I looked at the envelope, so tightly clutched in my hand it was nearly folded in half, and I opened it. The first paper I read was my birth certificate. I was born Ann Catherine, the daughter of Clara Howe and Vilem Pavka. I expected, then, that the second paper would show my name had been legally changed from Ann Pavka to Ann Parker. What I did not expect was the note attached to it. On it, my father had written: As agreed, Clare. *Was it something he had not wanted? Had my mother made the name change a condition of something he wanted? Had his own name, in fact, ever been legally changed?*

I sank into the purple velvet chair as far down as I could, until only my head was exposed above the high arms, at first just working on breathing in and out regularly enough so I would appear at ease to anyone who looked at me. Then I searched my life's story, separating memories into those that were real and those that were products of what I had been told. I could summon only a handful that stood alone, corroborated by what I had directly experienced and not tainted with the fear of having been fashioned for me. I fixed those few recollections in my mind and explored them thoroughly, looking for truth.

It unfolded like those last few minutes of putting together a jigsaw puzzle, when the remaining pieces that you had looked at so many times before, unable to see how they could possibly fit, suddenly made perfect sense, and your fingers couldn't move fast enough to put them into place.

I sat a bit taller in the purple velvet chair, able to depend on facts and to credit my own perceptions as truth. Reality blossomed, bright with detail. I had invented my family; rather, much of what I believed about my family had come from my mother's well-crafted stories. My father had not been a cosmopolitan man about town; he had been a lonely refugee who, above all, wanted to belong to a new country and a new family.

And my mother was not a sophisticate, at ease in the upper levels of society. Behind the pronouncements about what was proper and what was not acceptable was an insecure outsider, someone who was defending her position as one of the elite, probably more to herself than to others. The seemingly impromptu comments on décor, the arts, and everything else came after preparation and rehearsal. The hours she spent in Fifth Avenue department stores were as much to learn from what she saw as to shop, and when she named the artists of paintings we saw from a distance on museum trips, she had must have spent hours committing them to memory.

I remembered the evasions and half-truths that had covered chinks in the firewall between Gloucester and New York: my grandmother was referred to as enjoying a quiet life in the family home by the ocean, and the uncle who added to his income at the fish cannery by renting out the two small houses he owned was "in real estate." I had reconciled inconsistencies by disregarding facts.

My mother's single-minded pursuit of her perfect life had pushed me into the role of a supporting player in my own life. As the child of her ideal family, there had been little room for the real me.

I traced my reliance on facts and my faith in rational thought to that morning in the bank lobby. It was my emancipation from the blind acceptance of what I was told. I lost even the low expectations I had of religion, and skepticism became a hallmark of my personality.

I entered the world of science, and found purpose and pride there. I loved everything my commitment to science gave me, from the ability to make a life apart from my mother to my persistence in unearthing my family tree.

In the two minutes it took for a college professor to introduce the field of genetics, I decided that was where my future lay. That predictable chemicals are responsible for virtually every aspect of life, from how curly your hair is to how well you recognize faces, was magnificent. I followed my heart to advanced degrees in molecular genetics and a job with a Silicon Valley firm known for manipulating genes to do everything from engineering more nutritious strains of wheat to producing drugs that saved lives.

I loved my laboratory: the smooth cool feel of the stainless steel, the orderly arrays of bottles and Petri dishes, the sharp smell of disinfectant, the state-of-the-art equipment, most of which had not existed ten years earlier. I looked forward to holding my breath, listening to the whirr of the computer as it crunched the data. I enjoyed the process of culturing, mixing, heating, spinning, and examining, all the while understanding what was happening to the infinitesimal atoms I held in my hands.

I was proud of my work as a scientist, inserting a human gene for the production of an essential hormone into bacterial cells. I knew that I was part of something very special, adding small drops to the pond of human knowledge and changing the trajectory of lives.

It took exactly fifteen days to lose all that, and everything else.

Miriam Winthrop

7

I was so deep in thought that I arrived on the outskirts of Porto Velho without remembering the walk. I was going to look at the obituário of my great-grandmother, Maria Umbelina, and the daughter buried beside her. I rationalized the search by telling myself I might find a notation in the margin, something that could answer the question of why my grandmother was separated from the rest of her family. On some level, though, I understood that family history was contrived justification for returning to the records of people who had once walked where I did; I was actually searching for peace by escaping into their joys and sorrows.

Festivity was in the air. Houses were being whitewashed and flowers were everywhere, tufting large pots near front doors, cascading out of window boxes, and even blanketing the donkeys pulling the morning milk wagon to town. One particularly cheerful woman leaned out of a cart and handed me a thin branch with two large white hydrangeas bobbing near its tip. I returned her smile and offered a polite thank you, and her horse picked up its pace and carried her away.

The bustle multiplied as I neared the town square. Bicyclists wove their way through the narrow streets ringing tinny bells. Musicians played folk tunes. Young girls gathered in front of a store window, smiling at a line of dolls dressed in traditional skirts and blouses. Down a side street, two vintage trucks, polished to perfection with gleaming paint and shiny chrome, were packed with fresh flowers that people lined up to buy by the armload.

I took my time walking slowly along three sides of the square to reach the corner by the dock. There, fishermen unloaded freshly caught fish from enormous baskets, mended nets, and stood around talking and drinking steaming coffee. An outdoor market was setting up where the high retaining wall dropped to the shore. A small wagon filled with oranges marked the end of a line of tables piled high with food of all sorts, and mouth-watering smells competed for my attention: freshly baked bread, roasting meats, frying fish, honeyed cakes.

Two older women, wrapped in wool shawls against the chilly air blowing across the strait, flanked a cloth-draped wheelbarrow. They looked at me and nodded happily at each other when they saw me smile. At first, I thought they had set out toys for sale but, looking more closely, I could see the small, brightly colored objects were candies and tiny frosted cookies. There were crowns that glistened with candied green citron, scepters topped with glacéed cherries, Crusader crosses iced in Pico blue, and marzipan shaped into tiny fruits and nuts. I bought a sample of just about every confection and was handed a large paper cone holding my purchases.

As I strolled, I was drawn into the world of the village by the stories about family and friends I overheard. A network of social ties bound them together. It was a warm, safe place to be.

I followed the smell of coffee and the clatter of dishes to a café. It was a narrow building with four blue-painted tables against one wall and, at the back, a large wood table, around which a group of men were smoking, sipping coffee, and playing cards. They stared at me, and their banter slowed.

The one at the head of the table called out in the direction of a brightly-lit doorway, "Isabel! *Cliente!*" The other three glanced at me and then looked back to him. In his fifties, and by far the largest of the four in height and girth, he dominated the group, the others deferring to him as he restarted their conversation and passed platters of food, after taking the lion's share for himself.

I took off my hat and sat by the one window that overlooked the square and the beach. It was colder than I had expected, and the heat I had built up on my walk to the town was dissipating. I was grateful for the warmth coming from a huge cast iron stove, on which sat an assortment of kettles and baskets filled with warming bread.

A small woman in her sixties emerged from the kitchen, wiping her hands on the front of her apron. One of her legs was twisted out at a peculiar angle, and she had a pronounced limp. Her hairline was beaded with sweat, and strands of curly, graying hair had escaped the bun on the top of her head. Her fine-pored, rosy skin was a youthful contrast to a body afflicted by age and infirmity.

As she started toward me, the oldest of the men at the back table lifted his cup high and wiggled it at Isabel. A withered version of the leader, with the same sharp features and blue eyes, he might have been his father, although it was hard to be sure since many on the island shared kinship, the outcome of centuries of inbreeding in a small population. Isabel took a pot of coffee from the stovetop to the men before limping back to me. "What would you like?" she asked in Portuguese.

"Coffee, please." I looked around and saw the plates of food the men at the back were downing. "Eggs and sausage," I said, "and bread, please."

She looked at the same plates I had been studying and nodded, "*Linguiça* with eggs." When she returned, it was with a large cup filled with coffee that steamed the window, a platter of the smoked sausage and fried eggs, and a basket of bread. She waited while I tasted my food. The bread was unevenly toasted and the eggs were overcooked, but the coffee rivaled the best I had tasted, and I knew at first taste that linguiça would become a lifelong comfort food. Smoky, garlicky, and scented with paprika, it was filled with small nuggets of pork fat that oozed a red-orange oil I mopped up with my bread.

Satisfied that I liked it, Isabel took the chair beside me. "You are here for the *festa*?" she asked.

I shook my head to say no.

"Tomorrow is festa." When I didn't immediately signal my understanding, she continued, "You have festas in America, I know. My uncle went to America and came back to tell me." It sounded like that was the sole purpose of his return. She saw my blank look. "I can see Picoense blood in you. You have not been to the festas in America?"

"No." I had an impulse to apologize for my failure to know about them.

"What kind of Azorean are you?" she slapped her leg and looked disappointed in me.

"I didn't know I was from Pico until recently."

"Poor one." She patted my hand. "Don't worry. You will learn. On Pico, we have festas to celebrate, and to honor God and the saints. *Festa Vindimas* thanks God for our wines. *Festa Espírito Santo* reminds us of the rebirth that will come. In Porto Velho, we have a special festa for *Nossa Senhora* who watched over our whalers."

"Ah, yes, the whalers," I said. She took my response as interest, and I could admit that I did want to hear more. But it made me uncomfortable to think the men of my grandmother's family had been whalers as well as fishermen. To my twenty-first century mind, it was a cruel and shameful way to make a living.

"If you are still here in five weeks, come see the reenactment of off-shore whaling. Men from Porto Velho and other villages take out canoas trimmed in Pico blue, and they are joined by men from São Jorge in their green-trimmed boats.

Along the shores of both islands, onlookers cheer and wave, and the wind carries calls of *Blos! Blos!*"

I had read about the two very different ways to hunt whales. In the nineteenth century, large ships—often out of Massachusetts—went far from shore to find enough whales to satisfy the enormous demand for oil to lubricate the machines of the Industrial Revolution. By contrast, traditional Azorean whaling was done within sight of shore from canoas, very large rowboats, a practice that continued in the islands until the last whale hunt in 1987.

I could picture the man braced against the bow of the canoa, raising a harpoon attached to a huge coil of rope, as the whalers closed in on their quarry. Once speared, the whale pulled away at such great speed that the rope spun out quickly enough to generate tremendous friction. The first whaling job that young boys were given was to douse that rope with water, so the wooden boards of the boat didn't catch fire.

"Some remember when men used to cut up the whale's body right on the beach," Isabel went one, "and everywhere there were people taking away parts."

I liked listening to Isabel. It had been a long time since I had exchanged more than a few words with another human being and I found that, rather than dreading it, I actually welcomed the connection.

"At one time, our whales were used for lamp oil, for candles, for medicines, for perfume, even for—," she used a word I wasn't familiar with, "—*espartilhos*." Seeing that I didn't understand, she drew long vertical lines on her torso while sucking in her breath.

"For corsets." I said in English, sucking in my own stomach. She nodded, satisfied.

"The fat was melted down. Even the bones and teeth were saved." She stopped and got up, signaling me to wait.

When Isabel returned, she was cradling a large whale tooth. She laid the piece of scrimshaw reverently on the table. It showed a square-rigged ship, its sails filled with air as it moved in a strong wind on choppy waters, chasing breeching and blowing whales. The details were extraordinary, from the stitching on the sails to the tiny wreath of flowers that ringed the pointed end of the tooth.

"Fishermen can work at night," she explained, "but not the whalers who went far from the islands. Going after whales at night was too dangerous." She seemed to take pride in this. "At night, whalers relaxed by making these. They took the big needles used to sew sails, and they made the drawing. Then, they rubbed candle soot into the lines." She glanced at the men sitting at the back and whispered, "My grandfather made this one. He was a whaler."

I offered her the cone of confections I had bought, and we sat quietly for a while, tasting and watching the activity on the square. Isabel told me how after whaling lost its value, it had given way to thriving tuna and cod fishing industries. "My ancestors went to Gloucester, and many died when their cod boat went down, but there were captains who were born here and became American millionaires." Her thought might have seemed disjointed to anyone who didn't know about the life of a fisherman. There was danger, unrelenting work and uncertainty. Still, it could be very lucrative.

Two of the men at the back sat close together, hunched over the wood table and resting heavily on their forearms. In their sixties, they both had a typically Portuguese appearance, compact and dark, but the resemblance ended there. One wore a black-banded straw hat and a knit bowtie with his heavy cardigan, as dapper as anyone I had seen in town since I arrived. The other reminded me of homeless men; a grayed sweater, shapeless from too many washings, hung on his scrawny frame, and several days growth of gray beard surrounded his nearly toothless mouth. With hands wrapped around his cup of coffee, he was looking intently at Isabel.

He spoke out loudly, "Antos, your wife is talking about us." He looked to gauge the leader's reaction before continuing. "She is telling the American woman about how we were masters of the seas."

"Isabel gossips because she has too much free time," the large man laughed. He called out, "Isabel!" She was already on her feet, clearing dirty dishes from another table, and the men returned to their own idle conversation, without any indication that they even remembered my existence.

"It's true, Antos," the man with the hat offered. "We *were* masters of the seas."

Like many men their age, they spent a lot of time in their past. The one with the tattered sweater retold stories from his father. "Whaling ships would come for our men four or five times a year."

"They liked them because they were strong and worked hard," the man with the hat said.

"Hah, Little Joao! They liked them because they worked cheaply," Antos retorted.

"There was bad, but there was also good."

"Where was the good?" Antos called out loudly from across the table. "Three years of labor just for passage and, after they deducted the cost for the boat, and for the captain and the officers, there was almost nothing left to divvy up for the ones who did the most work and took the most risks."

The toothless man sucked his lips. "Once I saw a letter that Dark Manuel's great-grandfather got from his brother in America. I never forgot it. The captain was so bad he kept the boys outside on deck all the time. Too much sun, too much cold. A boy from Fayal died one night."

"But if we made it across, we left them and worked hard for ourselves," Little Joao said, defending his position that good had come of taking the chance and leaving to work on the American whalers.

"Some were lucky," Antos admitted. "Some in my family were. The captain signed papers for them to enter America, even let them live in his house. Now their families come back sometimes. But that would never be for me. This is where I was born; this is where I will die."

"It was different then" Little Joao reflected. "There were times when the Portuguese wanted our children to fight their wars. To escape, our boys had to be rowed out to whaling ships at night, covered with blankets so no one would see them, their mamas and papas on shore holding each other in the wind and the cold, crying and knowing they would never see their boy again. Government officials were everywhere, trying to grab the children before they left." His voice quieted. "Who knows? Maybe they would have been better off in the navy than on the whaling ships."

"Better? Never *better*. A fourteen-year-old boy drafted to the colonies for three years when his family couldn't pay for a surrogate! Low pay. Worse conditions. So many died of starvation. All for the glory of Portugal." Antos had all of them nodding in agreement. They dredged up bitterness over the bygone Portuguese land tenure system, and how the Portuguese Empire had left them to starve when the potato blight that most Americans associate with Ireland reached the islands in the 1830s. Almost two centuries later, they still resented how their ancestors had been treated.

I slowed my steps and composed myself as I drew close to the rectory. Along the way, I prepared a story about my return visit, but other than a man washing windows, there was no one around and the door to the rectory was open. The brass key ring was still hanging from the hook on the wall, so I quietly unlocked the door that led to the basement and returned the keys to their place.

I sat awhile in the records room, cocooned with the ghosts of my family, listening to muffled voices and floorboards creaking overhead, and feeling safe. Eventually, I brought the records for the 1910s and 1920s to the table and began my search. The priest who had made the entries had a proclivity for adding notes in the margins. *He died on the same day as his sister. She would have died in America but the boat did not leave until the following week. Fifteen relatives were present when he died.* Next to the only entry for January, 1917, he had written: *Pray to God he will be the last to die in war.*

He had written nothing next to the obituários of my great-grandmother, Maria Umbelina, or Francisca Simas, her only daughter to remain on Pico. I returned the slim books to their shelf and, in the dim light, I sent the entire stack tumbling down. A folded paper between the last page and the back cover of one book was shaken loose and skittered across the floor.

When I bent to pick it up, I could see the pin holes at one end where it had been posted for the community to read. In flowery calligraphy, it was headed *Desceanze em Paz,* Rest in Peace, and under that *Perdido no Mar.* I knew before reading any further that my great-grandfather had been lost at sea. Matias Cabral was there, along with the names of a dozen other family members I had assumed left for America before my grandmother and her sisters were sent. All had the same notation: *23 setembro, 1897, entre Pico e São Jorge, no navio* Boa Viagem. Their boat, *Good Voyage,* had gone down in that narrow strait I looked out over every day, and no one had made it to shore alive.

I remembered that whaling and fishing were family ventures, male relatives pooling their resources and working together on the same boat. If it went down, all the men in an extended family would be lost, and the women left behind would have a hard time surviving, especially at a time when the lucrative vineyards and orange groves were dying. My great-grandmother would have had no choice other than to send her daughters to America, one by one, knowing she would never see them again.

Early one morning, I heard the unusual sounds of a crowd gathering nearby. I stepped out of my house just far enough to see across Dairy Road to Two Trees, where the family from Big Meadow was joining a group from the village and my neighbors to the east. They all carried large two-handled baskets or burlap bags.

The olive grove behind the house was the object of everyone's attention. People stood several feet away from the trees, looking alternately at the ground in front of them and at a tall young man, bare to the waist and wearing a white cloth around his head. He seemed to be carefully considering the trees and the people as he chewed on the inside of his mouth.

A teenage girl caught my eye and waved shyly. I overcame my first instinct to turn away with the pretense of not having seen her. Instead, I smiled back. It was at the same instant that she tapped the shoulder of a woman standing beside her and pointed to me. They both called out and signaled me to join them. I shook my head, which prompted the older woman to leave the group and, to my dread, walk across Dairy Road and up the steps to the eira with a speed surprising to see in such a short, heavy body. Her hair was wrapped in several layers of cloth, the padding giving her head a disproportionate bulge at the top.

"Come join us!" she called out loudly as she approached.

"No. No, thank you." I took a step back and made a half turn toward the house.

"Yes. Come, American lady," she said in heavily-accented English. She put an arm around my waist and guided me to the steps. I protested but lost ground when the younger woman reached the steps and nodded rapidly, looking at me and pointing to the trees.

"What is happening there?" I asked in Portuguese.

"It is a big olive year," the woman said, propelling me across Dairy Road.

"A big olive year?"

Having reached the large group, the woman set me free and headed back to the position she had originally occupied in the grove.

I heard a quiet voice by my side, "The trees are heavy with olives." The young woman pointed to the low branches in front of us where I could see hundreds of small purple and green ovals. I marveled at the twisted tree trunks with their sensuously rippled gray bark. They had probably been there a hundred years and would live much longer.

"Trees do not bear every year, and usually there is a big crop only every six or seven years." She spoke slowly and used hand gestures, in a kind attempt to communicate with someone she thought did not speak her language well.

My reserved response, just a slow nod and barely audible *hmm*, was not enough to convince her that my question had been answered. She explained further, "Most years we get only a few olives from the trees. Those we just eat." She mimed chewing and swallowing. "Some years, there are a lot of olives. Then we make oil."

"I understand," I said.

"The wind has already brought down a lot of olives from the trees."

I looked down at the ground around the trees and understood why everyone was keeping their distance; camouflaged in the soil and fallen leaves were hundreds of the small, dark fruits. "At least those don't have to be picked," I said.

"It is harder to get them out of the dirt," she stooped low several times and held a hand on her lower back, "but we have to get them up quickly or they will be damaged."

The older woman rejoined us and handed me a small burlap bag, "For you," she said.

I waved her off. "No. It's fine. I don't need one."

"You will get your share. Come. Come."

I don't know whether it was her insistence or an impulse born of weeks of solitary pursuits, but I pushed aside the curtain through which I had been observing life and stepped into the communal venture. I accepted the bag and spent the next three hours pushing my aching arms and back to their limits, bending over the ground and filling first the bag I was given and then an empty basket with the tiny fruits.

After the ground was tediously cleared of the olives that had dropped, canvas was laid around the base of each tree. Men climbed to the highest branches, and shook them or beat them furiously with sticks, letting loose a rain of the hard fruits, which were packed into more bags and baskets until the trees were emptied of all but the most tenacious olives.

Everyone filled cups with water or wine, and rested on the ground. I leaned against the side of the house, both to stretch my back and to steady myself. My eyes were still adjusting to long vision after sorting through leaves to find olives, when a metal cup filled with water appeared under my face. I looked up to see the shy teen who had explained the presence of the large gathering on Dairy Road. I thanked her and emptied the cup in one swallow.

She smiled.

"What is your name?" I asked her.

"Jacinta."

"Thank you, Jacinta."

She refilled my cup twice, and we stood together resting in the shade of the house. I watched as a fallen branch was picked up and displayed by the owner—his head unwrapped to show a tangle of orange curls. Two men peeled off the bark, examined it closely, and negotiated for its purchase.

"What are they buying the branch for?" I asked Jacinta.

"It is beautiful wood for carving. They will make holy things to sell in Madalena." She walked over to another woman, who was scolding a squirming child, and returned with a rosary cupped in one hand.

"It's lovely," I said, bending over her hand to look closely. The wood beads and crucifix were a pale greenish-tan with dark veins.

"Olive wood is holy," she said seriously.

I gave a noncommittal *mm-hmm.*

"The dove brought olive leaves to Noah to show the flood was over and peace was near, so olive trees are holy."

At another time and place in my life, I would have been the first to point out the faults of her statement. Instead, I suppressed an urge to do as I might have in the past and talk about the pagan symbolism of olive trees in everything from King Tut's tomb to the Olympiads of ancient Greece. I just smiled and nodded. *Did I no longer care about holding the line against the irrational?*

"We give the church its share of the oil, and the bishop consecrates it for the ordination of priests—," Jacinta continued, "—and to baptize and bury ordinary people like us."

Ordinary people. She drew the line between ordinary people and extraordinary people in a different place than I did.

The milk cart from Big Meadow was pulled over by two donkeys. Most of the olives were dumped into barrels on the cart, and the remaining baskets and bags were added to the load. Everyone followed the cart down toward Porto Velho, a small procession of dirt-streaked, sweat-stained people. I followed. I might have told myself that I was just carried away by the group, but I wanted to know what would come of all my labor. A greater truth was that I was also enjoying myself.

Where the road took a hairpin turn and started its steep descent to sea level, we took a narrow path that led to a windmill, one of the legacies of early Flemish settlers who had come to the islands to cultivate woad as an alternative to Indian indigo. Set on a white foundation, the upper stories and trim were painted in cheerful reds and blues, making it look like a child's toy in the distance. A long stairway coiling around the outside of the building led to a tiny balcony, where a man leaned against the railing and reached out to the thin blades creaking in a brisk breeze coming off the Atlantic. He took off his hat and waved it high in the air to greet us, before joining everyone to bring the olives into the large room at the base of the windmill.

I watched from a distance until Jacinta appeared at my side. "Come. You do not have to work. You cannot bring much oil back to America with you."

By then I had realized that the communal efforts would yield oil to be shared in some way that was known and accepted by all. "I don't need any oil," I said, thinking of the vast store of food I had amassed at Casinha Goulart.

"But you must take your share," she said, with the look of someone who could not conceive of an alternative. "Watch from here." She guided me to wood crates against a wall. "We could just sell the olives to a processor, but doing it this way helps us to remember the way our ancestors made oil."

The olives were descended on, picked through to remove any twigs and leaves, and carried in buckets to an enormous stone trough at the center of the windmill's base. A millstone rolled back and forth over the trough, pressing oil from the fruit. Pits were removed and more olives were added until thirty or so buckets were filled with brown liquid.

Opposite me, wood hoops, one side covered with wire mesh, were laid on top of each other to construct a column. The crude oil was poured over the top and filtered to yield a cloudy green liquid that was distributed into an assortment of glass bottles.

In a division of labor everyone understood, the activity subsided and the men sat and corked bottles, while the women did the backbreaking work of clearing away pits and other debris from the floor. I wondered if the gender inequality was meant to reflect traditional roles, or if it reflected the way roles continued to be.

Several burlap bags filled with whole olives were brought to the center of the room, and everyone gathered around with anticipation as they were handed out. Jacinta carried over two small baskets and gave one to me. "The best olives!" she said. "These are yours." I lifted one to my lips, but she gently pulled my hand down. "No. No. You cannot eat them now," she whispered. "First, they must soak in salt water for a few days.

Then my mama puts them in jars with herbs and orange peel. So good."

"I'll try that. Thank you." My share of the oil was far more than I needed, so I brought home just one small, thick-walled bottle, leaving the rest to Jacinta. My first thought was that I would save it for a special occasion but, as I set it on a shelf in my home on Dairy Road, I thought sadly that such a time was unlikely to come.

I knew I had deceived myself when I said I was going to Pico to complete my family tree. In truth, as the plane moved eastward, undoing the miles my ancestors had taken a century to cover, I was fleeing people and places I associated with sadness, and ending a life that had become unbearable.

I began a discussion with myself, pitting the peace I had found on Pico by having no emotions and no expectations against the frail hope of something I only remembered as happiness. If I opened myself up to feeling, would I risk being overwhelmed by sadness? Was I still capable of feeling joy?

Guided by some subconscious mechanism I trusted, I slowly followed a finger of fog as it sank down Dairy Road. I was going toward the shore.

It was low tide, the best time to find what has been dredged up by the opposing forces of buoyancy and gravity. I walked the hard-packed sand between the tidemarks, looking for something that could bring back a barely remembered emotion, and tell me if the experience was worth the risking everything else that might come of allowing myself to feel again.

I studied what I saw, straining to feel beauty. I picked a perfect shell from the water and examined the symmetry of its ruffled rim and the pearly blush of its underside. It was beautiful, but I felt nothing extraordinary and returned it to its tide pool. I found a feather caught in a tangle of dry seaweed, and ran the soft down over my lips and eyelids, closing my eyes and waiting to feel more than the physical sensation. There was nothing I couldn't account for as anything more than the transmission of impulses by touch receptors.

I was so intent on my mission, I had ignored the old saying: Never turn your back on the ocean.

It was the freshening wind that made me look around. A dusting of sand was swirling on the road above the beach. The clouds of insects that had hovered over the sand were gone, and the shore birds had fled. An approaching storm was exaggerating the onshore breezes that came off the strait as the sea air cooled in the late afternoon and forced its way inland, usually doing no more than gently buffeting my house on the hill and swaying small tree branches.

As I passed Porto Velho, the sky darkened, and a light rain began to fall. Boats had disappeared from open water; small ones were being dragged up on the beach, and larger ones slammed loudly into the dock. Tall, gunmetal clouds moved in and white foam netted dark green waves. Gulls screamed as they tried to stay their course, plummeting and rising on shifting thermal columns, keeping their balance by dipping one way and then the other.

Keeping my teary eyes half-closed against the fine grains of sand that hissed against my pants, I tried to race the squall home. Even fastened from hem to collar, my heavy wool cloak offered little protection; bitter gusts worked their way through buttonholes and down the neckline. I pulled up the hood and put my hands deep in the pockets, leaning against a wind that pulled strands of my hair loose more quickly than I could clear them from my field of view.

By the time I made it to Dairy Road, I was out of breath. I turned to see a deep darkness over the strait, and it was moving toward me. The pelt of grass behind Big Meadow snapped up and flattened in the steady wind. The late afternoon chattering and peeping of the birds had been silenced, houses were shuttered, laundry had been taken in, and the dogs were nowhere to be seen. In the few minutes it took to reach the eira, murky clouds gathered overhead and the light rain turned to a downpour, penetrating the wool of my cloak. Lightening sparked as a gust slapped me hard, and I barely caught myself from falling.

Before I could slam the front door shut, leaves swirled into the room and rain wet the wood floor. I latched the door against the wind and heaped all my clothes at the far end of the front room, hoping to keep the wet-sheep smell out of my bedroom. Naked, I toweled off and wrapped myself in the wool quilt.

Outside the front window, bolts of lightning made whitecaps glow on the choppy, dark waters between Pico and São Jorge, and wind launched fat raindrops against the windowpane, making sounds like the insistent knuckles of little children pleading for entry.

On the eira, mandevilla vines twisted like the tentacles of an octopus in a stormy sea, and their waterlogged petals collapsed into amorphous lumps. I saw two caterpillars on a leaf. Then they were gone. Virtually all of their species on Pico were fated to die that night. By slim chance, a few would survive. Their genes might have given them greater resilience in the storm; more likely, they would happen to be in a place where they would not be torn loose from life.

The storm transformed the familiar slough. Creeks that I had crossed easily a few days before were swollen. The waterline was near the tops of the highest stones, and cool water seeped in around laces of my shoes as I forded, my feet adding sucking sounds to the burbling. I veered south, following the bank to a narrow waterfall that ruffled the otherwise glassy surface of a small lake, misting the air, and beading overhanging ferns fronds.

New shoots poked through tangles of dead underbrush, thirsty vines crawled up damp tree trunks, and meadows burst green with new blades of grass. Moss carpets were fringed with the light green threads that would start the next life cycle. Birds looked for their morning meal and squabbled over fallen berries, all chirping, twittering, whistling, peeping, and chattering.

In this place, life flourished.

I caught myself smiling, not a conditioned reflex or the pretense I had long assumed masked my hidden torment, but something that rose from deep inside and gathered to light my face. What I had searched for at the beach just a few days before had found me.

Would the happiness—if that was what it was—vanish if not grounded on Pico? Or was I romanticizing the island, simply because it was removed from where I had once been?

The contentment I had once found in my lab, I now found on my eira; movies had been replaced by sunsets so vibrant no movie could have captured them; time in doctors' offices had returned to time on my own. Rather than restaurant meals and gourmet take-out, I ate simple food that I treasured with all my senses. I found the same pleasure in sheets that carried the scent of the rosemary bushes they had been dried over as I had once found in perfumed soaps and lotions. In the past, friends had gloried in ever-changing lives, charged with new places, new experiences, and new people. The rhythm of daily life in Porto Velho was comforting in its predictability.

If I felt happier on Pico, why shouldn't I stay? Just as the life that thrived around the waterfall, perhaps I was a species of the Pico ecosystem, one who needed the land and water and air— even the people—to survive. Thoughts of living out my life on Pico filled me as I returned to my home on the hill above Porto Velho until, in midstep, the sweet lightness left me.

I had remembered that a residency visa required an independent source of income. I had none.

My time on Pico was limited.

Happiness was playing its perennial game of hide-and-seek with me, reaching out to poke me with playful giggles and then dashing away too quickly for me to follow.

8

"Time for sleep, Annie."

"I like listening to the ocean, Nana.

"When I was a little girl, I fell asleep to the songs of the ocean and the stream outside my bedroom window."

"I like that."

"Sweet dreams, my love."

In my dream, twin question marks were planted in the grass I walked on and floated in the sky above my head. I reached out to flowers, only to have them twist into question marks and crumble to gray ash when I touched them.

My heart thumped as a series of tremors juddered the house. I was still floating in the miasma between sleep and consciousness, my mind tugged between fear of the present and the insistent memory of having seen those question marks in the past.

I had remembered one of the records of Francisca Simas, the one sister who remained on Pico. Below her name, where each of her children's names would have been listed, there were pairs of question marks, rather than the two names that usually recorded the birth of a child. A familiar frisson ruffled me.

Francisca Simas had had five children. Although finding the descendants of one of those nameless children would be close to impossible, it was not unlikely that the family house might have been passed down for three generations.

The exciting possibility drew me up a foothill that overlooked the town, carrying binoculars, notebook, and a pencil. I stopped at one of my favorite spots on the island, a flat outcrop where I liked to sit after a hike and enjoy the view of Porto Velho. I walked back and forth several times to find the best vantage points and started to map the area. My only clue to the location of the family house was a brief conversation with my grandmother. She had lived close to both the ocean and a stream. The majority of houses in Porto Velho were at sea level; some, such as my own, were on the hills rising from the harbor. I estimated the area that was close enough to hear the push and pull of the waves as my grandmother had, and drew the boundaries on a fresh page in my notebook.

Squinting through my binoculars, I could see four roads running parallel to the shore at increasingly higher elevations. Dairy Road was the shortest of the four, and the furthest from the center of town. I named the other three: Near Road, Far Road, and Long Road. All were connected by switchbacks and steep steps cut into the hillside.

I started by sketching the coastline and a few landmarks— the town square, the submerged craters to the west, a line of trees probably planted half a century earlier to mark the boundary of a farm, and the sharp turn of the coastline to the east. Then I carefully drew the roads on my map. Large trees broke them into dashed lines, and left gaps that hid everything below their canopies.

Slowly I moved my binoculars across the landscape, making a small box wherever I saw a house. Many of the ones I could see were old enough to have been standing a century before, but I had no way of knowing about the ones tucked away in hollows or screened by large trees. And I saw no streams nearby.

I knew there were more houses and streams hidden from view, and I needed a higher vantage point. I thought of a long-abandoned farm that I had come across on one of my walks. At the back of the property was a telltale mound of vegetation that marked the place of an old well, and a hut so thickly covered with vines that it was just a soft hummock. Just beyond, a thirty-foot pyramid of stones towered over the farm, its triangular surfaces frosted with moss and decorated with plant life. It was one of the *maroisis* made by early settlers who cleared their land by laying down a solid square of stones and then climbing on top of it to lay down another smaller square, repeating the process again and again. Eventually, they had to scramble to the higher levels with rocks bound in cloth strapped to their foreheads.

I put on my makeshift backpack and started to clamber up. The sharp rocks cut into my legs and arms, and even my hardened muscles had to strain to pull myself to the top. I thought of all the bleeding fingertips and aching backs, of all the hope that had gone into clearing the land and stacking the stones, and of all the tiny plants that had been nurtured to provide food on that land. Had someone done all that and then walked away, perhaps to emigrate and reach for another dream? Or had that person been broken by the land and died short of a dream?

I looked down fondly on what I thought of as my neighborhood. I could see the flat blanket of green starting at the back of the Big Meadow house and spreading east behind

Bodgerville and Casinha Goulart. I could make out the milk cart returning from town and a line of bright white sheets drying in back of The Vineyard. Such strong emotion filled me that I felt myself lifting off the grass and gliding down to my home on wings of air. I didn't want to live anywhere but Casinha Goulart. I didn't want to lose my neighbors or my village.

The elements that had defined my life had changed abruptly; but the transformation in me had been so gradual I was only aware of it in retrospect. I couldn't remember the screaming of fire engines, the intensity of neon lights, or the smell of hot city pavement. Phone numbers, microscope settings, and log-ins, all once firmly fixed in long-term memory, had faded away. The muscle memory of negotiating rush-hour traffic had atrophied. I had forgotten how to live that life.

My life was on Pico.

The view from the top of the maroisis revealed many more of the older houses that were built at sea-level, closer to Porto Velho. I added those and sat back, discouraged. None were near a stream. Nothing had come of my efforts.

Then, a glint of light to the east caught my eye, followed quickly by two more. I swung my binoculars to the area and scanned to find the source, a broken thread of light reflecting off a stream that ran alongside Near Road. I checked the boxes that showed the houses along that road, stuffed everything back into my bag, and scrambled down.

I walked the length of Near Road twice, holding back, both from a fear of appearing ridiculous and from a reluctance to end hope. It was a quiet part of town, with small stone cottages lining a narrow gravel road. Most seemed old enough, but only three were close enough to the stream to hear its quiet rippling. At the first one, an older woman was pulling weeds in a front garden. As I walked up, she wiped her hands on an already grimy apron and stretched her back while she watched me approach.

The odds were no one would know about a family that had lived there a hundred years earlier, but I savored a brief fantasy of success in the seconds it took to walk across the road and smile. "Excuse me. Do you know the house of Francisca Simas Henrique?" I used every name I could think of to spark a memory. I added, "She was the daughter of Maria Umbelina and Matias Cabral."

"Yes."

I assumed her response was just an acknowledgement of my presence, but one of my Portuguese lessons repeated itself in my head: It is rude to say *yes* unless answering a question. It dawned on me that she was saying she did know the house.

I wasn't aware that I had reacted visibly, but she came over to me and put her arm around my waist. "Do you want to sit?"

"No. No. Please, where is it?" I said softly.

"You need to rest. You are very pale."

I took a deep breath and did my best to reassure her. "Really, I'm fine."

"Not the first, but the second house that way," she pointed as she spoke. I thanked her and walked away on shaky legs.

I passed the first house, anticipation starving me for breath. By the time I reached the second house, my knees were weak. I slowed and prepared for disappointment. I told myself that the chance someone still knew the whereabouts of one of Francisca Simas's descendants was slim, bordering on none. I stopped by the side of the road and watched the house from a distance, trying to divine something about its inhabitants. I could hear splashes and gurgles as a subterranean watercourse emerged from the porous volcanic rock and ran past the house.

The sound of my knocking alerted someone, and I heard a muffled voice coming from behind the house. I followed a narrow cobblestone walkway at the side to a shady patio overlooking the ocean. It was a peaceful cocoon, sheltered by tall trees that had probably tapped into the same groundwater that fed the stream. The lush growth absorbed all sounds but the burble of the stream and the distant shush of the waves. Retaining walls on either side were softened here and there by flowering vines, and an old well at the center was ringed by pitted and mossy stones. Overhanging leaves left a natural picture window at the far end that took in a flat stretch of milky-blue ocean and a ghostly São Jorge, opalescent-gray in the haze at the horizon.

There, a woman sat in a rocking chair. I took a few steps and stood by the well, absently stroking the moss. "Come closer," she said. "It's hard to hear when you are old, and I am very old." She cracked a smile at her little joke.

When I reached the chair, I sat on my haunches to look her directly in the face. "I am looking for the house of Francisca Simas. I am related to her. Her husband was—"

"José Henrique. I remember him."

I clenched my jaw to keep from crying. "Did they live here?" I patted the ground.

"Yes."

"Is this—," I had to stop to catch my breath, "—is this where she grew up?"

"Yes." She wrinkled her brow as if trying to remember something and added, "Her father built all this when she was just a baby."

I looked up at the house. I was where my grandmother had once been, outside the house where she had been born. When I turned back, the woman's eyes had closed. I touched the papery skin of a stick-thin arm and said softly, "I am Ann. Francisca was my great-aunt." Her eyes opened, but she looked confused. I repeated, "I am Ann."

She stretched her lips and showed toothless gums. "My name is Rosaria," she said, but the words sounded rote.

I searched for my answers slowly, knowing I was working against an aging mind. "What happened to José Henrique?"

"He moved to Lajes."

"What happened to Francisca? I waited. "Francisca Simas, his wife," I prompted.

"Francisca died. So young. She died." That I already knew.

"What about their children? What happened to their children?"

"Five children."

Yes. I knew. I wanted the woman to give me something I didn't know. "Do you know where their descendants might be?" I asked gently, trying to control the sound of desperation in my voice.

She shook her head slowly. "Descendants?"

I started from the beginning again. "Francisca Simas and José Henrique had five children. What happened to their children?"

"There was only Xavier." She kissed her fingertips and made the sign of the cross.

"What happened to the children?" I raised my voice. I was doubting everything she had said. There were five children. But there was only Xavier. "Do you know anything about their descendants?"

"How could they have descendants, my dear? They were children."

It was like one of those line drawings in which you can't see the figure everyone else does; then, when you finally do, it's impossible not to see it. I had dug out the area around Francisca Simas's grave and replaced the small square markers, cross side up in an orderly array between her stone and that of my great-grandmother. I had found four, no more. They belonged to four children who had died before they were baptized with names. They were children who could have no descendants.

"What about the fifth? What happened to Xavier?" I had startled her. She looked confused. "What happened to Xavier?" I asked more quietly.

She made the sign of the cross again. "He was a good father to many. Come. I will show you."

I stood quickly to make room for her. She shuffled into the house, leaning heavily on a walking stick. I followed. I watched her footsteps closely, ready to catch her if she tripped and started to fall.

The low rays of direct sun lit a large room, clean and tidy. The woman placed her walking stick on top of a large chest of drawers and steadied herself. She bent over and opened a drawer with shaking hands. When she raised her head, her eyes moved slowly from side to side and I could see she was disoriented, perhaps suffering from some type of dementia.

I held my breath until she nodded crisply and uttered a barely audible, "Oh." She took out a large packet of letters tied together by a length of lace, looked at them, and then at me. Her brow knit and again she nodded to herself. Her face was blank.

I was too close to lose. "Are those for me?" Without waiting for a reply, I took the envelopes from her. I looked directly into her milky eyes, and said slowly and clearly, "What happened to Xavier?"

A glimmer of light appeared in her eyes and faded again. I followed her back to the patio, where she sat and stared at the graying ocean.

I reached deep into the green flowered tin to pinch the tea. It was already half gone, as was my time in the house. The ritual of preparing and sipping it had become so tied to the respite I had found on Pico itself, I couldn't imagine going on without it. I poured steaming water over the leaves and set the cup at the far end of the table.

I took the letters from the pocket of my cloak. Damp had settled in the paper, and the heat from the fire vaporized a familiar scent to my nose, a blend of the witch hazel and lavender that my grandmother had used. At least, that was what I imagined.

I untied the lace ribbon, spread the letters on the table, and took a few steps back. There was no need to hurry. I sipped the hot tea and looked at the envelopes from a distance. George Washington's profile adorned the upper right corners in small squares of blue, red, or green. About half were postmarked *San Diego, California, U.S.A.*, and the rag paper on some of them had been softened and creased by many hands.

Dear Francisca,

   You cannot imagine this country of America! As the ship came closer to land, we crowded on the deck to see a magical city with buildings that looked like giant pillars of stone descended from the heavens, some topped with needles so tall they pierced the clouds overhead. We were taken by boat to an island built on landfill from the tunnels they are making to carry people on trains underneath the city of New York. Such a clever idea!

   Thousands waited with us to ask for entry, pressed close together, since a fire has destroyed the large building where immigrants used to go. So many languages were spoken, but even the little English we were taught by our uncles was not needed. A man from Fayal translated for us as we were checked by a doctor and questioned by customs officials. Luis Machado met us as arranged, and now we await our new lives in the house he has just finished building.

   Francisca, dear sister, I know you wanted to travel to America. You are the best among us for staying to care for Mama and Grandmama. Perhaps you will join us one day.

   Maria Rita
   4-1899

Dear Grandmama and Mama,

Maria Rita and I have arrived in America. From the ship, I could feel the connection to Porto Velho through the boards under my feet, that if only I could reach over the railing and push against the water, some small movement would be felt on the shore where my loved ones stood. As our island faded into the fog, the thread that joins us stretched thinner and thinner, but it will never be so fragile that it breaks.

This country is large. As we crossed it, I kept thinking that every hour takes us so much farther from home. We are now in a place in California called La Jolla. So many from Porto Velho are here, so I can find some comfort in seeing the faces of others who once walked our beautiful roads with us and knelt beside us in church. At dinner, I sit quietly just to bask in the sweet sounds of our language. Sometimes, it does not feel much different from home, except that you and my sisters are missing.

Maria Vitória
4-1899

Dearest Mama,

My sister tells me the sadness will fade but I cannot imagine any happiness away from my home. Early in the morning, I walk far from the land where all the exiles from Porto Velho are building their houses. I face east and scream my love to you. I imagine a whisper of my voice carrying in the wind to you.

Does Grandmama understand that we are not gone to a distant village from which we can return? Perhaps it is best that she does not know. She is already weakened by our absence, and I fear she will be with God soon. You and Francisca must be all for her now.

I will be married soon. My husband will be the brother of cousin Luis's wife. He is coming from Porto Velho soon with our dear sisters. They will bring news of our family. I miss you so. I pray to God every night that we will all be together again, even Grandmama. Tell her to find the strength for the trip, and we will take care of both of you forever.

Maria Vitória
5-1899

Dear Francisca,

 I am to be married to a cousin of Luis's wife, just like Maria Vitória. He is very old, almost forty, but I am told he has much money, so it will be good for me. Maria Vitória will marry one week later, but her husband will be younger. He will have his own tuna fishing boat, too.

 Luis says Maria Rosella and Francisca Rosa will join us in a few months. We are excited. I wish you and Mama could come to live with us.

Maria Rita
7-1899

Dear Mama,

 We are in California at last and so glad to have the journey behind us. California is also a good place, Mama. The land and sea here look much like Pico, but everything else is very different. A short cart ride away is the city of San Diego, with grand libraries, schools, and hotels, and trains that cross the city, not drawn by horses but by "electricity."

 I do not like the man who cousin Luis has already chosen as my husband. He speaks too loud and drinks too much. Maria Vitória says I must accept it, and Maria Rita tells me he will be away fishing so much that I will not mind.

 I think of how with one small turn of fate, my life would have been very different. If Papa had not gone to São Jorge that day, I might still be with you in Porto Velho.

Maria Rosella
3-1900

Dear Mama and Francisca,

I am working hard to learn more English. As Uncle Francisco wrote: The ones who know English will have a better life. *I have already made a small amount of money helping the children of a widower from São Jorge with their numbers. Luis says the man wants to marry me, but I have said no. No one is happy with me, but I do not care. I give Luis half of what I earn and tell him it is all I have. Then he is satisfied for a while.*

It is hard to accept we will not see each other again in this life.

Francisca Rose
5-1900

Dearest Mama,

Everyone speaks of looking to the future in this new place, but I am like you, Mama. My life in Porto Velho was more to me than inventions and comforts. I would rather have starved in poverty with you than lived apart from you.

Maria Vitória
5-1900

Dear Mama,

You are a grandmother! I have a healthy son who is named Joao. Papa would be so proud.

Maria Vitória is ill with pregnancy. Her husband and brother-in-law are building a house next to mine but the men are away fishing so much, it goes very slowly. When they are at sea, Maria Vitória stays with me, so she does not have to live in the tent.

Maria Rita
5-1900

Francisca,

 We are anxious for Emelia. Luis says only that she left Porto Velho but will not join us. Please write to tell us the news.

 All our houses sit next to each other by another ocean, so we can talk every day. We are both pregnant again. Maria Rosella is not happy with the husband Luis chose. They fight.

Maria Vitória and Maria Rita
4-1901

Francisca,

 We are very worried. Emelia has not arrived. Luis and Lula bought a dairy farm to the north in California and moved away. They do not answer us when we write about Emelia. What shall we do?

Mary Rita, Maria Vitória, Maria Rosella, Rose
9-1901

The frequency of the letters did not change as the years passed. They added a missing emotional dimension to the story I had uncovered: marriages and the birth of children; the construction of roads, boats, and houses; illnesses and deaths; Maria Rosella's divorce and her futile struggle to reclaim her children; the start and success of a tuna fishing industry; Rose's first steps in what would become a successful career; the deaths of the grandmother and mother they never lost hope they would see again; and assimilation into a new country. Through it all, the sisters had each other and, through it all, they wondered and worried about the sister who had vanished.

I reached for a knife and slit open the envelope of the one letter from California that had not been read.

> *Dear José Henrique,*
>> *We cannot find the words for this letter. Our dear sister Francisca taken by God so young. She suffered so in trying to have a child. Perhaps she felt that with the birth of Xavier, she had done what God wanted her to do in this life. Now she is with Mama, and we are without both of them.*
>> *We continue to search for our Emelia. Luis says only that she has had good fortune, and it is better for her to have no contact with us.*
>> *We wish you the best in your new life in Lajes with our nephew, Xavier.*
>> *Mary Rita, Maria Vitória, Maria Rosella, Rose*
>> *2-1913*

Three generations lived before me. Each saw immigration in a different way. My great-great-grandmother could not conceive of places unlike her own village. Her daughter chose to stay on Pico despite knowing what others worlds offered. Of the six sisters, only Francisca Simas was destined to remain where she was born, her curiosity unsatisfied.

Maria Rita, whose letters reflected the anticipation with which she approached shores of America, kept one foot in the culture of her birth and the other in her new world. Despite one marriage to a man more than twice her age and another that ended tragically, she had made a success of her life, raising ten children, and running two businesses.

I remembered the few records I had found on Maria Vitória. Only geography changed for her; she lived her entire life Picoense, never becoming an American citizen, teaching Portuguese at her church, and surrounded by mementos of the home she was forced to leave behind.

Maria Rosella came to America with as much eagerness as Maria Rita, but ultimately she was defeated by an abusive husband and a foreign culture she did not understand, losing her children and her life.

Rose was the most forward-looking of the sisters, an unmarried American career woman, long before that was widely accepted. Still, the letters showed that she and all the sisters kept Pico in their hearts—something my mother did not do.

In the generation that followed, my mother purged her heritage from our lives to cope with what she saw as the stigma of my grandmother's immigrant status. I was left rootless, disconnected from the essence of those who had created me. To moor myself, I had reached back and embraced the culture of my past.

I drained my cup of the last of the cooled tea and sat.

I recognized the smooth loops and lines of my grandmother's handwriting from the cards and letters she had sent me in the years we had together. In the upper left corner of each unopened envelope, she gave the return address of the Gloucester house she had claimed for herself and her children. On some, her oldest sister's address was simply *Francisca Simas; Porto Velho; Pico, The Western Islands*; on others, it was detailed with directions to the house and the names of relatives. I saw those were sent later, probably when the desperation to find her family was at its height, and her hope was at its lowest point. I arranged the letters chronologically, wiped my hands on my pants, and took a deep breath.

> *Dear sister,*
>
> *Did you and Mama give up hope of hearing from me? Are you both well? I am alone.*
>
> *All the years with Mrs. Garland, I only thought of the day I would be free to write to you. I am married now, worth it if only for the freedom to walk to the post office and mail this letter to you.*

Luis told me I was the fortunate sister because of my fair hair and green eyes, and because my English was best. Mrs. Garland was getting old and wanted a little girl. She was good to me except for not allowing me to write. So many times I begged for the money to buy a stamp. So many times I wrote a note and mailed it in an old envelope, hoping it would find its way to you and Mama without a stamp.

I pray to God I will hear from you soon.

Emelia
2-1913

Dearest Francisca,

I hope this letter finds you and Mama. Please write to me if it does.

I am afraid that Philip, who is my husband, will find a letter from you before I have the chance to take it from the morning delivery. He is Mrs. Garland's nephew and must know what was done to all of us. Now I fear I will never hear from you again.

Please answer soon. I am with child and still alone.

Your loving sister,
Emelia
3-1914

Dear Francisca,

Please write to me. I am so worried you and Mama are not well. I was shopping yesterday and heard two women speaking our language, so I went to them directly. I cried when they told me they are from the islands. They will ask about you.

Tell Mama she has a granddaughter, who has been named Estelle Mae.

As always, I send you my love.

Emelia

9-1916

My dear sister,
How can I go through the rest of my life not knowing where my family is? I only survived all the years in Boston by thinking of the day I would hear from you again. I miss you every hour of my life. Please, please, dear Francisca, write to me.
I have another child. Philip has little interest in him. He is not in the house much, and he drinks a lot. I remember how Mama never allowed drinking in the house except when Father Leandro came. He said her wine was the best on the island. I have so many memories but no one to share them with.

Amelia
7-1919

Dearest Francisca,
I have not heard from you. Are you well? Know that I always love you. Will we only be together again in God's house?

Amelia
4-1921

Dear Francisca,
Philip drinks all the time now. He has never been kind to me, but it is worse now. Our neighbors called the police many times, and I have talked to them, too. He left early this morning and I do not expect him to ever return. I am humiliated but far less than his mother. She is in the house from early morning to late at night, always saying the same thing: Do not tell anyone.

Amelia
12-1922

Dear Francisca,

> *Yesterday I met Philip's mother at the front door but did not let her in. I was shaking with fear, but I told her that she was not invited to my house. She wanted me to tell the police that Philip is a good man, and I said no. She threatened to have me removed from the house.*

> *Being a mother has given me courage. I told her to have the house put in my name by the end of the day, or I would walk all over town with the children and let everyone know what Philip has done. In exchange for telling the police that Phillip should not go to jail, a messenger delivered the deed to the house that day.*

> *It is only a small comfort, for I am mostly sick with sadness about you and Mama.*

> *Why do you not write?*

> *Amelia*
> *2-1923*

Dearest sister,

> *I have had my baby and chosen the name Clara Mae. I am alone with my children. I dream of having my sisters and Mama near to me, but I fear now that will never be. You will never be gone from me completely, though. I promise our past will continue in my descendants.*

> *Saudade.*

> *Amelia*
> *1-1924*

On the table, lives were compressed and ended with wounds unhealed, tears still fresh, hope unfulfilled. In my grandmother's life, the victory of a deed, the joy of births, the pride of citizenship, and the consolation of acceptance had all been framed by losses she was powerless to overcome. She had been taken from a place where she was surrounded by people who loved her to the isolation of living with people who knew nothing of her language or her customs, who did not offer the food she loved or celebrate holidays as she did. And her own family seemed to have turned its back on her. Any happiness that I might have found in uncovering what had happened to my grandmother was not possible.

I bundled the letters together and put them with my notebook. I picked at the tape on the inside back cover of the notebook and peeled it off to release the flat packet wrapped in two layers, first in its original paper, browned and brittle, and then in the snowy white rice paper I had bought. Inside was a tintype of my grandmother at twenty. There she stood, straight-backed, slim, and serene, her skin flawless and her thick, wavy hair caught up under a broad-brimmed hat trimmed with ribbon. Looking with new eyes, I could see the sadness behind her slight smile and in her gentle eyes.

The tiny shop in Porto Velho that was crammed with statues of saints and olive wood rosaries came to mind. Side by side on the wall with pictures of Jesus and Mary were pictures of Father Xavier, such an unusual name in the islands. "He is one of us, born right here in Porto Velho," the woman had said. I remembered thinking how much he looked like my grandmother. And the last thread in my family tapestry was knotted.

There would be no one to entrust the tapestry to. No trace would remain after I died. The last hope, the son of Francisca Simas and José Henrique, became a priest and certainly died childless, as I would. No one would care for the family graves. No one would give thanks for the sacrifices and the love. No one would remain to cherish the tintype of my grandmother, a beautiful young woman glowing with hope for a future that would prove so difficult. It would slowly corrode and disappear, as if it had never been.

Miriam Winthrop

9

"Who is the pretty lady, Nana?"

"That is a picture of me when I was very young."

"Can I have it?"

"It is yours to keep and to give to your child."

I had no particular interest in having someone special in my life when Lee and I met at a symposium on ethical issues in genetic engineering. Long before the first speaker was scheduled to start, we claimed our places in one of the conference rooms of a large and impersonal city hotel. As we revealed over dinner a few nights later, we had chosen our seats not to be close to the dais but so that on the way out, we could avoid a lobby crowded with television reporters who seemed to lack any understanding of our field.

While we waited for the speaker to begin, we advanced from brief, neutral comments to sharing subjective reflections. We frowned on those around us who voiced their complaints about the crowded, overheated room, and were among those who could ignore our glum surroundings when the first fascinating PowerPoint slides lit the room.

As we chatted between speakers, a concert played in my head. The comfort of solidarity with someone who held similar views. The challenge of intellectual dialogue, simultaneously listening with pleasure and gathering thoughts for the repartee. His wit and my own ability to match it with well-crafted remarks. The miracle of how I—typically reserved with those I did not know well—was so much at ease with him. And the even greater miracle of his attention.

The child of a petite Indonesian mother and a strapping Dutch father, Lee defined blended inheritance. My field of view was filled with his golden skin, dark-fringed amber eyes that crinkled at the corners, and the small patch of stubbled skin where his razor had skipped over the cleft on his chin. Even when he was not smiling, he looked like he was about to.

"Just yesterday, a woman writing a script for some crime show called to ask me how easy it would be for a criminal to clone herself." His laughter caught in the back of his throat.

"Don't tell me," I continued for him, "she wanted a twin who could be blamed for her evil deeds."

He laughed again. "She just didn't get it when I tried to explain that even if it were possible, by the time her twin was the age she is now, she would be twice as old.

"It got worse." He paused for effect, raised his eyebrows, and said in mock seriousness, "The criminal was going to name her clone *Dolly!*" The first mammal to be cloned from a single adult parent, *Dolly the Sheep* was the superstar of the cloning world in those days.

Our guffaws attracted more attention than either of us wanted, and we headed down a hallway with thick carpeting to muffle sounds and dim sconces to mask the spare, utilitarian furnishings.

I was still dabbing tears from my eyes when we reached the upholstered bench where we settled.

"Do you know why she was named Dolly?" Lee asked.

"No." I loved trivia, and I had already talked to him long enough to know the answer was going to be funny.

"She grew from a mammary gland cell," he said, trying to keep a straight face, "and the lead researcher said he was really impressed with Dolly Parton's mammary glands." Our laughter carried up and down the hall.

As we walked back to the presentation, which had already started, we found we had one more thing in common. We loved being able to apply the knowledge we revered to solve real world problems. Cloning was interesting; using it to save endangered species—perhaps even to bring back an extinct one—was spectacular.

During the lunch break, we both turned down the reheated coffee, warm Coke, and stale sandwiches left out on tables in the lobby. Lee said he would rather not eat than waste his appetite on food he didn't enjoy. I agreed and mentioned I was planning to stop at a great deli to get takeout for dinner, an idea I came up with on the spur of the moment, hoping he would respond as he did. A shift in his weight brought him closer to me. "I'd like to join you," he said.

The first afternoon session focused on mathematical models that were used to determine the relative contributions made by the environment and by genes, adding fuel to the nature-nurture debate that had found its way into social concerns, political matters, and legal decisions. Lee proposed an unsettling question to the speaker. It stunned me because it was what precisely what I wanted—but was too reticent—to say.

"How much praise is yours to keep, and how much condemnation is yours to own?" He had stood and towered over me.

"We can agree that there is an element of fortune—good or bad—in the world a child is born into, the adults who people his world, and the chance events that take place around him," he went on. I thought of a child who got the caring teacher or the abusive one, or another who witnessed a selfless act of heroism or a drive-by shooting.

Lee spoke with authority. "There are also elements of fortune—some obvious, some subtle—in the random assortment of genes a person inherits." Someone gave the familiar example of Down Syndrome that would deny a child the chance of a law career, and a another geneticist described a collagen variant that gave a girl the extraordinary flexibility needed to be a Thai dancer.

"How responsible is the violent offender when he is born with abnormally high levels of testosterone? How much credit can the seven-foot basketball player, the music prodigy, or the mathematics genius lay claim to?" Lee challenged the room. I had proposed similar arguments in published papers, but never in public.

In the next session, Lee argued in favor of treating medical conditions by altering DNA rather than by treating them with invasive surgery or toxic drugs. After the discussion had moved on to other arguments, I felt comfortable enough to whisper my own opposing opinion to him. Although we could cure disease and even better the gene pool by changing defective genes, doing so risked eliminating a collateral gene that might hold the key to surviving a nuclear holocaust or the next Ebola virus.

Our first date lasted seven hours, taking us from the search for a good place to share our baguette sandwiches through window shopping on Santana Row—the Rodeo Drive of San Jose—to coffee and pastries at a bakery, where the hints that it was time to go became a firm request that we leave. Through it all, long stretches of contentment were punctuated with moments during which I wondered at how happy I was.

I hesitated only once, when he asked the open-ended question: Who is Ann Parker? As an adult, I had voiced who I was many times, in language I periodically adjusted, sometimes to read like a line on a résumé, sometimes like a line in a personal ad. I was a geneticist who worked on the cutting edge of a new technology; I was a transplanted New Yorker who liked living in California; I enjoyed being with people who shared my passion for science; I liked being alone with good books and with the ocean. My life was both reflected by those phrases and molded to fit them, but the words were an insubstantial scaffold, and I remained only partially defined, a vital truth just out of reach. I replied, "You'll have to find out," when the truth was that *I* had yet to find out.

Lee was a good match for me in many respects. We saw the world in the same way, a place made awe-inspiring by the hidden worlds of atoms and the energy that made it up. We approached life in the same way, relying on data and applying rigorous reasoning to make decisions and determine values. That same way of thinking had led us to related careers, his in applied forensics at a lab less than a quarter mile from my own, and it had given us mutual respect. It was the respect that carried us through more and for a longer time than might have been true for other couples.

We dated for only a short time before—without a proposal that either of us could ever remember—we just accepted that we would be married, and started talking about what sort of wedding we wanted and whether we should buy a house right away. A long engagement seemed unnecessary.

Looking back on the early years of our marriage, time seemed elastic, days and nights, weekends and vacations, expanding to hold so much comfortably that, when it ended, I doubted it had all been possible. Sixteen waking hours stretched to accommodate full days of work in the lab, preceded by workouts, followed by dinners with friends, and interspersed with errands and coffee with colleagues. There was time for books, movies, restaurants, and window shopping. There were vacations when hours were spent snorkeling or touring architectural wonders, all without sacrificing anything else on long lists of planned activities. There were last minute drives to Napa or Monterey, when I happily lost myself in kayaking or antiquing, hot air ballooning or sampling wines. Somehow, time was accommodating.

Then time lost its suppleness. Like a shelf giving way, it happened quickly and in slow motion. I moved aside parts of my life to make room for the solitude that had become my refuge from unrelenting blows, the load shifted, and everything collapsed, leaving nothing but rubble, and I had no energy or desire to rebuild.

I had lived in a world where accomplishment was measured in academic degrees, tech savvy, and cutting edge ideas, a world peopled by scientists, dot-com successes, and thinkers who took pride in challenging the status quo and shaping a different world, and I was fiercely proud of my role in that world. A woman of my time, I lived on the cusp of a bright, new future.

Although some of my friends made forays into domesticity with bread baking or knitting, they were secondary to lives in front of computer screens and mass spectrophotometers. It was understood that more would have been a waste of intellect.

I hid the life I dreamed of. Next to research papers I had authored and micrographs of dividing nuclei, I kept a folder filled with ideas for family-friendly activities and recommendations about nutrition during pregnancy. I sometimes struggled to reconcile the two aspects of my persona—aspects that those around me might see as mutually exclusive.

When I married Lee, I saw our life together in well-defined stages, starting a family in our twenties, spending our thirties and forties enjoying soccer games, piano recitals, and school plays, watching our children graduate from college and marry in our fifties, and being doting grandparents in our sixties. In places, that mental armature was fleshed out with details that went beyond what might be expected of a young newlywed. I loved thinking about remodeling a 1950s bungalow to accommodate a growing family, the way to celebrate our twentieth wedding anniversary, and our first extended family vacation, crossing the Atlantic in a boat to reach the Azores.

Over the years, the relative proportion of time allotted to each stage and the importance I attached to it shifted, the child-raising years compressing as I passed out of my twenties and through my thirties. I gave up opportunities for fellowships, lost interest in the career path I had mapped, eliminated adventures to foreign lands, making adjustments—or so I told myself—to accommodate the key desire to have a child. Eventually, I could not imagine any happiness at all without children, and my idea of bliss shrank to singing lullabies, drinking from mugs that read *I love Mom*, hanging macaroni-encrusted Christmas ornaments, and passing on family stories to a large and loving family.

Even surrounded by people who inhabited the same limbo I did and could understand the shaky common ground we stood on, I felt like an outsider. In waiting rooms, other women talked among themselves about lives beyond trying to become pregnant, and chuckled over the indignities of producing specimens for analysis and the constant probing of their private parts. They seemed to have a nonchalance that in my mind reflected a lack of dedication, and when talk turned to the alternative of adoption, I told myself they didn't understand commitment and sacrifice; they were unwilling to endure what was required. I irrationally resented those who already had a child for taking up some of the available fertility in the world, and when one by one, each disappeared from the regular morning lines for blood work and sonograms, I hated them alternately for having achieved what I could not or for having given up. Every mother, every pregnant woman, became a declaration of what I was denied, and a condemnation of how I had failed in that, too.

I had no outdated notion that a child should come only from the tender expression of physical love and not from medical intervention. I was thrilled about the opportunities that existed, and I spent hours researching the latest advances, investigating fertility specialists, and calculating odds. My eyes skimmed over possible side effects and low pregnancy rates to focus on isolated cases of success. Intervention escalated. I turned over large parts of my life to taking pills, monitoring my temperature, biopsies, injections, surgeries, and ultimately IVF attempts, every detail carefully tracked in the notebook with the green-for-life cover.

Early on, Lee tried to cushion me from making too high an emotional investment. "If it's meant to happen, it will."

"What do you mean, 'If it's meant to happen'? You wouldn't say that about your car. If it's meant to run smoothly, it will happen."

He took it. "I just don't want you to be upset."

"I'm already upset, most of all by your attitude. You could care less. You don't even want a child."

He was calm. "I do. But my life will be fine without one."

"Fine. *Your* life will be fine. Well, that's the most important thing, I guess." I stomped away and spent the rest of the day feeling terrible about what I had said to the one person I could count on.

I told myself I had to conserve my time and energy, so I turned down invitations to dinner and begged off long-planned vacations. I stopped reading the latest bestsellers, no longer found joy in music, gave up planning gourmet meals, dropped my gym membership, and let weeds claim my garden. Cycles of hope and failure filled years. We faced the same two words every time: unexplained infertility. "Meaning *you* can't figure it out!" I once shot back.

When—as the doctors foretold—I miscarried, not once but four times, it was not as devastating as others might have thought. The first time, I confided in a couple of close friends and Lee told his mother. Everyone offered exactly the support recommended in magazine articles and blogs, telling us how sorry they were, telephoning daily for the first week, and then trying to distract us with invitations to dinner or the movies. The truth was I didn't feel in need of any sympathy. The miscarriages felt close to victory, proof that pregnancy was possible, and something I could point to at doctors' appointments as good reason to continue trying. Worn down and hardened, I carried on without emotional investment.

For a long time after medical intervention started to claim more of me than he could, Lee fought to save the peaceful, sane marriage we had once planned together. After that failed, he fell back on his kind nature and continued to serve my dream. Unable to take my anger out on doctors or bosses, I took it out on him. Nothing he did was quite right. To my mind, he wasn't concerned enough, never tried hard enough. By the time I started looking into adoption, doing it with my usual thoroughness and commitment, he was less than enthusiastic about having a child. I had started to lose him, because he had lost me.

Despite contrived rallies, our sex life was terminal. Pouring the wine or lighting the fire were only tasks to serve the greater good. There was little thrill in putting on lacey lingerie and, for Lee, little thrill in taking it off. He knew he was under pressure to fulfill his responsibilities at specific times, regardless of the circumstances. He eventually became irrelevant to my mission—or so he must have thought—valued as the contributor of something I could have just as easily purchased for less than $100.

Ultimately, I relinquished my self. Already vulnerable from abandonment and loss, the regimented struggle separated me from what had given me confidence and joy. My time in the lab was curtailed by races down the highway for early morning tests, emergencies I fabricated on procedure days, and feigned illnesses when it was time for an embryo transfer. My moods rose and fell as regularly as my chemically controlled cycles. I could not let my guard down. In the two weeks leading up to ovulation, a cup of coffee might interfere with conception. In the two weeks after, a glass of wine might cause me to lose a child I was carrying before its presence was even known.

As time passed, I ricocheted between optimism and despair so quickly, they merged. I got through days at work and evenings at home with my mind in the past or the future, a cloud of self-recrimination and desperation hanging over me.

It all seemed a small price to pay for atonement.

10

I passed the front of the Bodgerville cottage every time I started a hike toward the interior and every time I returned home. I always slowed to try to catch a glimpse of the occupants through the Dutch door, the bottom closed and the top open even when it rained. The house, oddly facing the hills and not the strait, seemed to be an afterthought in the landscape, two small buildings primitively cobbled together on a scrap of land wedged between Big Meadow and my own place. One roof was so low I could have easily reached up and touched it, and the stubby chimney was an archaic construction littered at its base with fallen stones. The only two windows were without glass and framed by rickety shutters, but even when they were open, the interior of the house was so dark I could never see what was beyond them.

The dogs were the most visible sign that Bodgerville was occupied, but there were others in laundry left out to dry, the smell of frying fish, and sounds that crossed the short distance between us. I knew young children lived in the house; I had heard crying and babbling. Late at night, a woman's ethereal voice sometimes drifted to me in the wind. I never caught the words, but I knew she sang of sorrows.

One day I saw her. A delicate-looking woman in her early twenties was casting grain in front of three chickens that pecked furiously at the ground and each other. I kept my eyes on her as I picked my way down the hill, returning from the waterfalls with that pleasant blankness I had come to crave, anxiety suppressed to leave a haze that knew little more than the motion of my legs and the sounds around me. She wore rough black pants, and her hair was tied back and covered with a white cotton scarf. Small-boned and fair-skinned, she reminded me of a girl in a Vermeer painting.

I raised my arm in greeting, slipping a bit on the rocks underfoot as I did. The woman stared at me like a peculiarity she was trying to resolve in her mind, and the children were clearly startled, the older one running to his mother and the toddler holding on to her pants. She waved back slowly, as if it was an unfamiliar gesture, and fixed me in her sights as I came closer, squinting to compensate for what must have been nearsightedness. The chickens also gathered near her feet, and clucking added to the crying of the two children. The encircled woman looked defeated.

"I'm sorry I frightened them." I gave her a half smile and waited. "My name is Ann." I waited, hoping she would respond with some recognition that I lived only a hundred yards from her. "I am renting the Goulart house for a while."

She seemed satisfied and pried the two children from her sides. "Welcome," she said with a slight nod.

"I thought I would say hello." I backed away, "I see you are busy."

Her response was quick. "Please don't go! Please have some tea."

I looked down at a still-full laundry basket. "Perhaps I could help you hang the clothes, first." She smiled, and tossed a handful of feed into a wood enclosure to draw in the chickens before closing the gate behind them. Together we snapped sheets and smoothed clothes, pinning them on a rope strung between the side of the house and a tree trunk, until the line sagged and the basket was empty. While we worked, I watched her older son who, although somewhere around six, had the same movement and language skills as his much younger brother, but was even more demanding of his mother's attention, balling his fists tightly and making short yelping noises when not immediately satisfied.

She introduced herself as Maria Cecilia, and invited me to sit on the cushion on a large boulder at the side of the house. Making several trips, she brought out a teapot, two mismatched flowered cups, slices of sweet bread, two jars with small amounts of jam at the bottom, a large wedge of deep amber cheese, and a small round of bright white cheese speckled with herbs. She seemed at a loss for what to say, and busied herself pouring the tea and silently offering me food.

"Have you lived here a long time?" It was all I could think of to put her at ease.

"I came with my husband after my first baby was born." She nodded at the boy who was sitting on the grass eating from an unsliced loaf of bread. She spoke as though she was confiding a secret, "My husband died last winter from an infection."

"I'm sorry," I said, and I meant it. "I didn't know you were alone."

She bit her lip and tears wet her lower lashes. "I take the children to see him every Sunday after Mass."

"Do you have other family here?"

"I am from São Miguel, but I have no close relatives left there." She looked out at the hill, lost in her own thoughts for a while.

In my mind, I ran through stock phrases but couldn't think of one that would offer any consolation.

"I will go back there to live anyway. I know a few people, so I won't be alone."

What she had said was an indication of what was uppermost in her mind. I realized her sorrow stemmed as much from an isolated life as it did from recent widowhood.

"I'm glad for you," I said, reaching for a knife and shaving some cheese from an almost brown wedge. I couldn't compare the taste to anything I'd ever eaten. It melted on my tongue and reminded me a bit of peanut butter, a bit sticky and nutty. "This is delicious," I said.

Her face changed, happiness reflected in soft gray eyes and a pink smile. "I make the cheeses myself. My mama taught me how to make them, and I learned even more myself." She explained how she traded with the Big Meadow family, using her skills and their milk to make cheese for them and to sell in Porto Velho.

"If you have more, I would like to buy some," I said, hoping she didn't realize my offer was more to help her than for the cheese itself.

She looked at the grass where both children were sleeping and said quietly, "Come into the house with me." The Dutch door led to a room with a bed in one corner and folded quilts on the floor next to it. The only other furniture was a small table and a dresser with short lengths of thick rope serving as drawer pulls. The top of the dresser was an altar, laid out with three statues of the Virgin Mary, a short vase with fresh flowers, and several candles burned to various degrees.

She pushed aside a long drape on the far wall that separated the room where they lived from the low-lying part of the house I had seen from the outside. "There are steps here," she said, as she descended into a dark room. "My husband dug this room when we moved here. It keeps the cheeses cool, so they last longer and taste better. We say, 'A woman's hands must be cold to make the best cheese.'" I saw my way down three steep steps and let the drape fall back. Maria Cecilia opened the shutters of the single window, lighting the room to show large metal tubs on the floor, an age-darkened table, and a wall lined with wide shelves holding rounds of cheese.

"You made all these?" I said in wonder, as I walked the length of the room, lightly running one hand along a waist-high shelf, touching waxy rinds and cheesecloth-wrapped packages velvety with mold.

She took in a short breath and broke into a wide, full smile. "Yes. These are my cheeses. I make four kinds. Here is *amanteigada*." She took a small white round from a shelf, unwrapped it, spooned out a portion, and offered it to me.

"It's delicious, like butter but with more taste."

"It is *gordura*, fat, and light, a good cheese to spread on bread. I will put some on a plate for you to take home."

I didn't want to insult her by refusing, but I was surrounded with clear signs of penury, and I didn't want to take even a morsel of what was almost certainly her only source of income. "Could I buy an entire round from you?"

Her mouth opened and for a few seconds she was speechless. "Yes," she said quietly.

I was carried away by a wonderful feeling I had forgotten. "Actually, I need a lot of cheese. I need to feed some visitors," I didn't miss a beat as I thought of an even better reason and congratulated myself on it, "and I would like some to give as gifts."

Her eyes glistened. "Yes. Yes. I have some cheese that is very good to give as a gift. It is *velho*, very old. I keep it five months before I sell it." She leaned over the lowest shelf, lifted up a deep yellow round, and put it on the table. "For hundreds of years, my family made cheeses for sailors, fresh to be eaten when they were in port, and *semi-duro* to take on long voyages. To make that, we heated the fresh cheese to take out the water so it gets harder, and pressed it with stones in these," she pointed to round molds with perforated bottoms.

She confided in me, "This is the secret that has come to me from my first ancestors on São Miguel: After we separate the curds and whey, we put the pieces in saltwater from the strait. Sometimes we add verdelho wine, too." She held her hand over one of the bottles on the table. "With every batch, I take some of my whey and put it into a bottle, so I can add a drop to the next batch." She looked me in the eyes and said solemnly, "Every cheese has some of the whey that came to me from my great-great-grandmother."

She sliced a sliver off the *velho* cheese, and offered it to me on the blade of the knife. It had a winey aroma, tasted a bit like smoky cheddar and, despite being firm, was also very smooth. I was already planning dinners of grilled cheese sandwiches, macaroni and cheese, and potatoes smothered with cheese. "Could I have a large piece?" I asked, marking it off on the wax with a finger.

"Yes…" And she tentatively added, "Ann."

It was dusk when I left, lightened with a joy I had no wish to analyze.

It was early, with the promise of a day yet to be discovered. Just after dawn, I left to find The Grotto of Towers, another proposed UNESCO world heritage site. I thought of Jack, who had driven me to Porto Velho on the day I arrived and had proudly shown me the plaque in front of "the beautiful manmade landscape" of the currais. I was different then, so flattened that I couldn't appreciate what that honor meant to him, or to me. Since then, warm pride had settled on my frozen shoulders, and love of Pico had prickled my deadened soul. I had become aware again, perhaps not as richly or as sharply as I had once been, more like the incomplete return of sensation to a limb deprived of blood for too long.

Gruta das Torres, a network of caves that perforated the lava rock of Pico, was in a hilly region to the west of Porto Velho. Ropes of magma had spilled down Ponta do Pico and cooled at the surface, while still allowing molten rock to flow through and out toward the ocean, and that had left behind a network of twenty-seven interconnected lava tubes. Through a vegetation-shielded entrance were cavernous spaces, some over five miles long, with skylights that let in enough light for trees, ferns, and mosses to grow underground. Magma had formed lavacicles that looked like icicles, splash stalactites that looked like pulled taffy, and small cylinders known as straws.

In the sixteenth century, when the island was settled, the caves were first feared as the realm of other-world spirits, and then welcomed as a source of groundwater and shelter for both people and their animals. Over the following four centuries, they were a haven to religious ascetics and warehouses for wood, coal, and wine.

If there was no one to leave the tintype of my grandmother to, it was best buried in the heart of Pico.

Looking for *Gruta das Torres*, I took a shortcut through a small forest. It came to an abrupt end with a slash of blinding sunlight at a grassy field that sloped toward a village and the ocean beyond. A well-tended path led me through neatly cultivated vineyards, so absorbed in sampling sweet grapes that I didn't see the buildings until I was in front of tall iron gates hanging from two stone pillars.

They marked the end of the path and the entrance to an extensive compound. Just inside, two nuns walked side by side in silence. They were wearing habits of a type I had only seen once in Italy when I was younger. Long, full robes swept the ground as they walked in step, bell sleeves hiding all but the very tips of their fingers, and white wimples leaving ovals of perfect, young faces exposed. I watched their pale grey tunics recede into the darkness of a chapel and heavy doors slowly close behind them.

Someone had approached me from behind, and I realized she had been standing beside me since I stopped. She was dressed to work in the vineyards, utilitarian black robes caught up in a leather belt and loose outer sleeves rolled up. Her apron was smeared with dirt, and she carried a pair of clippers in one hand.

She slipped the clippers into her belt and pressed a large wood crucifix to her chest with one hand. "I am Mother Espírito Santo. Come," she said, as she put her free arm around my waist and guided me through the gates to a small stone building. "You are interested in us?"

I said yes but didn't know why.

"Franciscans and Carmelites talk about how they brought the vines to Pico in the 1700s, and the Jesuits tell you how they perfected making wine from them," she said as we walked. "God was good to the brothers in the early days. The vineyards gave them sacred wine for the liturgy and...," she smiled, "for drinking themselves. Now, we are the ones who keep the tradition alive. When the vines on Pico began to succumb to the blight that would destroy almost every vine, the brothers were called home, and our mother house in Gouveia petitioned for the monastery vineyards. For the greater glory of God, we were granted this land and all its buildings."

I followed her gaze through the gates to a landscape as lovely as the natural ones on the island.

"The first group of novitiates started by burning the land, and they kept a few vines alive within the walls of the convent. Now, we participate in a project that uses modern techniques to grow the descendants of those original vines and bring back our wines."

In a tool-filled workshop, she hung her apron on a hook near the door and put the clippers in a basket. As she tidied the workbench, I felt a flutter of nostalgia. Her movements reminded me of how I used to do much the same in my own lab at the end of every day.

"We use our profits for the order and for our charity work." She pointed to a motto painted on the wall above a scarred table. "*Ora et Labora.* Pray and Work. First you pray, then you work for the order and for the people."

Back outside, Mother immersed her hands in a rainwater-filled barrel and scrubbed them with a wood-handled brush tied to its side. She walked through the compound, closing doors and shutters, and stopping to observe other nuns as they swept the large courtyard, took stiff brushes to a wine press, and removed laundry from clotheslines. Each woman made the sign of the cross as we passed, but Mother's was the only voice to be heard.

The grounds were lush, watered from enormous cisterns and a well dug directly through the basalt rockhead. The order seemed to grow quite a variety of produce. Two elderly nuns filled a basket with green beans as curly and thin as corkscrews and placed it beside a pile of yams. They exchanged smiles and nods with Mother. I sensed that they had a different relation with her, perhaps because they shared a long history, or perhaps because their age afforded them some leniency in the rules.

Tropical air was moving in from the ocean, carrying with it salt that mingled with smell of herbs from the garden and roasting meat from the largest building. "The wine cellars are underground," Mother Espirito Santo said as she ushered me through a door at the side of the chapel and into a small anteroom with a table holding a box of thick white candles and a dish of long matches.

I took off my hat, and she handed me one of the two candles she had lit, before leading me down steep steps that burrowed under the chapel. To my left, the wall of the stairwell was painted with large grape leaves and bunches of fat purple grapes. I read the words along the top. *My Father is the grower of the vines. I harvest His love.* I found her at the bottom, surrounded by barrels of wine and hundreds, maybe thousands, of bottles lining the walls.

She pried a plug from one barrel, dipped a ladle into the cuvée and filled two tiny glasses on a table. "*Verdelho*," she said, "is the basis. *Boal* is the sweetness. *Alicante* is the fragrance." She inhaled deeply and held a glass to her candle.

"I understand," I said to let her know I had followed her. Apparently, she took that as an indication that I thought she had finished.

"No," she continued. "There is more. *Malvasia* gives soft fruit. *Cerceal* gives acid. Then," she looked at me sternly and wagged a finger, "only then we have balance."

I was taken back to a wine tasting tour in Sonoma with Lee, when I had heard a variation on what Mother had said.

"And most important? We add our prayers."

I felt no urge to question that. It was the truth of her world, and the truths of my world had not sustained me in a long time.

She picked up a bottle and turned it to show the label, a miniature of a man with a long, dark beard standing next to a young woman wearing a loose veil. "Jesus gave wine its importance when he made wine from water in Cana, so our wine is called Cana."

"The label is beautiful," I said, looking at the bottle.

"Sister Marta paints them for a few bottles that we give as gifts from the order. She is old and cannot move well, but she paints like an angel. Here," she ran a finger over a small raised cross on the neck of the bottle, "José Moniz makes a special mark for us when he blows the glass. Manuel Leal and his sons make the barrels for the wine to ferment and age. Their cousins make the iron hoops to hold them together. You see, our vineyard gives jobs to our people.

"You know our wines are famous?" Here she waited for me to answer.

"I have read about them."

Her response reminded me of how Isabel had reacted after I told her I had only heard of festas. "*Read* about them?" She tightened her lips and shook her head slowly. She handed me a glass of the berry-red wine, took a sip from her own glass, and then motioned to me to do the same. "Tasting is better than reading," she said.

I took it and gave my thanks. Trying to do what I thought was expected, I savored it slowly, holding it to the light, sniffing the aroma, and sipping. The warmth spread down my throat and a blend of flavors rose. It was good, but I lacked any ability or even the vocabulary to describe it properly. I just kept saying, "This is good," until I had drained the glass under her watchful eye.

"It is good. The brothers sent it all over Europe, even to the czars of Russia." She stopped talking suddenly and began to hurriedly tidy the cave, rinsing the ladle and glasses by pouring water from a pitcher over them and onto the dirt floor, and hammering the plug back into the barrel of wine she had opened. "Come. It is time for vespers."

The sound of the chapel bells grew louder as we went up the stairs and opened the door to a swirling warm breeze. She circled back to the front of the compound and faced me. "It is late. You will stay with us tonight." She closed the gates and locked them with a large key on a ring hanging from her belt, and that did not disturb me at all.

I followed Mother as she quickly walked back to the chapel, beating the dirt from her habit. Abruptly, she slowed her steps and lowered her head, and we joined other nuns who stood in the chapel. She nudged me into a pew at the back, took the hat from my hand, and covered my head, all without making eye contact. As everyone stood to sing hymns and psalms, knelt to pray, and sat to listen to Mother reading passages from the Bible, I did the same.

"We read from James 1:2-4," Mother started. "Consider it pure joy, my brothers, whenever you face trials of many kinds, because you know that the testing of your faith develops perseverance. Perseverance must finish its work so that you may be mature and complete."

My mind had wandered, as it always had when I sat in church, letting what had no meaning for me give way to the musings of my mind. But that evening, Mother's words penetrated my cocoon, and they angered me. I *had* persevered. *How much longer was I expected to go on?* My dreams had already cost me everything, including the hope that I could ever realize them.

Mother built on her theme with a reading from Corinthians that ended, "We were under great pressure, far beyond our ability to endure, so that we despaired even of life."

I *had* despaired of life. To survive, I had done what had been done throughout human history, something that perhaps was hardwired into our genes to allow the continued existence of the species. I had turned away. But I had gone further. I had decided not to feel anything at all.

The prayers and hymns grew fainter, and I dozed off until I heard Mother whispering in my ear. "It is time to leave."

The compound was cleverly laid out, so only the public places were visible through the gates. Once across the close, a house came into view, as lavish as any I had seen on the island. A small gate opened onto an inner courtyard, tiled in Moorish mosaics. Pink clematis was trimmed to circle the broad base of a fountain that splashed at the center, and the corners were planted with varieties of roses, their fragrance scenting the unusually warm and humid breezes. The buttery light that came through the large arched windows on the ground floor was welcoming. Beyond a polished door was a large room kept cool by thick stone walls and mesh screens that allowed air to circulate. Its plastered walls rose to a high ceiling with dark beams, thick Persian carpets covered the floors, and paintings hung over furniture that glowed with beeswax I could smell as I passed the heavier pieces.

No one spoke, so I did not. Mother put a hand on my shoulder to guide me to the dining room. She indicated that I was to take a seat next to hers at the head of the table. After weeks at Casinha Goulart, the thick chair pads took me by surprise and, for the first time on Pico, I thought wistfully about comforts I had done without.

There was a clear hierarchy at the table. Postulants, wearing simple gray dresses and white scarves, sat on a bench at one end of the table, and three novitiates in their early twenties sat between them and the nuns. Across from me were the two elderly nuns, one of whom led the community in a short grace, ending with a firm, "Amen."

A young lay girl, probably hired from one of the nearby villages, poured a deep ruby-red wine and carried in platters of roast pork and vegetables. Salt cellars with tiny silver spoons were passed around, along with a small jar of cracked peppercorns. Dinner itself was eaten in silence but, after the table was cleared and the postulants were dismissed, plates of dried figs caked with sugar and wedges of melon in a rainbow of colors were passed around, and conversation began. It wasn't as I might have expected. Rather than the senior nuns leading a pious discussion on religion or matters related to running the convent, there was a relaxed exchange of ideas about the business of winemaking, the gray area between helping others enough and helping them too much, and the role of pleasure, all flavored with wit and a bit of gossip. Mother spoke of their hardships and triumphs in the past year, and asked everyone to pray for a successful Festa de Vindimas to celebrate the wines God had given them.

When smaller groups of two and three formed, Mother turned to me and offered an overview of the community. I could tell where she was going as she highlighted the rewards of their lives and moved on to the organization of the order.

"For six months, you live as we live, to see whether you are right for us and we are right for you." It seemed reasonable, but I wondered how many actually left at the end of the trial period. "Then you agree to remain in the same motherhouse for as long as you are needed, and you become novitiates, entitled to all our privileges." She emphasized the last word. I knew what she was suggesting.

Signaling the end of the meal, she rose from the table and looked down at me. "It is a good life, a life of service and meaning." It was true. A convent—just as a monastery—could be the backdrop of a meaningful, peaceable life. Part of the price would be one I was already paying: the chance to shape a fuller life. For me, the rest of the price would be a renunciation of the convictions on which I had rested my life.

After evening prayers in the chapel, the young postulants and novitiates stopped to bow their heads in front of Mother, receiving her cupped hands on their wimples and a murmured blessing, before filing out. The rest of the nuns walked with me back to the manor house and up the stairs to the second floor, where heavy oak doors on either side of a wide hall opened into small bedrooms. One by one, I heard the doors latch. With the ironwork on the windows, the nuns were safe for the night.

I removed my shirt and skirt, used the chamber pot, and fell asleep immediately. Sometime in the middle of the night, bells sounded and I awoke thinking that I could hold onto the tintype of my grandmother a little longer.

11

I hit the ground before I realized I was falling, sky and ground whirling around me, my body plummeting downhill, tumbling onto sharp stones, rolling over scree. I was in free fall. I clawed at passing rocks but didn't stop until my shoulder crashed into the edge of a low outcrop on the hill behind my house.

I had survived, I told myself, in the same instant that razor-sharp pains struck from every part of my body, each one competing to claim the greatest attention. My shoulder screamed in agony, and one ankle was already crushed in a vise of rapidly swelling tissues. I tried to get up, only setting off more pain and waves of nausea. I scanned for someone to call out to, waited, and looked again. I was alone. "I don't need anyone," I whimpered and lay still.

I tasted blood where my teeth had gouged a flap from the inside of my cheek, and I felt the wet of more blood on my shoulder. I knew I was badly injured. I knew I had only myself to rely on. With a detachment I would not have expected, I calmly blinked away sweat, swiped hair out of my eyes with the back of an aching hand and, fixing my eyes on the eira far below me, tried to crawl, dragging my limp arm. I came close to fainting.

Drizzle turned to rain, and I began to shiver. Little by little, I twisted my body and wriggled closer to the rock. Bracing one leg against the outcrop and using my less injured arm, I pulled myself up. I could see the ocean.

I collapsed to the ground. I felt my heartbeats slow and weaken. The world pulled away from me, sound distant, sight narrowed to a pinpoint. I accepted that this was another unwinnable battle. I had failed to bring life to my descendants. I had failed to atone.

When I arrived on Pico, I was disconnecting from the life I knew. Here on the hillside, I was disconnecting from life itself. It was just a matter of drawing my last breaths, and how perfect to do that on Pico, close the ocean and my people.

Dim sentience.

I was in bed, cocooned in rosemary-scented quilts, without the will to open my eyes.

Someone was moving around the room, shadowing the light from time to time.

Moonlight changed to sunlight. I opened my eyes. My clothes lay in a pile on the floor, bloodied and ruined. A man stood with his back to me. I closed my eyes.

I was propped up in my bed. Something warm and wet moved tenderly over my face, and my skin savored the feeling.

I was alone. I listened to the scrunching sounds I made by squeezing the quilt with one hand, and felt the pain of stretching the tiny muscles of my fingers. My ankle was tightly wrapped. I started to count the throbs and fell asleep.

I pulled apart my eyelids. Leaning against the wall close to the bed was a long branch stripped of its bark and forked at the top, where it was carved into twin bunches of what were immediately recognizable as daffodils. A cane.

A cup of cold tea was on the table next to me. I reached for it and was immediately knifed by pain. I sat back and rested before thirst compelled me to try again. I slowly stretched out my good arm, grabbed the lip of the cup, and emptied it in one swallow. It left a sweet, minty aftertaste in my mouth, and I relaxed into sleep.

In the afternoon, I heard activity in the front room. Someone tapped on the bedroom doorframe and pulled the curtain aside. Tall and plump, she was in her fifties and gave the impression of competence and practicality with neat, plain clothes and hair pulled back in a braided bun. She came closer, circled me with strong arms, pulled me up so I was sitting rather than lying down, and she reached for the quilt folded at the foot of my bed to wedge behind me.

I was confused. I couldn't work out who she was.

"You need food." Her voice embraced me. She left, and I heard the clang of metal and the clink of porcelain. When she returned, she was wearing a long white apron and carrying a deep bowl steaming with the aroma of meat and vegetables. She set the broth on the table by my bed. I looked at her, thinking thank you but not able to say it.

"It is still hot." She dipped a spoon into the soup and lifted it to my lips. "I am Rita. I am Francisco's mother."

I stared at her blankly.

"He carried you here from the mountain. You were hurt."

I nodded very slowly, snatching at disconnected memories of the moment I hit the sharp rocks and the view of the ocean before I closed my eyes for what I thought would be the last time. A few spoonsful of soup stirred me from my half-dazed state with a small flutter of energy. I raised my head slightly and formed the words *thank you* before sinking back onto the pillow.

She continued to talk as she slowly fed me. "The doctor says it is best for you to stay in bed until you regain strength. You should not get cold. I will help you to dress."

I realized I was naked under the covers. She must have followed my thoughts, because she explained, "You were wet from the rain. Francisco cut your clothes off. Do not worry. I can stitch them together again."

After a while, the warm soup made me drowsy but I fought sleep, opening my eyes again and again to make sure Rita was still there. My last thought before I fell asleep was that I loved her for wanting to salvage my clothes.

For days, I had no thoughts beyond Rita, no desire other than to see her again, no past to regret, no future to despair. When the hydrangea petals outside my bedroom window blushed pale against their dark foliage, another day had dawned, and I knew she would come soon. When the setting sun bled into the clouds and washed the world outside in rosy light, I knew I had to endure another night without her.

Alerted by pain from damaged tissues, and restricted by torn tendons and ligaments, I slept fitfully, locked into one position. Each time I woke, it was fully, and oftentimes I panicked at the thought that I might not see her again. *How would I find one Rita on an island filled with Ritas?* I relied on her to comfort me even when she was not there, lulling myself to sleep again by imagining her walking into my room again.

When direct sunlight filled the front room, I started to listen for her arrival, but she moved with such graceful lightness, I rarely heard her footsteps on the wood floors.

Instead, I was usually surprised by her appearance in the doorway to my bedroom. She showed her Flemish roots, with a high forehead, green eyes, and auburn hair, always cleanly parted in the middle and pulled back in a bun. Although she had the sprays of lines at the corners of her eyes that come from a lifetime of smiles and worries, her skin was fine-pored and remarkably unblemished for an older woman. She always wore a cotton skirt and white blouse, sometimes personalized at the neckline with embroidery in glorious colors. On chilly mornings, she wrapped her shoulders with a shawl, sun-bleached everywhere but the brightly patterned places where it was usually knotted.

I resisted when she said I should be taken to the doctor in Madalena, and fought her over having one of the island's visiting nurses come to me. Those suggestions came with risks. If I was told I had healed, I might lose Rita. If I was told I needed professional care, I might lose Rita.

I became her child. As I recovered, she fed me, led me to the bathroom, and bathed me. She softened my scabs and massaged my bruised skin with salves, and she tenderly repositioned my ankle and shoulder under poultices that warmed them. Her touch alone relieved my pain. She brought broths, and later rich stews, in a small blackened pot always covered with the same faded blue plate, a lightning bolt crack across its center. She lifted small spoonsful to my mouth when I was at my weakest and encouraged me to feed myself when I could. And I grew stronger.

Sometimes she brought her daughter, a quiet child who looked very much like her mother, and sometimes she brought her son. With his olive skin and black hair, I assumed the boy took after his father. He was in his teens but—with sparse hairs on his chin and a deepening voice that cracked from time to time—soon to be a man. He never stayed longer than the few minutes needed to obediently follow his mother's directions to restock the firewood or carry in the food she had brought.

Between sunrise and sunset, the shadow of the roof's overhang on the living room floor moved steadily from left to right, and day by day the pace slowed as I spent more time awake and alert. Rita stayed less and less as I healed, leaving me to fill time alone in the rocking chair.

When she was in the house, I kept her in my sight, anticipating each step she would take, alert to the tone of her voice, determined to be the good patient. When she lit a fire in the stove to warm water for my sponge bath, I struggled to unbutton my nightgown. When she took jars of cream from her basket, I told her how much I liked the rose-scented one. When she laid out my change of clothes, I was reassured that she still cared enough about me.

One day, I watched the steam rise and dampen Rita's face as she filled a deep bowl from the kettle. Her hands wrung out hot cloths that she used to gently wash me in the same way she had always done. She wrapped my injured shoulder in bandages, tucking in a few leaves with little hairs that prickled and raised a pink rash on my skin. She told me they would help loosen the joint, and a complete lack of scientific evidence made no difference to me.

After my bath, she slipped my arm into the sleeve of a fresh cotton nightgown and left me to finish dressing while she emptied the wash water. "The Goularts put a beautiful bathtub and toilet in there. They have lasted over seventy years," she said when she returned. I nodded.

Just a curtained alcove of the bedroom, paneled from floor to ceiling with heavy wood boards, the bathroom was barely large enough to hold a free-standing tub and a toilet. No one I had known would have considered it even adequate, but Rita saw it with different eyes. She appreciated the painted vines that grew up the outside of the bowl, ending in blue flowers on the inside, but said nothing about the exposed pipe that carried cold water from an opening in the ceiling.

"Try to lift your arm a bit," she directed. I winced at the smallest movement. "You are just afraid. You can do it. You must start to move it, or it will never be good again." She slowly lifted my arm and carried it back down several times.

She handed me the cane. "Where did that come from?" I asked.

"Francisco made it." I could see she was proud. "Everyone says he does the best woodwork on the island, maybe on all the islands."

"It's beautiful." I looked at her, the words not coming for a moment. "Thank you, Rita."

She opened the front door and called out, "Umbelina." Her daughter came through the door immediately, and I was struck again by how lovely she was. She had her mother's green eyes and fair skin but for the first time I saw the oval face and full mouth of Rita's son. Her two light chestnut braids were held in place by neat lace bows at the ends, and she had decorated them with a few of the yellow daisies she carried.

"These are for you, ma'am," she held out a bouquet, "They are to make you feel better."

"I am Anna," adding a terminal "a" at the last moment to make my name one that she would be more familiar with. "Your mama is helping me because I hurt myself."

"I know. You fell down the mountain, and Francisco found you and brought you to the Goulart's house."

I hadn't thought of the question before. "How did Francisco know where to bring me?" I asked Rita.

"Luisa from the dairy," she pointed in the direction of Big Meadow, "is a friend. She told us about the American woman who had moved into the Goulart house by herself."

"I guess I'm more a stranger than I thought."

"And more a neighbor than you thought," she said, looking directly at me.

I felt bad; if anything I had been taken care of as a neighbor not a stranger, in the way I imagined family cared for one another. I was the one who had resisted any ties to the community.

As always, Rita sat with me while I ate what she had brought, sometimes silently, sometimes talking about her family or village life, but never asking questions about my life. When I had wiped the bowl of stew clean with my last bite of bread, she lifted herself from her chair, made eye contact with her daughter, and nodded.

Umbelina smiled and asked, "Where is your brush, ma'am?"

"I think your mother left it on the table in my bedroom. And please call me Anna."

She returned quickly with the brush, and I felt her fumbling with the tie Rita had put in my hair the day before.

"Let me help," I said, reaching my good arm around to my back.

"No," she circled my wrist with thin fingers and returned my hand to my lap, "Mama said I was to do it." Her voice had the same lovely musical quality as her mother's. I allowed myself to enjoy the rhythmic tugging, as she brushed my hair slowly and deliberately.

I turned around. "Tell me about your family, Umbelina." I liked having a reason to look at her face, with its fleeting features of youth.

"I have a Mama and a Papa and five brothers. I am an aunt eight times. Zeca and Cajó live with their families. Manuel lives in Portugal now."

"Manuel went to Ericeira three months ago," Rita explained, "and his family joins him next week." She tightened her lips and nodded to herself, an acceptance of the inevitable.

"I had my children in batches," Rita explained. "The first three were Francisco, Manuel, and José Carlos, who is called Zeca. Ten years later I had Carlos Jorge, who is called Cajó, and Jorge Carlos, who is called Joca, and ten years after them, I had my dear Umbelina."

"Francisco and Joca live in Porto Velho with Mama and Papa and me," Umbelina offered. "Joca is too young to be married and have his own house, and Elena died a long time ago, so Francisco is alone. Mama keeps telling him to marry again and have children, but he says to stop talking about it."

"You did a good job, my child," said Rita.

"She did." I turned to smile at Umbelina. "Thank you. It felt very nice."

"I am going to bring in some wood," Rita said, walking out the door.

She returned with an armload of branches. After setting them to the side of the hearth, she reached into the bulging pockets of her skirt and took out several small oval potatoes. "You have a nice potato patch near the cistern," she said. "Umbelina will dig up more for you tomorrow." I didn't know I had a potato patch.

As she usually did, Rita stayed for an hour after settling me in for the day and made us cups of tea with dried herbs she took from envelopes in her basket. Sometimes we sat in silence, and sometimes she explained what we were drinking and why it was good for me. I found I did not like *camomila*, which she made to relax the cramps I was getting in muscles that had atrophied, but I loved the honey-sweetened mint tea and the elderberry infusion that were supposed to help me breathe more easily. She handed me a large cup of sweet cinnamon and licorice tea.

"This is delicious. What is it for?" I asked.

"It is to enjoy," she said, smiling.

We laughed together.

They both returned early the next day. Umbelina went directly to the wide sill beneath the front window. She seemed deep in thought as she unrolled a piece of paper and flattened it with small stones at each corner. I looked at Rita, but she kept her gaze steadily on her daughter, who held a thick pencil over the paper without making a mark.

"She likes art?" I asked.

"She draws lovely pictures." Rita walked over and started stroking her daughter's hair. When she spoke, it was clearly for

Umbelina's ears. "She does many things well. Her bread is the best." Umbelina looked up at her mother but smiled only slightly.

"I tried baking bread once," I said, hoping to divert the child's attention. "It was terrible. Not at all as good as hers is, I'm sure." Lost in her thoughts, there was no sign that she appreciated the compliment.

"Then you will come to my house, and we will all try together," Rita said, looking at her daughter.

She walked over to me and lowered her voice, "Joca wants to emigrate, probably to America. She will miss him, but much more, she is worried that Francisco will go, too. He is very special to her. When she was a baby, his voice could quiet her. As soon as she could walk, she toddled after him. I had to pry her off his leg so he could go fishing; even then, after he left, she would keep one eye on the sea until he returned. To him, she is a sister, a daughter, someone to cherish, someone to pour his love into. They are of the same type. It is a good love."

I wanted to let her know I could feel her pain, to console her, but all I could think of saying was, "I'm sorry about Joca leaving."

"I will not be alone. I will have my Umbelina, the child of my heart...at least for a while."

"What do you like to draw, Umbelina?" I asked.

"People, ma'am." She perked up a bit. "Could I draw you?"

"No, my love," her mother said. "I am going to help Anna with her bath now."

She bent over her paper again, still not making a mark.

I had an idea. I reached up to the mantle and pulled myself from the rocking chair. I took the tintype of my grandmother from under my notebook. Holding it by the edges, I carried the photograph to Umbelina, along with several blanks sheets I tore out of the notebook. "Would you like to draw this lady?" I asked.

She drew in a breath. "Yes," she said reverently. "Yes, please." I propped it up against the almost empty green flowered tea tin, and watched as a remarkably true likeness of my grandmother's face started to appear, capturing her gentleness and her strength, and the hint of sadness that was always in her eyes.

Rita busied herself at the stove. When she had finished, she said, "I am leaving this for you, so you can eat it after your bath."

I looked at the small pot and felt a stab of jealousy. She was going home to be have dinner with her daughter. "I can take care of myself."

"You cannot take care of yourself."

"You don't have to do this."

"People take care of each other."

"You must have a lot of your own work to do."

"I have work, and I will do it later today."

Rita prepared for my sponge bath. She lifted the dressing on my arm and laid her hand lightly on my skin. Her touch reminded me of my grandmother, and I longed for her as I had when I was a child, her warm arms, her sweet smell, her soft voice saying she would see me *in the morning bright*.

My grandmother always rose early and napped in the afternoon, so—on days when I wasn't invited by relatives or neighbors to join their families at the beach—I often had two or three hours to myself after lunch. I liked spending that time in the attic, accessed by lifting the corner of a long, heavy drape and ducking underneath to the bottom of a steep staircase. The hot, musty air swirled with sparkling dust when I disturbed it, and prickly sensations of exploration and discovery accompanied me into a cavernous space, lit only by a few dim bulbs and two cloudy skylights. I cleared my way by snagging cobwebs with a wire hanger that I brought from the wardrobe in my room, cocooning one end of it with the sticky spider silk as I waved it in the air in front of me.

I rummaged through boxes, crates, and trunks with over fifty years of belongings left behind by ten or more people who had once thought them worthy of keeping, and who had probably entirely forgotten about their existence. I sat cross-legged in front of whichever container caught my interest and sorted the contents. There were cut-glass perfume bottles with beautiful stoppers, baby clothes wrapped in shredding gray tissue, small plaster statues of saints padded with excelsior, a china donkey with a broken ear, a teapot separated from its handle. Rough shelves against one wall held piles of sheet music with my mother's name written across the top, Playbills for Broadway shows she must have taken my grandmother to, and hundreds of paperbacks with yellowed pages that detached from the dried glue in their spines when I cracked them open, and glided away on the heavy air. At one time, the magazines must have had special meaning for whoever had stored them there: a 1937 issue of *Life* with FDR's picture, a *Popular Sports* issue devoted to Lou Gehrig, several issues of *Photoplay* that promised to identify the Hollywood actress with the best figure.

My favorite finds were painted tins. I sat under one of the skylights and wiped away layers of dust with the hem of my skirt or a sleeve to reveal the hidden picture. A spray of bright flowers decorated a tin of bath salts. A rainbow of forty colored pencils opened to a few stubs. A plate of assorted cookies was held by a disembodied hand, while a scrubbed and smiling boy looked on with anticipation. I would work my nails under the edge of the lids and bit by bit pry them open. Usually they were empty, but—real or imagined—when I pushed my nose into the corners, I could always catch a whiff of the chocolates or tobacco they had once held. Inside a container for *Cremo Oats* were bundles of black-and-white photos with rippled edges. Looking back, I know they must have been pictures of my own family. I wish I had taken them.

On rainy days, when going to the beach wasn't an option and not enough light came through the attic skylights, I went around the corner to the Gloucester landmark, *Our Lady of Good Voyage* church, and spent time in the cool, dark vestibule. Just inside the front doors, pamphlets were laid out on two narrow tables, glossy with beeswax. They expounded the importance of keeping my virginity, explained how to know if you had a calling to the priesthood, and assured churchgoers of a place in heaven if they raised good Catholic children. The tables were presided over by racks of prayer cards. On one side was a saint or the enthroned Madonna, usually a High Renaissance painting with luminous color and lush drapery. On the other side was either an account of the saint's life or a prayer asking the saint to intercede with God for help with a wayward child or an alcoholic husband, deliverance from disease, or other issues that held no interest for me.

Sacred to others, I collected the prayer cards as pieces of art, sometimes making the expected donation of a nickel and sometimes not. Back in the hot, still air of my bedroom under the eaves, I sorted and re-sorted them, arranging them on the white chenille bedspread by gender or age at death or simply by how much I liked the paintings. Occasionally I said the prayer on the back, in much the same way that, as a teen, my best friend and I recited the incantations in a book on magic that we got when touring *The House of Seven Gables* in nearby Salem. I had little faith that the prayers would lead to anything.

Occasionally, I arranged the collection according to how the saints were martyred. The one who always found a place at the top of the array was Saint Sebastian, a handsome young man shown contorted in agony, his body dripping blood from the piercings of many arrows. He was called the saint who was martyred twice. The first time he was shot through with arrows for encouraging two Romans to remain faithful. After being left for dead, he was nursed back to health, only to be martyred again.

When I was a child, I took his story as a parable of second chances. As an adult, I remembered that his cruel death had only been postponed.

With only three landlines, and cell phones years in the future, the arrival of the mail was a highlight of the day in my college dorm. My box was never empty. My mother wrote daily, and the care packages she sent from B. Altman & Company were filled with enough to treat everyone to an evening of Italian cookies or Belgian chocolates. In my freshman year, she sometimes arrived unexpectedly on a Friday afternoon to take my close friends and me into Boston to see a popular musical and have dinner at one of the best restaurants in the city. She was, as always, an extraordinary hostess, making each one feel like the center of her attention. Once introduced, she not only remembered everyone by name, she remembered the details of their lives, asking on future visits whether an older sister had chosen the date for her wedding or how a grandfather was recuperating from heart surgery. She brought small gifts, a bar of scented soap or a box of toffees, sometimes hinted at including my friends on future stays in the Hamptons, wrote them references for au pair positions in Europe, and introduced them to the eligible sons of families she knew. She made me the envy of all.

I went to my mother's alma mater. Once there, I wondered how that had happened. I had wanted to go to Yale, where women were being admitted for the first time. My mother said the choice was mine, but it was her responsibility to make sure I fully understood everything I had to consider. She described the ghetto that surrounded Yale and how crime had a way of spreading into the nearby campus, and she told me about the difficulties of being a girl at a traditionally all-male university. She just didn't want me to be disappointed, she said. Every decision to apply despite those drawbacks led to another discussion. It wasn't until I was in my thirties that I understood I had convinced myself I didn't want to go to Yale because it was easier than listening to another discussion.

My mother would not have been as happy dropping me off if she had realized that her alma mater was far from the college she had attended. No longer the exclusive domains of a privileged few, the social upheavals of the 1970s had made campuses more diverse, had allowed women the vision of using their education to do more than bide time until marriage, and had put brave new ideas out there for all.

Science was the exciting, new frontier, and a modern building with gleaming labs and large lecture halls reflected that. It was in those rooms that I realized I had no interest in the life my mother led. When I told her I was majoring in molecular biology, she seemed genuinely bewildered by my choice. "I just don't think of it as a something a girl would study," she said. My plan to do a summer internship at a lab in Boston led to many long talks. "What's wrong with the art program in France?" my mother asked. "Are you worried you won't fit in there?" When I was not swayed by her arguments, she reminded me that I was wasting my birthright, all the advantages of my upbringing, and every sacrifice she had made.

One evening on Pico, after Rita had gone, I looked down at the constellation of punctures on my skin, finally healing under her tender care. The image of Saint Sebastian formed in my mind, and I remembered the words that were my mother's final volley whenever I did not come around to her point of view: *You are lacking something.* Perhaps it was a measure of the hurt those words carried that they had remained hidden from me in a way the memories I struggled to confine were not. I had not even flinched when she said them. Their sharp arrows had bypassed consciousness and had been locked away—until I saw my own wounded skin lit by a Pico sunset.

I sat back, barely breathing, and I heard my mother clearly. *You are lacking something.* I could never protect myself from that assault, because exactly what was lacking was never made clear. As my mother assessed my shortcomings in the politely restrained voice of a lady at a society tea, I could not rise above it by reassuring myself her thoughts were not rational. *You are lacking—,* she looked up like she was trying to find the words for the deficit in my character, a flaw so terrible that words did not exist for it— *something.*

Now, holding tight to the eira wall, I could not return those words to their place, and other arrows streaked out. *Do you know what you are, Ann? You are an ingrate. You got the best of everything and never appreciated it.* I knew I had been raised with everything she had wanted. She had dressed me in clothes from Saks when she had worn dresses sewn by her mother. She had watched a limousine take me to school, after growing up in the only family on her street with no car at all. *I sacrificed my life for you.* As child, I had asked myself many times what sort of child I was to hurt my own mother, a mother who had done so much for me. *You are a disappointment, Ann.* I always accepted that I was a disappointment, but I had seen no way not to disappoint and still be whole. I could not make myself happy in the place my mother saw as her great gift to me.

The wounding began in earnest when I told her I had been offered my dream job at a start-up outside San Jose. Now, as the evening stars appeared above Porto Velho, I heard those recriminations as if for the first time. Sitting across from me at dinner, standing over me as I packed, and riding with me to the airport, she had recited my character flaws and elaborated on my poor judgment. As I struggled to pull out of quicksand, her hands kept pulling me back in. She only wanted the best for me, she had reassured me in a motherly voice, when I asked her why she hated me.

My mother's words followed me to bed that night, and her voice whispered to me.

You never could make wise decisions, Ann.

I'm used to being alone; you turned your back on me long ago.

You are a coldhearted child. Your father never liked that in you.

Your grandmother would be ashamed of you. That was far more cutting than owning those words herself.

Leaving became one thing I did not fault myself for. Long before I was aware that it was true, I knew in some part of my being that I had to escape or die myself.

When I called to tell my mother about Lee, predictably she tried every familiar approach to prevent the marriage. After close questioning about him, she implied that he must have had reasons other than love for wanting to marry me. After asking about his family background, she said I was far too good for him. She asked, "Do you really want your children to grow up in some mixed-breed family?"

For three weeks afterwards, I made nightly calls that were never answered. I put an invitation in the mail. The wedding would be on the beach at Lover's Point in Monterey, and would be followed by brunch on the patio of a nearby restaurant. I made a reservation for her at the best hotel in the area and rehearsed introducing her to Lee and his mother. I wore a dress she had bought me, hoping it would please her.

She did not come.

Whether it was habit, a vain attempt to mend fences, or just a fear of breaking the fragile thread that connected us, I never stopped calling, at first every few days and then, as my calls were increasingly picked up by voice mail, on Sundays. Finally, I called only on holidays. Most of the conversations were monologs during which I chatted as though everything was fine between us; when she did speak, she was brief and cold, and she kept up her attacks. I never knew whether she intended to punish me or to prod me into doing what she wanted. She may not have known herself.

I began to keep an account of our conversations, with dates and verbatim accounts of what she said. I was very clear with myself about why I did that. I wanted evidence. I wanted to be able to look back and not hold myself responsible for what happened between us.

Her last request was that I not attend her funeral, and her will stipulated that I receive nothing.

Miriam Winthrop

12

I awoke to rain. For the first time since I fell, I did not immediately think of discomfort and limitations. Moving tenderly, I felt no deep aches, no sharp twinges as healing skin broke free of scabs, and I reveled in the absence of the one sensation that had overshadowed all others, and the rebirth of pleasure in moving my body.

I sat up in bed, testing my injured arm, and stood slowly, waiting for the pain that came with putting weight on my legs. With a small reserve of energy beyond what I needed to simply get through the day, I walked around the house and looked over the rooms that seemed more like home than any place I had lived since I was twelve.

All morning, downpours followed brilliant sunshine, and blue skies followed rain. Between cloudbursts, I went outside to the eira, its stones still wet, and I breathed in the grassy, salty, minty, piney freshness that came after a rainfall on the island.

I thought about walking along Dairy Road, but pictured myself stumbling on a rock and hitting the ground hard again. Instead, I was content to watch the fairytale landscape and my neighbors, and to sip the spicy cocoa that Rita had left for me.

Rita came at midday. Before I had the time to notice that she brought nothing with her, she announced, "You will come to my house today. Carlos and the boys are back from fishing, and Nossa Senhora was good to us. We are having a celebration."

I was taken by surprise. I wasn't ready, I thought with rising panic, not ready to meet people and socialize. I wanted time to consider what I should do. With another person, I could have easily found a reason not to go, even if it was one without any truth to it. Nothing came to my mind; even if it had, I doubt I could have lied to Rita. I looked down at the yellowed bruises on my leg and stammered, "My ankle hasn't completely healed yet," hoping she would be the one to confirm it was too soon for me to leave my house.

"You will be fine."

"How do I get there?" I said anxiously. "I don't even know where you live."

She smiled indulgently and said, "We will walk down together as soon as Umbelina comes back from playing with Bárbara. You will lean on me and on your cane. Until then, go dress yourself."

It was happening so quickly. Then, just as it occurred to me that I could simply tell Rita I was too tired or in too much pain, a hard-to-reconcile thought crossed my mind: the prospect of meeting new people interested me, perhaps even excited me. I wanted to know what her house was like, plain and small like my own or large and homey, and whether I would like her husband. I wondered what I should wear, who would be there, what I could say to them, and if I would be accepted.

When I was dressed, I looked up at the drawing of my grandmother that Umbelina had given me and searched the face for a sign of approval. She did seem happy.

I hooked one arm around Rita's waist and took the pressure off my right leg with the cane that Francisco had made. I was quiet as we walked down the steps and along the road to Porto Velho. Mounting anticipation and almost three weeks of confinement had left me shaky and slightly out of breath, so we went slowly, Umbelina and her friend from Big Meadow diverting themselves with short side trips off the road to pick flowers that caught their eyes.

As we got closer to the maze of streets off the main square, I wiped my sweaty palms on my skirt and smoothed my hair. Near the center of town, both girls raced ahead and climbed a stone staircase built into a knoll running along the southern edge of the town. "Francisco!" Umbelina cried out as she wrapped her arms around her brother, who looked far taller than his modest height from fifteen feet below. He was in his mid-thirties, his face a blend of his mother's and the more Mediterranean features I had seen on his youngest brother: large dark brown eyes with flecks of gold, dark chestnut hair, light olive skin, and a broad forehead. His beaten leather hat fell off as he lifted his sister high in the air, smiling. She giggled gaily, tousled his hair, and poked the flowers she was holding into his curls, laughing even more.

"Francisco," his mother called up to him, "come down and help Anna."

He hesitated a moment, then put his sister down gently.

"I'm fine," I said, reverting to type, despite having noticed there was no handrail and knowing it would be a struggle. I had always been anxious to keep a balance between what I received and what I gave, wary of either ulterior motives or being used when the two were not equal. It was a lesson I had learned over and over from my mother. When she felt she gave more than she got from me, I paid a price that exacted too much from me.

Rita just looked at me and shook her head slowly. She kept her eyes on me until I meekly said, "Thank you. Help would be good."

Francisco reached the lower steps and kissed the top of his mother's head. Looking at me, he said, "Never argue with my mother. It will be wasted breath." We all laughed.

"Francisco is a good man. He was glad to be there to help you," Rita said, almost reading my mind. "And he is glad to be here to help again." She went ahead, leaving me to take the stairs leaning heavily on her son. We didn't follow her into the house. Instead, I was led between two tall hydrangea bushes at the side of the house. Children's voices and laughter quieted as I walked into a flat grassy area where scattered knobs of bedrock served as seats and tables.

Rita appeared at the side door of the small house and motioned to me to come to her. She put her arm lightly on my shoulder and announced loudly, "This is Anna. She will be sitting in the shade at the back." Immediately, three young boys cleared that area, and Francisco guided me to my designated seat on a retaining wall at the back. He seemed to search for something to say. Finally, he asked if I wanted anything to drink.

"No, thank you, but the food does smell good." It did. The aroma of freshly baked bread from inside the house and meats being grilled over a wood fire outside made my mouth water.

In time, others filed between the hydrangea bushes, adding sandals, clogs, work boots, and other shoes to a pile left at the edge of the grass. Women brought bowls of food and stacks of plates that they put on a large board of wood set on two roughly constructed sawhorses, and a few of the men carried jugs of what I assumed was wine to a far corner of the yard.

Francisco stood by my side, not talking but reluctant to leave me alone. Rita signaled him from the doorway, and they exchanged a few words. He returned to me. "Would you like me to introduce you?" As I stood, he cupped my elbow in his hand and guided me toward three people standing nearby. He stopped suddenly before reaching them and said with some surprise, "I don't know your name."

"Ann." I corrected myself, "My name is Anna."

"That I know," he said gently, "but what are your other names? Which family do you come from?"

"Parker."

"Parker," he said slowly, smoothing over the Rs so that it sounded more like 'Paoka'." And what are your parent's names?"

"My parent's names?" I heard my guarded tone and regretted it.

"So I can introduce you."

"My mother was Clara; my father was Vilem Pavka." I owned the names without my mother's shame, and I was proud of myself.

I was formally introduced to everyone, Francisco noting their connections to his family. Their lives were so entwined, the distinction between nuclear family, extended family, and the rest of the community blurred. I was in a culture where the usual identifications of college degree, professional position, or neighborhood meant less than what I was used to, so—especially since so many had the same first names—I found it did help to distinguish among people when he noted where the person was born or lived. The group was notable for its variety, very young and very old, dark and fair, tall and short, dressed in workpants and suits, but everyone seemed perfectly at ease standing together, talking, listening, and laughing.

Rita's husband, Carlos, was a large, weathered man with a thunderous baritone and a cap of thick snow-white hair over aggressive black eyebrows. He seemed to dominate every group he joined as he moved through the gathering, the amiable host, the patriarch, the well-respected boat captain. Seeing the family together I could appreciate how Rita had taken the edge off the raw masculinity the boys got from their father, giving her sons varying degrees of refinement and warmth.

Rita's mother-in-law had her own place close to the side of the house and an enormous fire pit, which she tended from time to time. As Francisco brought me to her, I said, "It's amazing that your grandmother does so much."

"She is like my Mama: it would upset her if she could not feed visitors." He explained that she insisted on making part of every meal. "She says that when she cannot, she will feel she has nothing left to contribute."

His grandmother put down her oversize fork and returned to her chair. I looked down on the flowered scarf that barely covered a pink scalp with sparse white hair, and I waited to be introduced. Francisco did not speak until she looked me in the face.

Despite not seeing or hearing well, she was a lively woman and did most of the talking. Giving us news about the upcoming birth of her first great-great-grandchild brought spots of color to her papery white cheeks. "My grandmother always prayed she would live to see yet another generation," said Francisco with tenderness.

She was soon on her feet again, turning the sausages and fishes, and telling stories of days past that were related in ways only she understood. She had a vivid memory of people and events that dated back several generations, and others were drawn in as she talked about the villages buried by volcanic ash, the priest who sang opera in the streets, and the birth of two sets of triplets in a single week. For those around me, her stories would flow into the generations to come.

"Having her here with us lets us visit many lives," Francisco commented as we walked away.

His face broke out in a wide smile when he guided me to a man about his own age, who stood at the center of a group of laughing people. "This is Anna, the daughter of Clara and Vilem Pavka. She is from America and lives in the Goulart house near the pasture," Francisco introduced me.

"Baltazar." He grinned and bowed extravagantly from the waist, a man whose presence far exceeded his small stature. I liked him immediately. Much like Francisco, he was thoughtful and charming, but where Francisco was somewhat reserved, he was outgoing. He talked about the people around us with a sharp humor that came from familiarity and affection.

"Who are you related to here?" I was trying to get the knack of introductions.

"I am *exposto na roda*," he said, and he and Francisco shared a laugh.

Francisco saw that I was puzzled. "Babies used to be left at convents or churches on a *roda*," he explained, twisting his hands in the air to show something making a half turn around and then coming back to where it started, a gesture I couldn't decipher.

The two men exchanged glances, quickly scanned the yard, and settled on a spot for me to stand. "Come. Come. Watch." They were enjoying themselves. Francisco went inside the house, appearing a moment later at the side window, holding up a loaf of bread. "This is baby Baltazar!" he said dramatically.

Baltazar went to the other side of the window, laughing. "That's me. Also, my mama is not married. What will she do?" He took the bread from Francisco, held it over his stomach with both palms, and mimed a heavily pregnant woman waddling around near the window. "What will I do?" he wept in falsetto voice. By this time, the two men had attracted attention. Rita was by the firepit, shaking her head in disapproval, but all the children were shrieking with laughter.

"Ah! What do I see here? It is the Convent of Nossa Senhora. Ah! And here is," he looked at me and said clearly and slowly, "the roda."

Francisco's hand appeared at the window holding a large plate that he swiveled out under Baltazar's chin. Much to the amusement of almost everyone, Baltazar let out a scream and cried, "The baby is being born!" Then he put the loaf of bread on the plate, and Francisco's hand rotated the imaginary Lazy Susan back into the house. My own laughter ended with a deep sigh that released all tension.

When Francisco returned to the yard with the prop baby, Baltazar put a nearby shawl over his head and tore off a corner of the loaf. "Mother Superior is hungry," he explained. That remark did not amuse some onlookers, particularly Rita, who lifted a single finger in warning, immediately making both men drop their smiles, apologize, and go into the house.

When they returned, it was without the bread and the makeshift veil.

Francisco explained, "In the past, villages were so small, usually people knew if a woman who was not married was going to have a baby, but sometimes she could hide at home or under *capote a capello*." I could picture the long hooded cloaks introduced to the islands by the Flemish. "After the baby was born, the mother took the baby to the roda or left him near the house of relatives, *exposto*—out of place—hoping they would care for the child and she would see him grow up."

Baltazar said, "Do you understand? I was given for adoption. I do not know who my mama is. It was a Catholic children's home, and the priest named the infants."

"And the priest named you Baltazar?" I asked.

"Yes. Before, priests often gave the babies the second name of the most important family in the area—"

"—because sometimes because the father was the squire's son!" interrupted Francisco.

"Or the mother was his daughter!" chuckled Baltazar. "But the old priest who baptized me liked to choose unusual names for the expostos. Mine is the name of one of the Three Kings."

"Your Majesty!" Francisco said grandly, setting off more titters from the guests.

Francisco pressed his lips together to keep words from escaping. "Babies today are lucky," he started reluctantly. "In the old days, most died. It was a matter of chance that someone heard the bell on the roda to let the nuns know a child was there. Then the *pai dos engeitados*, the father of the abandoned ones, who was in charge of caring for the expostos in the city where he was born, had to find an *ama* to give him milk. If the child was lucky enough to live to be four years old, the convent would give him away as a servant."

"Lucky? Four years old? A servant?"

"Oh, yes," Francisco nodded. "When people didn't want to pay the tax for the amas, there was no one to feed them and they died. Even when there were amas, most expostos survived only a few days, and almost all died before their first birthday."

My horror was followed quickly by profound sadness.

"Some saw the *filhos da igreja*, the children of the church, as gifts to God. They said that was how God gets his angels, so they let the babies die without actually killing them."

I stopped in my tracks. "No...," I whispered, almost to myself. "Oh no."

"I've upset you, Anna." He put an arm around my waist and guided me toward my seat on the wall. "I'm sorry."

I felt a wave of nausea. It wasn't only from the thought of unwanted, neglected children. I was crushed to find such an ugly scar on my idyllic refuge. "It's just not right, Francisco. A punishment like that just because their mothers weren't married?"

He hung his head. "The shame was so great, Anna."

We had reached the wall. I was suddenly very tired. In the moments it took me to settle back into my place, I stopped myself from protesting that such cruelty would not have been tolerated in most of the world. It had been. I thought of four-year-old slaves picking cotton, children sold to weave carpets, infants thrown into dumpsters. I felt a veil of depression distance me from everyone else.

Francisco moved closer to me, looking concerned.

I was quiet, examining how I felt. This time what had separated me from joy was a veil not a wall, and I was able to do as Baltazar himself had done, to shed it and live with the happiness I could gather from around myself.

I sat back and eavesdropped on conversations, thankful that Francisco was content to quietly sit beside me. The adults in the yard had sorted themselves into small groups of either men or women. I could see that bartering, whether for goods or services, was a way of life. The jars of honey one large woman brought attracted a lot of attention, and I overheard her make deal after deal. "I have more jars than I need. You can have one for forty eggs and the return of my jar next week."

"Forty eggs? I am already giving twenty to Brígida next week. What about one jar for ten eggs this week and twenty more next week?"

"Fine. You can't live on just honey."

Someone else tasted the honey she had drizzled on squares of bread and left on the table. "This is the best you have ever made, Maria Luisa."

"The bees made it," she replied with a smile, "I just helped them clean their house."

"And you have a village of houses to clean!" a man called out from another group.

"I can send some of my mother's sausages for this," someone said, "two sausages for each jar."

"Just return my jars," she said, and another deal was made.

Around the yard, others exchanged cheeses, jams, pickles, wine, and promises of help with picking fruit. The tempo of conversation picked up as people drank and relaxed. The last meats and fishes were pulled off the grill and stacked on a platter, the makeshift table filled with food, and everyone inched closer and closer until Rita called out, "Dinner!"

The men ate heartily and drank freely, drawing wine from the jugs that had been brought in. Most of their discussions centered on fishing or how tourism was both helping and hurting the island. Their conversation grew more animated and punctuated with loud laughter until, as the women were clearing the table of what little remained of the food, the men quieted and drifted off to doze under nearby trees.

Long after we had finished eating, Francisco sat beside me on the retaining wall, getting up only once to refill his plate. I wondered if he stayed because his mother told him to or because he wanted to. His antics with Baltazar aside, I still saw him as a quiet sort, truly comfortable only with those he knew best. He exchanged no more than brief comments with nearby men and responded to my compliments on the food with nods or smiles. His manner was different around Umbelina and Bárbara, though. When they carried over bowls heaped with warm berries baked in sweetened cheese and spices, he rubbed his hands together devilishly. "Ah! Two bowls for me."

"No," they chimed in unison.

"Why not? I have two eyes to see them, and two nostrils to smell them, and even two sets of teeth to eat them. I really think they are both for me."

"No," they giggled.

"Yes," he teased them. "Which one should I eat first?" He carefully examined one and then the other. "This one has more berries. This one has more cheese."

The girls held the bowls tight to their already stained blouses and turned around laughing when he tried to reach out for them.

"Alright. Alright. One bowl can be for Anna, and I can have the other bowl together with your sweets for my dessert."

"No!" Their shrieks brought Rita over. The apron that had been spotless was streaked with grease and smudged with charcoal, and her ankles were swollen. I could see beads of perspiration on her face and the strands of hair that had escaped her usually neat bun. The long day had tired her.

She positioned herself between me and the low sun that streamed between the tree trunks. "After you finish the berries, it will be time for you to go home," she said with enough kindness to ease the fleeting panic that I had offended and therefore lost her. "You have had enough activity for the day, and it will take a while to get up the hill."

"I am a bit tired," I said. Being tired was a weakness I rarely admitted to. That, too, could put me in the position of being the one who needed to receive more than she gave.

She seemed pleased, nodded, and collected the empty plates and cups around us. "You will walk with Luisa and," she looked at her son, "Francisco will help you."

He got to his feet and ran fingers through his thick curls.

"I had a good time," I reached out to hug her. She held me close and I swallowed the lump in my throat. "What would I do without you? I love you," I said silently.

The girls walked more slowly on the return trip, trailing Luisa who stayed close by my side. The setting moon looked impossibly heavy to remain suspended above us, a splendidly textured silver globe cupped by a bright crescent. How different that same moon would have looked from the place I left behind—just a thin arc, its fullness obscured by city lights and its richness by city eyes.

Francisco had offered his arm to me when we descended the steps to the road, and I held on until we reached the eira, as much for the support as for the feeling of security that came from his strong muscles.

"Here is the secret to making good piecrust."

"I promise not to tell anyone."

"This is a secret that you should tell."

"Why, Nana?"

"When I tell you, part of me is in you. And when you tell your children, I will be in them, too."

Out of breath and straining sore muscles, I returned from a failed attempt to reach the rainforest. The sound of children's giggles came from behind the hydrangea bushes on the far side of the eira. Bárbara, dark and petite, and Umbelina, the tall, fair child who took after her mother, crawled out on hands and knees, and stood. Each held one side of a fabric-wrapped bundle they extended to me. They looked at me and cupped their hands to whisper in each other's ears before walking closer to me, Bárbara leading the way, fidgety with excitement.

"We made something for you," they said in unison. After untying several lace ribbons, the two fumbled with scraps of cloth, extracted a large tile, and lifted it to show a colorful scene.

"I painted my house," Bárbara chirped happily.

"And I painted your house," Umbelina added more quietly.

I looked at an expanse of green grass with dark purplish figures I took as cows; on either side were the two houses, to the right Big Meadow and to the left Casinha Goulart, fringed with blue hydrangeas that rose to a white sky. Umbelina was clearly the better artist. My house was rendered in great detail, the eira in the foreground decorated with the pots I had found in the shed, topped with delicate pink blooms that existed only on the tile. A painted cup of tea rested for me on the window sill.

"Papa brought the paints from Madalena when he took the milk," Bárbara said with wide eyes.

"And he got a brush, too, a tiny brush," squeaked Umbelina as she put her thumb and forefinger close together to show just how small it was.

"It is so beautiful!" I held the tile up to the light and looked it over, commenting on everything I saw and making sure to compliment each girl equally, before placing it carefully on the wall.

"There's more, a senhora," said Bárbara.

"Yes. There's more," repeated Umbelina.

Bárbara reached into her pocket and pulled out a thick slice of bread, crushed flat along one side. "It's for you. I made it myself. I'm the only one who knows Mama's secret for making bread."

I accepted. "Would you like to have some tea and sweets with me?"

Umbelina nodded solemnly, while Bárbara burst into a happy, "Yes. Yes."

Remembering *Ladies' Tea* that my grandmother and I had shared, and that I had imagined sharing with my own daughter, I spread slices of sweet bread thickly with jam, cut them into small shapes, and put them on a plate. I made three cups of tea and invited the girls to come in, where we spent half an hour tasting and sipping.

Several times, I caught them eyeing my notebook and exchanging glances. I looked at them and raised my eyebrows. Bárbara spoke first. "Could we have a piece of paper, ma'am?"

"Of course. And a pencil? Are you going the draw something?"

Umbelina smiled and shook her head. They both started giggling. "We want to know who we will marry!" Bárbara said.

"And the paper will tell you?"

They explained how. We tore a sheet of paper into twenty-three squares, wrote one letter of the alphabet on each, and folded them in half. Then the girls ceremonially immersed the folded papers in a bowl of water and hung over it, holding hands and staring. As one piece unfolded, they gasped and reached in. "*I*! It's an *I*!" exclaimed Bárbara.

"Who is *I*?" Umbelina asked her friend.

She screwed up her face and thought hard. "I can't think of anyone," she said very slowly. By that time, the second letter—an *A*—had unfolded. "*IA*," she said. "I don't know about the *I*, but the *A* means I will marry someone called António."

They repeated the prognostication with another alphabet of folded paper squares, and Umbelina got the letters *M* and *U*, which opened up many possibilities. With their encouragement to do what I silently wanted to do myself—I stared into the water at the letters they had put in for me. *S*, *F*, and *E* unfolded at the same time.

My mind worked differently. Bárbara's letters spelled *ai*, or alas, making me think she would not marry; Umbelina's letters spelled *um*, one, so I thought she might find her one true love; my own letters spelled out both *se*, if, and *fé*, faith. If I married again, it would be to faith? If I had faith, I would marry? I thought of Mother Espírito Santo and the convent. I thought of Francisco.

Science still structured my thought processes. I filled my lungs with air and pictured oxygen molecules crossing membranes. I stretched my legs and pictured the assembly and disassembly of proteins in muscles. I felt the heat of the sun on my skin and pictured the transmission of impulses along neurons. Knowing the mechanisms for what my body was doing gratified me, and added to the pleasure of being able to move again.

I walked down Dairy Road and cut across a field to the back of Rita's house, where the usual chores were in progress. She put aside the basket she was filling with young leaves of chard and came toward me. "You are much stronger, Anna." Her round cheeks were pink and her hairline damp. She quickly wiped her hands on the skirt of her apron, put her arms around me, and held me close. "Do not do too much, too quickly," she scolded gently.

"I am just walking," I heard defensiveness stain what I said and immediately wished I could take it back. Rita was not finding fault with me. Rita was not my mother. In my shame, I was silent for a few seconds.

Unfailingly good-natured, Rita asked, "Do you need something, Anna?"

"Yes. Please. I would like to take Umbelina out for the afternoon."

"She would enjoy that. I could put some food in a basket."

"I thought I could buy something special in town. It would be a little celebration." As I said it, I hoped my tone would put behind us my reaction to her concern for me.

I was surprised by shrieks behind me and looked around to see Umbelina and Bárbara holding hands and dancing in circles. "A celebration!"

"Umbelina, it will be like a festa, a festa just for us!" Bárbara said.

"Where are we going, ma'am?" asked Umbelina, as always the more subdued of the two.

"I thought we could go to the beach on Fishhook Bay." This was followed by hugging and fluttery giggles.

I made merry with the girls for the next few hours. We selected sausages wrapped in crisp pastry, tomatoes warm from the vine, and a large paper cone filled with spun sugar candies. We made our way to the shore and sat by a stone pool that high tide had filled with warm saltwater. There, we looked for shells and decorated ourselves with long strands of dry seaweed. All the while, I was disturbed by my response to Rita's concern.

I was no longer a master at hiding from my fear of expecting the best from others.

The three of us returned, wind-disheveled, sunburned, and dusted with fine black sand. The activity and the hike back uphill, carrying the treasures we had collected and the clothes we had shed, slowed all of us. Perhaps as much from reluctance to face Rita as from exhaustion, my legs felt heavy when I climbed the last set of steps to her house. While the girls brushed sand from their skin and shook it from their clothes, I followed the sound of voices between the two hydrangea bushes at the side of the house to find Carlos, Francisco, and Joca sitting on the grass, working on small fishing rods and fashioning hooks out of thin wire.

"I thought you men went out to catch tuna not sardines."

The three of them laughed with me. Joca was the one to explain. "We are going to Fayal soon. There's a stream there with *truta* that Mama loves. We'll bring her some when we come back."

Rita appeared at the side door. "I thought I heard a familiar voice. Did you all enjoy the beach?" I was still holding leftovers from lunch, an assortment of shells tied up in a shirt, and a half-empty cone of candy that spilled onto the grass when I shifted my position. She looked past me with a disapproving stare. "Francisco! Why are you sitting there? Get up!" He was on his feet before she finished speaking. "Take those from Anna. Her shoulder is not completely well."

I started to say that I was fine but stopped myself. Francisco caught my eye and, with a barely suppressed chuckle, said, "I will put these by the door for you." The message was clear. When Rita has spoken, you do as you are asked. Carlos looked at both of us and grinned—but only for a moment.

"Come, Anna. You must be thirsty." I followed Rita into the kitchen. I couldn't tell whether the tension I felt was in the air or just in me.

She set two glasses on a heavy table, darkened with age and marked with the life of a large family, and brought over a jar filled with a deep pink liquid. I looked closely at the petals floating on top. "Hibiscus," she said, as she squeezed the juice of an orange into each glass. "You cover the flowers with hot water and leave it to cool." She dribbled in some honey and topped it off with the tea.

My glass glowed coral in an afternoon sunray. I absentmindedly stirred the tea and took a sip. It was tangy and sweet. "I like this." I was waiting for a sign that I was forgiven, a sign that I had not lost her.

I silently sipped my drink. As in Casinha Goulart, one large room took up most of the space on the first floor of the house, stretching from the kitchen, past an enormous fireplace to where we sat by a window. The similarity ended there, though. Rita's home was welcoming and cheery. Curtains filtered the bright sun, flowered cushions softened the chairs around the room, and large braided rugs covered the hard floor. Mint was rooting in a glass on the windowsill. Hats and jackets hung on hooks by the door. A small table held an unfinished cup of tea and a plate with only crumbs. A stuffed animal—probably belonging to one of Rita's grandchildren—lay discarded in a corner, next to a basket that trailed a ball of blue yarn. The clutter was a reminder that people lived there.

One chair stood out from the rest of the furniture. The golden wood, threaded with undulating brown veins, seemed to glow from within. With nearly invisible joints and the silkiest of finishes, it was a work of art. Grapevines grew up the legs to leaves on the backrest, and the arms were embellished with tiny flowers. I couldn't resist running my fingertips across the surface.

"Francisco made that for me," Rita said with pride.

"He did?" I was astonished that something so lovely had been made by someone I knew.

"He bought the wood a very long time ago. The men made such fun of him, spending his money on something so expensive, something so useless. But what do they do with their money? They smoke. They drink." She shook her head slowly.

"For a year, he wouldn't let me into the room he shares with Joca, while he worked on the chair. I couldn't even clean and with boys—" she remembered with a grimace, "—a room can get very dirty."

She opened a small tin on the table and offered it to me. "How are you feeling, Anna?"

I paused. "My shoulder aches a bit." I took a sugar-crusted orange candy from the tin and chewed on it. "Delicious." I was distracted, trying to work my way to what I wanted to say.

"It is also made from hibiscus petals. You heat sugar and water, drop in the petals, and then cover them with more sugar."

I was quiet. "I really appreciate ... I may not show it ... I know you always want the best for me."

The next day, I saw Francisco through the window, leaving Big Meadow with a large net bag. I was no longer in the habit of starting my day in front of a mirror or adjusting my clothes in preparation for meeting people; still, I quickly brushed my hair and smoothed my blouse before rushing outside and calling to him.

I was at the end of the cash I had brought with me. It had lasted far longer than I had expected. My needs were simple. The island filled my days with all the diversion I wanted, and much of what I ate came from the stock on my shelves. For everything else I had Rita and her family. But I needed money for something else, and for that, Francisco could help me.

He seemed pleased to see me. "Good day, a senhora," he greeted me formally.

I looked down at him and exhaled. "Francisco, could you do me a favor?"

He put down the basket and took the steps in twos. "What would you like?" His smile was like his mother's.

"You said you were going to Fayal soon."

"Yes. It will be a short trip, just two days at sea and one by the river." His voice was a masculine version of Rita's, mellifluous and deep.

"Could you do something for me while you are on the island?"

"Of course." He stepped closer.

I lifted my hand and signaled him to wait. In the house, I opened the drawer of the small table and took out my earrings, large silvery pearls set in inverted cones of braided gold. Back on the eira, I opened my hand to show Francisco. "Do you think anyone on Fayal would be interested in buying these?"

His eyes opened wide, and he bent over to examine them without touching. "Yes. They are very beautiful." He stood up and looked at me with some concern. "Are you sure you want to sell these? They must be special to you."

"Other things mean more." I hesitated but just for a moment. "I am sure." I picked them up and held them out to him.

He nodded solemnly. "I will do my best for you, Anna."

"Are you looking forward to going back to sea?"

He didn't reply at first. "I ... I am different, not like my brothers. I do not want to live a life on the ocean. Everyone teases me. I was my mama's first baby, and they say she treated me like the little girl she wanted. They say she was too gentle with me, and that is why I do not like doing what they do."

"Not everyone likes the ocean, Francisco."

"No. No," he corrected me. "I like the colors of the water and the shapes of the waves, but I like it from a distance. Out there," he glanced at the strait, "the ocean dominates everything, and you cannot escape it. It will always be the master. No one ever knows when it will rise up next, or what it might send down to end your life."

I thought of my great-grandfather and nodded to let him know I understood.

"There are boats so heavy one hundred men could not lift them, and the ocean can reach up with waves the size of mountains and send them to the ocean floor. People only claim a thin line of shore. To the ocean's eyes, we are an inconsequential speck, not to be considered as it does what it wants."

"It isn't always that way." I didn't know whether I was defending the ocean I loved or trying to help him make peace with his lot in life. He thought I was making a distinction between the fierce and the placid faces of the ocean.

"Even when the sea is kind, life on it is not. We live crowded together for long, cold days of doing the same thing over and over again, away from family, away from comforts you are not aware of until they are not there. And we can never forget that a gentle sea can become a monster without warning. I saw a rogue wave break over a Fayal canoa. The boat hovered on top of the swell and tilted, pouring every man into the icy water. Every time our boat was lifted up, we could see a man still alive, floating past the bodies of those already dead, but we could not reach him. He knew he was going the die, Anna. I saw him make the sign of the cross, so weak he could not reach far from his chest." Francisco turned to face the São Jorge strait, and I looked out with him. "That is ten miles, just ten miles. There are thousands of those miles out there."

I hadn't seen sadness on Francisco's face before, and it made me wonder how many other people had sorrows they hid, as I had done with my own. I tore myself away from my own thoughts and asked, "Do you have to fish?"

"What else would I do?" he said with a note of weary resignation. "Here, a man can farm or raise cows, but I do not have land. In my family, the ocean is our land."

"I saw the chair you made for your mother. It is one of the most beautiful pieces of furniture I have ever seen."

He self-consciously rubbed his hands together. "That is another thing I am teased about. Men make furniture for their homes, even to sell, but it is made to serve a purpose."

"Something beautiful has a purpose. The chair gives your mother pleasure—the shape of the tiny flowers, how the wood glows, how smooth it feels." He thought, and I waited for a response.

We were close enough for me to see the details of his face. His skin was at the same time smooth, from his mother's fine-pored complexion, and rugged, from years on the ocean. Exposure to sun had given him wrinkles around his eyes and across his forehead that made him look older than his thirty-five or so years. One iris had a thread of yellow running across the dark brown background and a thin white scar divided his right eyebrow in half, a flaw that distinguished him.

He swallowed. "I like working with wood. I like thinking about how to use it to create something as close to perfect as possible, making the form I want appear and seeing the wood live again."

"What's wrong with that?"

He shrugged. "That does not make a living on the islands."

"Would you want to go somewhere else?"

"I thought … I might go to America." He considered something before asking. "What is America like?"

"There is more land—much more land—and, of course, a lot more people." Excitement percolated through his usual reserve when I described the size and variety of America's terrain, but my picture failed when I tried to tell him about how life might change for him. "You might know the people around you, but you might not. I think it is most unlike Pico in the cities. People have come from many places, so they have different ways of doing things, different ways of talking and dressing and eating. Everything can seem faster, and you could be too far from the ocean, or from forests and fields, to get to their beauty easily." I realized I was painting a bleak picture, but I knew most of my experiences would only give him a misimpression. "There are many more ways to earn a living than fishing or farming. Perhaps making beautiful furniture?"

He seemed to consider everything I said carefully. "I could find work and learn English. Then I could bring my family to me."

I searched for something positive to say, but I couldn't help myself. "It can be hard without family."

"Immigration is difficult to arrange, and once done, is hard on everyone. Mama and Umbelina would miss me," he said with resignation.

"I'm sorry, Francisco," was all I could think of saying. In him I saw the hopes, fears, and sadness of immigrants at any time in history.

He sighed. "The priest says man must suffer, but I wonder why that must be so."

"You're a bad Catholic, Francisco," I teased.

I guess I am," he said seriously. "I know there will always be times in life when men suffer, but isn't that a reason to try not to suffer at other times? Life should not be a constant fight."

13

Rita and Joca trudged up Dairy Road, both carrying far more than I had seen them bring before. Instead of a colorfully embroidered blouse and skirt, the only clothes I had ever seen her wear, Rita wore a drab black dress with a row of buttons that ran up from her waist to her neck, her bright chestnut hair the only touch of color against a pale face.

I started down the steps. "Is everything alright, Rita?" I knew it wasn't.

She motioned to her son. "Go ahead with the baskets and wait for me before going in." My heart thumped. "Luisa …," her voice cracked as she pointed in the direction of Big Meadow. "Her daughter is dead." She stifled a sob, tightened her lips, and tried to compose herself. I didn't know what to say. I reached out and put my arm around her shoulder.

Luisa and I are cousins, second cousins, but—"

"—but still family."

"We are the same age. We played together as children. We sit together at church every Sunday."

"I'm so sorry." I wanted to let her know I understood how Luisa must be suffering. Suddenly, I realized who had died. Memories of Bárbara came to me with such clarity, the whispering when she and Umbelina gave me the painted tile just days before, the intense delight as she licked the jam off her bread, the giggling when she splashed me with water at the beach. I saw her small, happy face framed by two shiny black braids poked through with flowers.

"No! What happened? She was just here. She was fine. She was fine." I saw the small pieces of paper unfold. *A* and *I*. Alas.

"She was trying to reach some peaches. She climbed to the roof and up the tree. It wasn't very high, but she fell badly." Rita took a deep breath. "She died a few hours later," she wept.

"She was so young," I said, as though some universal law of fairness is violated when some get a century of life and others get almost none.

"She was eight—," her voice broke again, "—almost exactly the age of my Umbelina."

"Come. Sit with me." I guided her inside to the rocking chair where she had nursed me so tenderly and sat her down. I dragged a chair from the table and sat close to her. I knew the loss of her friend's child was devastating, but somehow I also knew there was more to Rita's grief.

"Luisa and I have twin lives." She stopped to compose herself with a deep breath. "We were born the same month, and we lived on the same road in town when we were young. We were together so much, we thought we each had two mothers and two houses. We married cousins the same spring. After she married, she and her husband lived in her parents' house, just as Carlos and I did in mine."

I nodded and patted her hand.

"Our first sons were born about the same time. When her husband's brother died, they moved to his house up here." I knew that in such a small community, the distance was immaterial. They would still have seen each other often. "Our families grew together, with boy after boy after boy. But we both wanted girls. Boys go to the sea with their papas, go to their wives' families, or leave the island and are rarely heard from again. Girls stay with their mamas, learn from their mamas, and mark their own children as they were marked by their mamas.

"We were always pregnant at the same time. I remember kneeling in Mass and praying to God: if there is just one girl to be born, let it be mine."

"But you both had girls."

"Yes. We both had girls in the same week, and we became even closer. Our daughters played together. We made clothes for them together. We imagined our lives as grandmothers in our daughters' homes."

I knew what she thinking. "Umbelina is fine," I told her.

"She is fine *now*," Rita emphasized. "What happens to Luisa, happens to me. It has always been that way; I can't explain it."

"It's rare for a child to die." I knew there was little comfort in what I said.

Rita got up, wiped away her tears, and smoothed her dress. "Bárbara's death just reminds me that I could lose my Umbelina. That's all." Her face looked strong again. "I need to bring Luisa some food." She looked at me. "It isn't the food, you understand. We always bring something. It is our way of saying, 'You are not alone. You will always have someone who cares when you need it.'"

I did understand. "Could I come?" I asked, reaching for the red flowered tin of tea.

The milk cart was not by the shed but out on Dairy Road, freshly whitewashed and rimmed with black bows. Beside it, a priest talked to three older men. "Tomorrow morning, Father da Serra will lead Bárbara to church for the last time," Rita explained, swallowing hard, "and from there we will all go to the cemetery." She harshly wiped away the tears that had filled her eyes but not yet fallen. "It is white ..." she tried to compose herself, "because she was an innocent child." Her last words rushed out in a single deep sob.

The front room at Big Meadow was smaller than I had thought; much of the first floor was devoted to storage rooms that I had glimpsed when someone went in to get wood or an extra chair. It was hot with so many people. They whispered among themselves. In a corner, Carolina and Beto, Bárbara's cousins who had brought me the basket of food when I first arrived, sat playing with other children.

I remembered Bárbara's mother, Luisa, from the party but would have known her simply by her resemblance to her daughter. Like many, she was clearly of southern Portuguese descent with a shorter, rounded body and dark eyes set in pale skin. Black hair had escaped a bun at the nape of her neck, long strands snaking down her back and over her shoulders. All I could think was that we would never know how like her mother Bárbara would have been when she got older.

Luisa sat at a large table in front of the fireplace, propping herself up on her elbows, her head in her palms. When she looked up and saw Rita, she gave a small gasp. Her dry eyes started to glisten with unshed tears. The friends embraced and both wept deeply. Two teenage girls stood beside them, wiping drippy, red noses and eyes with their sleeves. Francisco was there, too, talking to the men I had seen loading milk cans onto the cart just the day before. I stood slightly in back of Luisa and solemnly said the only thing that came to mind, "I'm sorry for your loss." It sounded cold to my ears but my grief was so true I couldn't think beyond platitudes.

The terror I felt when I saw the small coffin on a side table pushed me to Rita. I grabbed her sleeve and plastered myself against her. She followed my gaze and looked back at me. "Bárbara is not there." She saw my distress. "Do you want Francisco to walk you back to your house?"

I hung my head and quietly told her that I wanted to stay.

"Good. We are going to make a lining for the coffin." She went to confer with an older woman who was slicing bread at the back of the room.

I remembered something Bárbara had said. *I'm the only one who knows Mama's secret for making bread.* And I remembered my grandmother entrusting me with her secret for making piecrust. *When I tell you, part of me is in you.* With the death of a child, the secrets, stories, dreams, and struggles of many generations can also die.

The older woman brought a length of fabric from a storage room, while Rita picked up a sewing basket by the fireplace. Luisa became aware of what was happening and stood. When she saw the cloth being laid out on the table, she let out an agonized cry and went wild, thrashing her arms and whirling around to confront everyone at once. "You think that because I wasn't there I didn't see it?" She looked at the space in front of her. "I see her! I see her reaching. The peach is within her grasp. Her fingertips brush it. She smells it."

Luisa screamed, harsh and loud, and put her hands up into the air. "She's falling. She's falling slowly. She's grabbing at branches. The bark is scraping her sweet skin." She whimpered, "She's scared. My baby is so scared." She choked on a sob deep in her throat, then stopped. She lifted her head to the rafters, listening with a horrified look on her face. "I hear her hitting the shed roof. The sound. The sound. Can you hear it? A hollow thud, like God beat his drum. Just once. And silence. I know. I know my baby is gone from me."

Rita wrapped her friend in a tight embrace, nearly pushed off her own feet as Luisa fought her, absorbing the energy and calming her with soothing words. She made eye contact with several of the mourners and the room began to clear.

Luisa shuddered and took a deep breath. She cried silently for a while, then brushed aside the cloth on the table. "No. No. Not that," she said with resignation. She unwrapped the shawl from around her shoulders. "Bárbara liked to sit in my lap and snuggle into this. She said it smells like me." One of the women tried to wrap the shawl around her shoulders, but Luisa resisted.

Rita intervened again. She took the shawl, guided her friend back to a chair, and sat beside her. "We will make it together," she said soothingly. Her friend nodded. "Anna will help," she said looking back at me.

I brought the sewing basket to the table, where Rita had already spread out the shawl. It was a soft, tightly-woven silk printed in gold and green paisley, not the right colors for Bárbara, I thought for some reason. I saw Luisa stroke the shawl gently, the way Bárbara might have done as she nestled in her mother's lap, the way she wished she could still do for her daughter. Rita directed the effort, layering the shawl over a piece of an old quilt before handing out threaded needles. I watched carefully, so I could follow what the others did, and we sewed along the edges of the shawl before making crossed lines of stitches to hold the stuffing in place.

When it was finished, Luisa placed the quilt in the coffin smoothing the wrinkles until she thought it was right. She went into a small adjoining room. I could see her child's body on the bed. With some effort, she picked her up. No one offered help. Everyone accepted this was something she wanted to do herself. When she reached the coffin, her husband lifted the girl's dangling legs over the edge, and Luisa gently laid her only daughter on the shawl and tucked her in. Her husband reached over to cover Bárbara's face, but Luisa pushed his hands away firmly, leaving a pale oval swaddled in the dark gold and green paisley. She put her hand gently on Bárbara's chest and whispered words too softly for anyone to hear.

Rita put her arm around her friend's shoulder and said, "Bárbara will be waiting for you when your time comes."

It was hard to fill my lungs with enough air, and a tight band constricted around my head. I walked out the door and home alone, stumbling over small stones in the dark.

Early in the quest to have a child, when it was still an adventure and easy to believe that the reward was just slow in coming, Lee and I decided on Leanna as the name of our first daughter. We told ourselves it was good choice, his name and mine joined, soft and strong at the same time. "Leanna Lindt," we would say over and over. It sounded perfect.

Perhaps to spare himself—or me—the pain of fruitless emotional investment, perhaps because he saw no point in choosing names that would never be used, he lost interest in them over the years. Names became mine alone. Madeleine, chosen for Proust's *In Remembrance of Things Past*, was followed by William, my father's name, and then Hope. They existed for only a few weeks, desperately multiplying cells, unformed and unaware, but the details of their unlived lives comforted me through the injections, the frantic races to beat the clock back to my lab, and the fear of their deaths. Thinking of due dates and pink-or-blue nurseries reminded me of what I struggled for. Each one had moved aside to make room in my heart for the next, and they remained only as the children who might have been.

Laurel was my child. It was not a name I had ever considered but when it came to me, it seemed God-given. The first link Google brought up was for *Laurel azorica*, a tree that had once covered Mediterranean lands but had been largely replaced by other species—except on the Azores, where it thrived. When I read that the laurel wreath symbolized victory in ancient Rome, I was convinced the cosmos had sent me a message: this child was meant to be.

At the very moment her eight-cell embryo was placed in my care, I felt she was stronger than my other almost-children. The home pregnancy test was so vibrantly pink, and the blood hormone levels a few days later were so high. Even with all the knowledge that science and eight years in the pursuit of fertility had given me, I was unprepared for the reason. The ultrasound showed three babies. By then, I was too tired and too worn down for fantasies. All I could do was try not to feel love.

After a second ultrasound, I met the news that one heartbeat had stopped calmly, thinking that there would be more of everything for the two who remained. Lee and I were distant but still living together when they reached the earliest stage at which I could have prenatal testing done. I made the first available appointment for a chorionic villus sampling, which could tell me how healthy my babies were.

"I have a CVS scheduled for tomorrow. Can you drive me?" I asked Lee.

"I suppose I can take time off work," he said. To my ears, it was a grudging offer. "When did you make the appointment?"

"Just yesterday. It was the only one I could get," I lied.

"Mm-hmm," he said abruptly. "What time?"

"Ten tomorrow morning." I wanted to call him out for not caring, but I didn't want to risk losing his support. My children needed it.

"I'll make arrangements." He returned to his study, where by that time he spent most of his time, listening to music until long after I went to bed.

We awoke to a storm. Trees were down everywhere and the main roads were closed in places. Lee must have known that nothing but more tension would come of trying to dissuade me, and I found him waiting by the front door, swinging his car key back and forth on a finger.

I had learned to leave my body. From the time I lay on the gurney to the time the nurse approached us in the waiting room three hours later, I was aware of little. "Mr. and Mrs. Lindt?" I stood. We were the only ones in the large waiting room. Apparently no one else had felt the need to make it through what was being called *the storm of the century* for a non-urgent appointment. Lee stood, too. She held out a manila envelope. "The final results will be sent to your obstetrician, and she will go over them with you."

I wasn't listening to her. I tore open the envelope and read the preliminary report. Normal. So far normal.

"Did you want to know the sex of the baby? We don't include that in the take-home papers in case you both want to be surprised."

I hadn't caught on to what she was saying. The *baby* not the *babies*. "Yes," I said, without waiting for Lee to answer.

"You have a girl."

"A girl!" I had a girl.

In the car, I read everything carefully. There was only one heartbeat, only one child. Only Laurel.

Laurel was mine alone. Four weeks after the CVS, Lee told me that, regardless of the outcome of my pregnancy, he no longer thought we could be happy together. I knew his own discontent had been growing, and for a long time part of me had wanted to release him from the torment I was putting us through. He moved out a week later, calling before he left work every day to ask if I needed anything. Then, he accepted a job offer in Boulder. I knew the legalities of divorce were only a matter of time.

On the day before he left for Colorado, he stopped by to give me his new contact information and to let me know he would be "financially responsible for the child." As I closed the door on him, I fell to my knees and sobbed aloud, "We still have each other, Laurel. We'll always have each other."

I followed her development the way ground control tracks the trajectory of a rocket. I knew hour by hour which body part she was forming, how long or heavy she was, what milestone she had passed.

I had ignored that *Laurel azorica* is an endangered species. I was calm when I saw the pink stain on the tissue at twenty-two weeks, relaxed when the doctor told me that time would tell if it was a problem, resolute when I was asked to come in almost daily for ultrasounds and blood work. Even after her heart defect was diagnosed, I didn't accept it as a major problem. We would get through everything with the help of medical science.

At twenty-four weeks to the day, the cramps started suddenly. I checked myself into the hospital. Reading the admission printout upside down, I could see Lee's name was still in the records as my emergency contact. Neither of the numbers listed was still active. I had alienated or ignored my friends to the point that my own phones had not rung with a personal call in months. I was disconnected from everyone except Laurel.

For the rest of my life, I would remember the ceiling tiles overhead, the sound of gurney wheels spinning, the smell of newly opened packages of plastic tubing and disposable gloves, the distant announcements over the P.A. system, the bad oil painting showing a pioneer family crossing the prairie in a covered wagon. Every day, I said to Laurel, "Just one more week, my child. Just hang on one more week."

She was born suddenly. There was no time for an epidural and no need. It was so fast, and she was so tiny. She was no trouble at all.

Laurel and I were wheeled to a new room together. As the two nurses who had accompanied me from the delivery room were settling me into bed, a doctor I had never seen before opened the door. One of the nurses patted my shoulder, and then they both left quickly. The doctor introduced herself as the on call neonatal specialist.

Laurel's condition was grave, she explained. "The problem with her heart is more serious than anyone anticipated."

They're just trying to cover themselves. They don't want to be held liable on the off chance that something goes wrong.

The doctor's voice penetrated my thoughts. "She would need surgery to have any chance of surviving the night."

I have faith in medical science. After all, that Laurel has a life at all is because of medical science.

The doctor pulled a chair up to the side of my bed. "There would have to be many surgeries over the next few months," she said quietly.

We will take them one by one. I was already imagining our victory celebrations after each hospital stay brought my daughter closer and closer to complete health. "When would the first one be?" I asked.

I read the doctor's face. She did not think the surgeries were a good idea. Defiance flared in me. *You don't want Laurel to have the surgeries, you hardhearted bitch. You don't care about this child. She's just another anonymous birth to you. But she's a person. We both fought hard for this chance at life.*

The doctor lowered her head and took a deep breath. "The chance of surviving any one of the surgeries is very slim." She looked at me sadly, "Very, very slim."

I looked at Laurel, sleeping peacefully on my chest. I shook away images of her tiny body riddled with needles and tubes. "But there is a chance."

"Yes, there is a chance."

A scientist never says never.

"If she survived, and I want you to understand that is a big *if*, there would be a long and painful recovery. Every time."

I hadn't taken my eyes off Laurel. I was trying to look into her soul, to know what she would want me to do. I brought her closer to me and held her protectively. *No. No. No. I cannot let you go.*

I felt my resolve slipping. *How can I put you through that? How can I let your only experience with life be pain and cold lights and the smell of disinfectant? How can I make you suffer, all to give me my chance at happiness?*

Still holding her, I felt invisible hands taking her from me. I relaxed my grip.

Darling, darling child, this is the only gift I can give you.

I caressed her downy fair hair with a finger, and watched her delicate skin turn dusky blue. Even then, she didn't make it hard on me. For a few hours, she breathed peacefully, a warm, light bundle, until she left.

My sweet child, I am so sorry.

I turned away the grief counselor and called a neighbor to take me home, saying Lee was unexpectedly out of town. I shared nothing. No one was entitled to any part of my child.

I arranged with the family undertaker in Gloucester to bring my baby home, turning down any sort of religious service and settling on going directly to the cemetery, where I laid her next to my grandmother.

For three weeks, I had called into work with tales of the flu followed by strep throat. By that point, I had done so little with my research that I had made no progress in over two years. I had noticed the tight-lipped nods in the elevator and the barely raised eyebrows when I explained my absences and late arrivals. I knew that my pretenses had not fooled anyone.

The day I returned, I spent much of the morning in a recently renovated ladies' room at the far end of my floor, standing in the corner, my face to the wall, gagging on the same new plastic smell as in the delivery room where Laurel was born. I never noticed the blinking light on my phone.

Late in the afternoon, a representative from HR appeared in my lab. "We have been trying to contact you." That was the first time I looked over and saw that I had voice mail. I knew why she had come. I looked at her blankly.

She handed me an envelope. "We had hoped to sit down and have a discussion with you sooner, but this is the final date to let employees know if their contracts will not be renewed." She waited for me to say something, but I didn't care enough. "The information is all is the envelope, and HR is available for any questions you might have." Again she waited. Again I said nothing. I was actually thinking that I would not have to submit any more monthly expense reports. "Someone is waiting to help you carry your things to your car. Goodbye." I took her extended hand and let her shake mine.

There was relief in accepting that I was destined to not realize my dreams. I didn't have to struggle for anything. I didn't have to feel anything.

I was walking to Rita's house, lost in thoughts about whether or not I wanted to abandon the life I had known, and the way

I might support myself if I were to stay on Pico. I found myself at the bottom of the hill, with no memory of a single step I had taken to get there.

Although I could read the time of day in sunlight and shadows, in the movement of fog banks across the strait, and in the whistles, trills, and hoots of the birds, there was little to tell me the day of the week. I hadn't noticed any of my neighbors on their usual Sunday morning walks to town, the pleasure of a work-free day on their scrubbed faces. I looked ahead to see groups of people streaming toward the church, dressed for Mass in clean shirts and fine cotton blouses, and carrying baskets of food to share with family and friends after the service. I felt like an intruder who had stepped into a private and faintly embarrassing situation. I hurriedly turned around, avoiding eye contact with an elderly couple supporting each other as they slowly passed me.

"Anna!" It was Umbelina, coming down the steps from her house and waving. She turned around and called out to the others, "It's Anna. She's going to church with us."

Rita appeared at the top of the steps, shielding her eyes against the morning sun with a hand. She smiled and nodded in approval, while tying a scarf around her head. Francisco appeared behind her briefly, brushing his thick curls back with his fingers. He looked down at me, and returned to the house. In moments, I was surrounded by Rita, Carlos, Joca, and Umbelina.

"Anna," Umbelina tugged on my sleeve, "guess what? Papa is the Emperor! Papa is the Emperor!"

"This is not the time," scolded her mother. "We are late. Walk. Everyone walk," she ordered. She put an arm around my waist. "You are well enough to go to Mass, Anna." It was halfway between a statement and a question. I said nothing. Swept up by being part of the family, my usual resistance to all things religious never made an appearance.

I was the last person in a pew occupied by the extended family: three of Rita's four sons; two daughters-in-law, Josefa and Clara; and six grandchildren whose names I could never keep straight. Rita reached behind Umbelina to put a large handkerchief on my loose hair, and then patted my shoulder and smiled at me with love. Just as the priest entered and everyone rose to their feet, Francisco slipped in beside me, smelling of soap and the lavender Rita always tucked into freshly washed laundry. As almost all the rest of the men, he wore no jacket, and I could feel his warmth through the layers of cloth between us.

I sat back and scanned the congregation, trying to identify the people I saw. I was familiar with my neighbors and recognized others from the party at Rita's house. I found myself counting how many people I did know—and getting excited as the number reached into the thirties, then the forties and fifties. If I remained in Porto Velho, I would have a place in the community, part of a whole. One after another, the people I loved had left me. I knew I would be left again in life, probably many times, but in Porto Velho I would not be left alone.

I barely listened to the priest, until Umbelina started swinging her legs and whispering excitedly to her mother. I saw everyone sit up and pay closer attention. "Today we celebrate the *Império do Divino Espírito Santo*, the Empire of the Divine Holy Spirit." Here and there, people blessed themselves or bowed their heads. The priest lifted a Bible overhead. "Joachim do Fiore prophesized the Third Age, as foretold in the Book of Revelations. In Europe, our Franciscan brothers were persecuted for speaking of this, but here they were welcomed, and we have kept the truth alive!"

A few murmured, "Yes, we have."

"Our beloved Santa Isabella," he stood aside and raised his arms to a crown set high on a pedestal beside the altar, "told us that if we honor the Holy Spirit by caring for everyone, the Third Age will come." He faced the congregation, "And when it comes, we will have peace."

Everyone around me made the sign of the cross, so I did.

After Mass, I strolled around Porto Velho arm in arm with Rita. She took me to a short dead end road near the church. "This is our *Imperio*." The tiny building looked like an oversized Barbie dollhouse. Pink trim set off the door and the scalloped arches above multi-paned windows. "It is the hall of the *Irmadade*, the brotherhood that does good works. In there, everyone is equal and everyone is together as one."

Except women, I thought to myself. It was far easier to discard the substance of my former life than it was to relinquish how it had formed me.

"It is where we keep replicas of Santa Isabella's crown, scepter and orb. Every village has them." Rita pointed to the top of the flat façade where a plaster statue of the saint stood. She was wearing a crown and a cape filled with white roses, and carrying a scepter and orb. "When she was a young queen, the king caught her sneaking bread to the starving people in her cape, but when he pulled it open only roses tumbled out. It was a miracle."

The church in Gloucester flickered in my mind's eye, and I remembered a statue of Santa Isabella wearing a crown, roses mounded at her feet. The tradition of honoring her had been important enough to survive in the immigrant population.

"Santa Isabella founded the first Holy Spirit brotherhood to help the poor. In her honor, we feed the poor on the seven Sundays after Easter."

Umbelina caught up with us. "Bárbara's papa was the last *mordomo*. He cut a lot of straw into pieces, and one piece was shorter than the others. Everyone in the Irmadade chose a straw, and the one with the short straw got to be the mordomo this year!"

Rita explained that the mordomo organized celebrations on several consecutive Sundays. Members of the brotherhood, also chosen by lot, were given the special honor of displaying the crown and other relics in their house for one week before a procession returned them to the church. "The poorest among us is supposed to be crowned Emperor but in Porto Velho, we are all poor, so the brothers choose."

Carlos was to be Emperor and the last to have the great honor of hosting the relics in his home. With that title came a special role in the procession to church and the parade that followed Mass. It also meant a significant obligation for Rita, who would be responsible for the community banquet that symbolized giving food to the poor and reminded everyone to take care of each other.

Rita led the way along a path that rimmed the western edge of town. Close to where it ended, she took off her shawl and laid it on the ground. She, Clara, and Josefa crisscrossed the area, gathering withered blossoms from rose bushes and putting them on the shawl. Umbelina wandered away, and I stood by the shawl, occasionally lifting its ends to make a pale brown mound at the center.

I looked out over a landscape drenched in light. To the south, hills dressed in swathes of color—purple grape hyacinths, pink thistles, yellow buttercups and field clover—lay ruffled above broad pastures. On the northern edge of the island, where the transition from the mountain to the narrow coastal plain was abrupt, the land dropped off sharply to a glittering sapphire strait.

The scene reminded me of another place, far removed in time and place, and it crossed my mind that there had been such breathtaking sights in my other world. I had fallen into my life on Pico, so relieved to be free of endless disappointment and sorrow, so reassured by being moored to a family and shielded from loneliness that I had willingly wiped out my other life. There was good in Porto Velho; there had also been good before.

With that realization came my first real consideration of the flaws in my sanctuary. Everything was not perfect. The separation of male and female roles persisted on the island, particularly in villages like Porto Velho, and the isolated, idyllic setting was shadowed by deprivation, uncertainty, and lack of opportunity.

I remembered that Bárbara had died a few hours after falling, and I pictured those hours filled with gleaming hospital corridors, trauma units, microsurgery, and drugs engineered in places I had once been part of. I wondered if she would have survived her fall there.

Most of all, it was disheartening to accept that the world of science which had defined me and fulfilled me was too far removed to be part of, and I felt the loss of what I once had.

As we returned to the house, I scanned the yard for Francisco but didn't see him. "Does the whole family gather for Sunday dinner?" I asked Rita.

"It's different every week. Sometimes, it is only the five of us, but we can be fifteen or twenty."

"She's always prepared, though," said Clara, taking a pot of beans from the basket she had been carrying.

Josefa went directly to the oven, took out a large blackened pan, and lifted the cover to check the dinner that had been left cooking all morning. "Given the choice, my children would want to eat here every day."

I heard the sound of men's voices outside, and my attention wandered. Rita said to me, "Francisco will be here soon. He usually spends some time by himself after Mass, working on his wood or just going out on his boat."

"His boat?" I was remembering his feelings about life on the sea.

"He keeps a small rowboat by the dock. He likes to go around the coast." She put a few peppercorns into a stone pestle, crushed them, and stirred them into the bowl of yellow squash Josefa brought to the table.

Francisco came up behind his mother, put his fingers to his lips to keep everyone quiet, and hugged her. He carried a paper-wrapped bundle. She turned around, patted his cheek, and gave him a taste of the squash.

"I didn't scare you?" he asked.

"After your brothers, there is nothing that can scare me." She looked at what he held out for her and unwrapped about a dozen tiny cookies. "Where did you go?"

"Prainha."

"You didn't take the boat?"

"No. I thought we could all leave early tomorrow and go to the crater."

I was watching, enjoying the exchange between the two of them. Rita glanced at me and then at Francisco. "Perhaps Anna would like to see the crater," she said to him.

"Ah ... yes." He turned to me and asked, almost reluctantly, "Would you like to go out in the boat tomorrow, Anna?"

For a moment, I was caught by his gold-flecked eyes. "Yes," I said quietly. "Yes. Thank you."

"Can I come, too?" Umbelina was by her brother's side.

"Of course," he said, lifting her high in the air. "You are my very favorite sister."

She giggled. "I'm your only sister, but you're my favorite brother."

"Umbelina," Rita said sharply, looking at her and then at Clara and Josefa.

Francisco put her down, and she said soberly, "I'm sorry."

"Go wash up and tell everyone dinner is ready," Rita directed her son.

After Sunday dinner, Umbelina untied her mother's scarf and rolled the rose hips onto the table.

"This is a special treat," explained Rita as she and her daughters-in-law picked through what they had gathered.

"And Mama knows the best place to find them," said Clara. She brought the kettle to the table, and steam condensed and trickled down the windowpane.

"Now the fun part," said Umbelina when Josefa got out two wood spoons. "Last week, I was the best squasher." She placed the back of a spoon on a fruit and pounded it with her little fist. When all the fruits had been crushed, Clara scraped them off the table, put them in the kettle, and returned it to the stovetop. As the tea steeped, the last of the dinner was cleared, dishes were washed, and leftovers were distributed.

Rita poured four cups of ruby red tea, rose-scented and steaming, and we sat on the steps until the grandchildren started to gather, ready to be taken home by their mothers. When we were alone, sipping refilled cups of tea, Rita said, "I think I will stay home while you and Francisco go out in the boat," and she gave me a curious look, as if she was trying to remind me of something.

Suddenly, I remembered what had brought me to Rita's house that morning. I wanted to invite everyone to dinner the following week. Offering her a day free of food preparation—and the entire family a festive meal—was all I could think of to give back some of what I had been given. "Rita, I would like to make dinner for you and your family." I looked for approval on her face, and found more—an expression of pride.

We decided on the following Saturday, just before the busy week when the family would host Santa Isabella's crown and Rita would oversee preparing a banquet for hundreds of people.

"I'd like Luisa and her family to join us," I said.

"I don't know if she will come." I hadn't anticipated that uncertainty. "I talked to her this morning," she explained, massaging her temples. "She is not doing well."

"I'm sorry. It's too soon ..." I couldn't finish my thought.

"It is more than that. Grief is to be expected, of course," Rita explained, "but she blames herself for what happened."

When I found words, my voice was weak. "Why would she blame herself?"

"Bárbara had climbed on the roof to get peaches before. Luisa told her it was dangerous. That day, she heard the sound of footsteps overhead, but she didn't go out. She wanted to put the bread in the oven first. Then she heard her scream."

I said nothing.

"She doesn't talk about it, but I know my friend. She thinks that if she had cared enough, her daughter would still be alive."

I understood.

14

I looked out over the strait. Although still early in the morning, overnight showers had given way to sunshine, and the sky was deep blue all the way to the horizon. Even behind me, over the inland areas that were always the last to clear, only a few cottony puffs decorated the top of Ponta do Pico. The still, warm air promised a good day to spend on the water. I was mulling over whether walking to Rita's would make me seem too anxious, when I heard Umbelina's laughter bubbling up the slope to the main road. Soon I saw the top of Francisco's head as he turned onto Dairy Road and walked up the hill toward my house. I went inside, knowing Umbelina's slow pace and excursions would give me time to finish dressing.

I had just pulled my hair back when I heard a light knock. I opened the door to Francisco.

His biceps straining the sleeves of a clean white shirt, he lifted up two large iron pots heavy with an assortment of cooking utensils and plates. "Is it alright if I come in? Mama thought you might want these."

Umbelina arrived as we were adding what Rita had sent to my meagerly stocked shelves. The basket she carried was heavy, and she needed both her arms to lift it a few inches off the ground, knocking it forward first with one leg and then the other. I thought of Carolina, who had brought me a basket from her mother when I was new to the island. Remembering the way I had welcomed that other girl saddened me, both because I had not shown her any of the tenderness I showed Umbelina, and because I had not been able to feel any tenderness myself then.

Francisco took the basket from his sister, and asked, "Is this a good day to go out in the boat, Anna?"

I didn't turn around. "Yes. It's such nice weather, and Umbelina would like …" I scolded myself. *Whether or not you go, he could take Umbelina.*

She came over, put her arms around my waist, and squeezed tightly. "We're going to the crater, but Mama says we must dress warmly. *It gets cold on the water,*" she parroted her mother, wagging her finger at me. We all laughed.

Francisco came near and spoke softly, "I didn't know if you wanted it to be secret, so I didn't want to say anything until we were alone." He took my hand and closed my fingers around a roll of euros. "This is for the earrings."

I turned away quickly as I whispered my thanks, taken by surprise at the feeling that had risen in me when he held my hand and put his lips close to my face.

Used to having to keep up with Lee's high energy and long-legged strides, it was relaxing to stroll alongside Francisco. On the way to the dock, Umbelina, the ever curious and independent child, explored roadside pockets of wildflowers, while Francisco and I chatted about my upcoming dinner party, expressed admiration for Rita, and shared our mutual love of dogs. Although his manner was far from effusive, I found I could read his emotions in the timbre of his voice and the look in his eyes.

When we arrived, the dock was slick with blood and slime, and cold black eyes stared at me. Most of the fish had been gutted and frozen at sea, but some flapped helplessly as they were dumped from nets and barrel-sized baskets onto the wood planks, before being opened up by the fishermen. The still, warm air was heavy with the smell, and I choked back bile as I hurried through the tangle of unwashed men and dead fish, holding on to Umbelina's arm with one hand and Francisco's sleeve with the other.

It was a relief when he finally pushed his boat away from the dock. He apologized for the scene on the dock. "I wanted to reach the dock between the early boats and the late boats."

"Why are some early and some late?"

"When you fish, you can return early with fewer fish, or you can stay at sea and catch more fish, but risk losing all the customers who have already bought what they need. It's hard to know the best choice to make." He was talking about more than bringing in the catch.

"We are going at high tide. The lower the water, the rougher the sea. The boat is small, and Umbelina does not swim well." He must have thought that would concern me and added, "Don't worry. I stay close to the shore, even on a calm day. You will be safe."

I felt completely safe. I had gotten my lifeguard certification while at college and had renewed it every two years until it was squeezed aside by my all-consuming desire to have a child. I was inordinately proud of being in the same group as strong ocean swimmers and Baywatch beauties.

I didn't say much as we approached the partially submerged crater just off the coast and sat back, content to listen to the rhythmic splashing of the oars and let the air skimming off the surface cleanse and soothe me. These were dangerous waters, even for those who knew them well; I could see jagged spikes of rock just beneath the surface, which Francisco skirted by using an oar to push away. He tugged on one of his sister's braids and warned her not to lean too far over the edge.

Francisco maneuvered the boat close to a lava formation that looked like a miniature cityscape rising out of the ocean and threw a rope around one of the wet skyscrapers. From there, we could look over the crater rim at a temporary aquarium brought in by high tides. It was not an environment for fragile organisms; they had to survive the hammering of waves and desiccating low tides. In the absence of large predators, however, they thrived, so the water held a rich diversity of life. Sea lettuce, surf grass, and hardy brown algae fed a teeming ecosystem. We watched quick-moving shrimp and crabs, snails that crept past, purple sea stars that moved so slowly we could not see their progress, and bluish anemones that would only release themselves from their substrate when threatened with imminent death, wriggling away to start life in a safer place. Unlike other tide pools I had known, there was a large population of fish. Carried in by waves; many died in their new environment; some lived out their lives in a place they could never leave; a few would be carried out by another tide.

"Do you ever fish in the crater?" I asked Francisco.

"There are many more fish out there," he told me.

"But you don't know where *out there* they are."

"Of course I do." He pointed to an area about equidistant between the Porto Velho harbor and where we were moored. "The birds tell us." I looked and saw a swirling mass of black and white gannets plunging into the water.

"Do you want to bring home some fish?" I looked at the fishing tackle stored under the sternsheets.

He was considering it. "Mama would like the fish." He thought. "No. Better to go when Joca is with me. The boat will drift too much."

"I could take the oars, if that's what you're thinking about."

His smile was very close to a laugh. "It's a small boat but a heavy one, and not easy to control in the ocean."

I realized he was probably right, but I wanted to meet a challenge and show I could. I sat beside him, put my hand on his back, and nudged him onto the bottom boards. After a minute of settling my hands and rotating the oars into position, I took a stroke that barely broke the surface, and then tried two more. The oars were not for lightweights. The shoulder I had thought was completely healed throbbed, and even the other shoulder had strained to make the strokes. "How long would it take to get to the fish?" He didn't look up. "Francisco?" I thought he was hiccupping. He was trying to control his laughter. I joined in, then Umbelina followed, and soon we all had tears running down our cheeks.

Umbelina returned to trailing her fingers along the surface, occasionally combing out strands of seaweed and popping their air bladders before tossing them overboard.

"How long will you stay with us, Anna?" Francisco asked.

My answer was truthful. "I really don't know." I added, "I would like to stay." I was going to add *forever* but stopped myself. "Do you know whether you will go to America?"

"My answer is the same as yours: I don't know. There is much here I love. I would not have my family and neighbors in America. And this is the place of my birth. The sound of its music, the taste of its food, even the feel of its soil is mine. I can look at the sky and know if it will rain tomorrow—"

"—or look at the ocean and know where the fish are," I finished for him. We were both quiet for a while.

Almost to himself, he said, "If I stay, I could lose something I do not even know could be mine. Do you understand?"

I nodded and offered another perspective. "To reach for something better, you risk losing what you already have."

He only tightened his lips and sighed, doing battle with himself.

I didn't want him to leave. Just once, I wanted to be able to count on my world staying as it was. I didn't want to live my life braced for the next disruption, the next loss, the next fragment to shatter. I wanted to be close to someone who would not leave me alone. That shouldn't be too much to ask of life.

I whispered silently to him, "Stay. Stay and be with me," and in that short moment I imagined a lifetime of peace on Pico, safe and loved as part of Rita's family.

Although rich in community, for most on the island, life did not allow for much more than the necessities. There was enough food, but the honey that was traded at Rita's gathering, the cookies that Francisco brought home, or the cone of candies I bought for Umbelina and Bárbara were seldom-enjoyed luxuries. For my dinner party, I had decided to offer my guests every special treat I could lay my hands on.

Rita's family had fish or sausages nearly every Sunday, so I went to the butcher to see what poultry I could buy. A coarse, stubbled face gave the man a soiled look, and his apron was marked with fresh blood and old, rust-colored stains. Stout and soft-bodied, bushy black hair edged the neckline and armholes of his sleeveless shirt. Grinning and bobbing his head, he pointed to a string of plump, fresh sausages hanging from the ceiling and explained why they were the best on Pico. To establish good relations, I asked for two, and cringed as he licked his fat fingers before picking up a piece of newspaper to wrap sausages I would never eat. I thanked him, then explained why I had come. He agreed to get ten ducks from a farm on Fayal and deliver them on the morning of the party.

I left orders with shopkeepers in Porto Velho for bottles of wine, new candles, and several kinds of pickles, cheeses, and tea. At a cart in the square, the farmer offered to have her son gather the earthy mushrooms that grew wild in Gruta das Torres, and she directed me to another woman, who proposed harvesting tiny potatoes early. I left a large sum of money with one shopkeeper who was going to Horta to restock, and he agreed to spend it all on the best imported food he could find.

His was the first delivery to arrive on the morning of the party: a tin of Turkish delight, jars of brandied peaches, two boxes of marshmallows, a large savarin, a plum pudding from England, and an assortment of nuts.

The rest of my orders followed one after another for the next hour. I lined up the bottles of wine on the eira wall, and the pickles and cheeses on the shady windowsill. I carried in bags of vegetables and boxes with candles, tea, and sugar. As I arranged the desserts on the table, I looked through the front window and saw the butcher and a young boy deliver ten dressed ducks.

I knew I had a problem.

Just then, I heard Umbelina's knock and looked up to see her grinning face peeking through the front door. I held out my arms, and she ran into them.

"Mama sent me to help you today." It was great fun for her.

"I am so glad you came," I said. "I do need the help. I have a problem."

"Uh-oh. A problem is not good," she said seriously.

"No, it isn't. I don't know how I'm going to cook all the ducks in one small oven. Even your mama's pots are not large enough."

I was startled by Francisco's voice by the front door. "You could cook them on a fire outside."

Surprise at his presence lingered, so my reply was slow in coming. "It's a good idea, but I would still need something that was large enough to hold them."

"Do you have a washtub?"

I remembered seeing one in the shed. Umbelina and I emptied it of rope and cobwebs, and scrubbed the enamel tub by the cistern, while Francisco cleared an area beside the eira to build a fire. Using small branches as spits, we held the ducks over the flames until they were crispy-skinned, and then put them in the washtub with onions and mushrooms that Francisco helped to chop. Umbelina was in charge of adding herbs and orange segments to the cooking stew.

"With your mother's cooking skills I didn't think you would have any experience with this sort of thing," I said to Francisco.

"Mama sends some food with us when we go out fishing, but we usually have to cook for ourselves at sea. It's very simple, fried fish and potatoes, but we learned well."

We nestled the washtub in the embers, and he moved aside a leather-wrapped bundle to sit on the wall and poke at the coals.

"What's that?" I asked.

"Those are Francisco's tools," said Umbelina. "Nobody can touch Francisco's tools," she said firmly. "He was going to carve wood today."

I turned to him. "Oh. I'm sorry. I didn't mean to take your time."

"I can carve wood any day. This is a special day."

"No. Go. I know how much you enjoy it."

He stood and came closer. I felt a breathless rush that had faded from my life years before. "I want to be here," he said slowly and firmly.

I nodded in acquiescence. "Where were you going to carve?"

"I go to a field up there," he pointed to a spot on the hill behind The Vineyard. "There's a small meadow with a large flat rock at the edge and—"

"And oak trees to shade it. I know that place. I love it. It has a view of the ocean."

"That's where I was when I saw you fall."

It seemed a lifetime ago.

The desserts alone had filled the table inside, so Francisco removed the large shed door and set it on top of the wall at the corner of the eira, leveling it with small stones tucked in strategic places and making our banquet table steady with makeshift legs. I laid out the plates, glasses, and forks that Rita had sent, and brought out the olives I had picked and left marinating in lemon zest and rosemary. Finally, I pulled up a bunch of the mint that grew wild by the road, rinsed off the leaves, and put them on the table to end the meal as was usually done.

By noon, Umbelina had decorated the house with flowers. At the last minute, I put the tile she and Bárbara had painted for me between two of the pots on the eira wall, and I wedged a bouquet of candles into each pot. I stood in front of them unable to find words to send to two children, Bárbara and my Laurel, who I had loved but known for too short a time.

I left our version of duck à l'orange to cook slowly in wine, while I went to wash and change my stained, smoky clothes. I had worn the same long skirt, pants, and cotton blouses for weeks. For the first time since I arrived, I carefully thought about what to put on. At the back of the wardrobe, I found the pale pink silk shift from SoNa that I had thought would serve as a nightgown; with black pants and a shawl, it was elegant. I made two thin braids on either side of my forehead, pulled them back to hold my hair off my face, and left the rest loose. The little makeup I owned had been in my long-forgotten suitcase, so I made do with some salve rubbed on my lips and a couple of slaps to bring color to my cheeks. Without my earrings, I had only my grandmother's onyx ring for jewelry. I closed my hand around it and thanked her for saving my life by bringing me to Pico.

I walked out into the main room and asked, "Umbelina, could I have some of your flowers for my hair?"

She stared. "You look like a queen, ma'am." It was so heartfelt, I felt beautiful.

Francisco looked sideways at me a couple of times, and then stared openly himself. "Yes," he said scratching the top of his head. "Yes. Very lovely."

Everyone arrived together. Rita, Carlos, their sons, daughters-in-law, and six grandchildren came up the hill just as the Big Meadow family walked down Dairy Road. Even at a distance, I could see Luisa's reluctance to come. Each time she slowed or turned her head to look back, her husband wrapped an arm around her waist and pressed her forward.

We brought chairs from the house for Luisa and Rita, and the very pregnant Josefa sat in the rocking chair. The rest of us were comfortable on the eira wall, softened with quilts and pillows from the house. Grace was said, Carlos opened bottles of wine and poured it into cups, everyone filled their plates, and the children finished before the adults had all settled in.

Even with over twenty people, it was a quiet meal. Luisa seemed to be working hard to listen to what we talked about, but she said nothing. Others tried to fill in the framework of what I knew about their families with more intimate details— or so it seemed to me—and the questions asked of me reflected what was important to each of them. It had been years since anyone cared enough to ask about me, years since I was comfortable enough to open up. I felt accepted. I felt loved.

Clara, whose more adventurous nature and interest in emigrating was confirmed by her sister-in-law, asked me about my people and my town in America. Most of what I said described Gloucester and my grandmother. I told them about a fishing town in America where there were many people whose ancestors had been born in the Azores, where Portuguese was still spoken in some homes, and where women made *massa sovada*, sweet bread, for feast days. I told them how I had loved living with my grandmother in a house on a hill overlooking the ocean, and some of what we had done together when I was a child. I said little about my life after that.

"Are you…have you been married?" asked Clara.

Francisco's eyes rested on me for a moment before quickly looking away. I tried not to let him know I had seen. "Yes."

"Do you have children?" asked Josefa, whose life happily revolved around her own.

I thought of the customs and immigrations forms I had had so much difficulty filling out as I flew above Pico. This time, the answer was easier. "I had a baby girl," I said steadily. "Her name was Laurel." It comforted me to think my child was now not unknown to everyone but me.

I looked at Luisa, dressed in black as she probably would be for the rest of her life; she reached into her pocket, and I could see her work the beads of her rosary under the thin fabric. Francisco started to say something, then stopped and took a long sip of his wine. Rita reached out and rested her hand on my arm. I covered it with my own hand.

Josefa and Rita talked about the different personalities of each of their children, and how they had seen signs of the adults they would become at an early age.

"What you put in them, they carry with them for a lifetime," Rita said.

"It is usually what our mamas put in us," commented Josefa.

Again I remembered what Bárbara had said on the day she and Umbelina gave me the painted tile. *I'm the only one who knows Mama's secret for making bread.* And again I remembered my grandmother's words when we made piecrust together. *When I tell you, part of me is in you. And when you tell your children, I will be in them, too."* Not being able to pass that on seemed another way I had let her down, another way I could not atone for what I had done to her.

"Why did you come to Pico?" Carlos and his sons usually sat apart from the women, and even then he rarely spoke, so his voice took me by surprise.

How could I explain why I had come? The reasons I would have given others, the reasons I had given myself, or the truth as it existed when I arrived were all possible answers. I offered an incomplete answer. "It was a difficult time in my life." Everyone seemed to know enough not to ask what the difficult time was. I imagined they thought I had lost my husband to death or desertion.

I tried to explain further. "I wanted to visit the place I was from ... the place my grandmother was from. I thought it would help me keep a promise I made to her."

"What did you promise?" Umbelina asked from across the eira.

My words came slowly, because I was remembering the reason. "She had wanted to find her sisters, and I promised her I would do that for her."

"Did you find them?"

I had found them but too late for my grandmother.

Rita spoke. "Whether she found them or not, the promise was a gift to her grandmother. She entrusted her search to Anna." She turned to me. "That alone consoled her."

I swallowed the lump in my throat.

Rita started to praise Francisco's good nature, his commitment to family, and his moderation in all things. It was then that Luisa made her only comment of the evening, "His mama wants to see him happy with a good woman, Anna." The men took this as a cue to leave, and soon I smelled the tobacco smoke coming from the side of the house.

The discussion moved on to the ways in which the women themselves had been changed by their children. Josefa had once been extremely shy; Rita had been a tomboy; Clara had not wanted children at all.

The men reappeared, Carlos holding two small guitars that had been brought from Big Meadow. I could see the similarity to the ukuleles that had first come to Hawaii with Azorean immigrants. He and Clara's husband played, and the rest of the men joined in a mournful song about a widow lamenting the loss of her husband at sea. The melancholy lyrics and minor key of the *fado* immersed the rest of us in private thoughts. "We are forever separated in life, but we will live together again in God's house," they sang. No one made eye contact for a few moments after they finished. I glanced at Luisa, and she was nodding.

I no longer questioned what they believed. If it eased their lives in some way, if it made them feel safer or gave them hope, what was the point of finding fault? Sometimes, I wanted to feel the way they did. I wanted to believe I would see Laurel and my grandmother again. But I didn't.

A smoky purple haze was settling to the east. With only a half moon to light the way, it was time for those returning to town to leave. Everyone conspired to have Francisco stay behind. Josefa was concerned I would fall again while cleaning up. Rita wanted her son to bring back her large pot after I had washed it. Clara pointed out that he needed to extinguish the fire. Even Carlos said that having a man nearby was always helpful. Umbelina was repeatedly denied requests to stay with us.

"It's chilly tonight," Rita looked pointedly at Francisco and then at the shawls we had both left on the back of a chair.

He wrapped mine around his own shoulders with a grin on his face. "My mama always takes such good care of me." He put Rita's shawl around her shoulders, kissed her on the forehead, and went to say goodbye to everyone else.

"Francisco," Rita called out after him, leaving him to finish her thought. He took my shawl from around his shoulders and wrapped it around me. It carried his warmth and the smell of lavender and brine I always associated with him.

After loving embraces, I waved as the families walked down the steps to Dairy Road. "Thank you, Rita, Luisa, everyone, for coming and sharing dinner with me, and …" I wasn't sure how to express something so significant. "… everything," I ended, almost to myself.

With the leftovers carried away to give Rita a brief respite from cooking, there was little to do, so Francisco and I finished just after darkness fell. I saw him to the top of the stairs, and we stood side by side looking out at the soft gray silhouettes of trees against a moonlit fog. What followed was a congenial silence that neither one of us felt the need to end with words.

In the dark, our hands brushed against each other. I started to tremble and hoped he would think it was because of the cool night air. *Settle down. You're a grown woman. Even if he has some small, passing interest in you, you do not want this. You could never do the work you love here, and you cannot separate him from his family.* Yet, when our fingers touched again, I instinctively wrapped mine around his.

He wrapped his arm around my waist, and it felt very different from the way he had steadied me on the day we climbed the steps to the party at Rita's house. I turned to him, ran my hands down his muscled arms, and hugged him. He pressed his hands against my back and drew me closer, and I lay my head on his chest for a few moments listening to the thudding of his heart, until he pulled away, murmured goodnight, and quickly disappeared down the steps.

Alone on my side of the door, I saw a single sugar-crusted marshmallow left on the table.

"Can we have hot cocoa tonight, Nana?"

"Of course, my love."

"With marshmallows?"

"Anything for my Annie."

My mother was visiting friends in Boston. I was alone in the old house with my grandmother. Light snow was falling, and hoarfrost covered the trees in the backyard. A stem from my Uncle Russell's rose bush had worked its way into the warm space between one of the kitchen's sash windows and its ice-glazed storm window, and a deep pink flower bloomed against the feathery white rime.

We spent the day together, preparing for the upcoming Thanksgiving feast. As we chopped, mixed, baked, and tasted, we planned an evening that was to include a dinner of stuffing balls and pumpkin pudding, watching *The Carol Burnett Show* on television, and braiding each other's hair.

I was still stirring sugar and spices into an enormous green-glazed porcelain bowl filled with apple slices, when my grandmother finished lining three pie plates with crust.

"Are the apples ready, Annie?"

"Yes, Nana, all done!"

She inspected. "Perfectly mixed. Your apple pies will taste just like mine one day."

"But I don't know how to make piecrust like yours."

"Here is the secret to making good piecrust."

"I promise not to tell anyone."

"This is a secret that you should tell."

"Why, Nana?"

"When I tell you, part of me is in you. And when you tell your children, I will be in them, too."

As she filled the pie plates, she told me what she had learned from her mother. I had never felt as special or as loved. I was the one she had chosen to entrust with the secret. I would always have a part of her with me, and one day I would have children and part of her would be in them, too. I knew how much it would mean to her; she seemed most content when she talked about passing on family traditions.

I brushed the tops of the pies with milk and sprinkled them with sugar, as she had just taught me.

Large snowflakes were drifting down outside the kitchen window and even with the oven on, I could feel the cold outside. I was looking forward to snuggling together on her chair and getting warm.

"Can we have hot cocoa tonight, Nana?"

"Of course, my love."

"With marshmallows?"

"Anything for my Annie."

It was only when I was with my grandmother that what would make me happy was most important.

After the pies were in the oven, she put on boots and buttoned her long wool coat. "Do we need anything other than marshmallows, Annie?"

"Just marshmallows, Nana."

"I'll be back before the pies are done, my love."

The old house was drafty and getting colder, so I curled up on her favorite chair and wrapped myself in the afghan she kept on the arm. Soon I was at the edge of sleep, a blanket of snow muffling the sounds of the neighborhood. I imagined the same scenes I had run through in my mind countless times since learning my grandmother had lost her sisters. I would find all five of them and bring them back and make her happy. I would go to the library. I would find their names in phone books. I would call them one by one; I knew exactly what I would say. I would meet them at the train station in Gloucester. Then I would walk them up State Street and into the house, where my grandmother stood in the kitchen. And she would see them and know I had brought them to her.

A caramel-butter-apple smell came from the kitchen. I peeked through the oven door at the three pies, syrup bubbling through their vents. As darkness fell, I watched the pies go from gold to deep brown. I turned the oven off and left the door open, too frightened to take out the hot pies myself.

Finally, I heard my Uncle Russell's heavy boots on the wood floor of the entrance hall. "Annie!" he called out.

He found me in the kitchen, and looked down at me from his great height. "Ma—your grandmother—fell on some ice downtown. They took her to the hospital."

I knew. I knew positively what he was going to say next.

"Ma's passed on."

He waited for some reaction. There would never be one that anyone could see.

The day I graduated from high school, I went into my father's study; I wanted to imagine his pride in what I had accomplished. The small room had been purged of nearly all personal belongings soon after his death, but over the years I had found some pictures, medical records, his last datebook, and a few other mementos tucked into the pages of books or forgotten at the bottom of drawers. I always returned them to the place I had found them, reasoning that if they were moved they might be discovered and destroyed.

I waited until my mother had left for the evening, and I sat in my father's comfortable desk chair, wrapped in the flannel shirt I had found neatly folded in a large inlaid box in the bookcase. I did what I had done many times, and I idly looked through the treasures I had discovered. I would not understand the reason I was drawn to the study until I was well into adulthood. It gave me something tangible as reassurance that my father had really existed, and that I had not imagined all the good I associated with him.

I took a beautifully embossed silver cigarette case with the initials *V.P.* from the curio table. Inside I found a thin rectangle wrapped in yellowed paper, on which my father had written *Nana*. It was the tintype of my grandmother as a young woman. I would never know how he came to have it or, with any certainty, why it was concealed where it was, but it was clear he had cherished it. By then, I had hidden my feelings about my grandmother's death completely—even from myself—for over five years. I had not shed a single tear for her or for myself.

I immediately recognized her gentle eyes and slight smile, and a powerful moan rose from deep inside me. I wept without stopping for what must have been close to an hour, some of my sobs so loud they surely would have aroused attention from neighbors had I not been cocooned in the wood-paneled study.

It was not a complete catharsis that allowed me to come to terms with what had happened. I suppressed any emotional connection to my grandmother's death again that same night, but the heartache returned more readily and less sharply several times over the decades, accompanied at times by sorrow over the death of a father who had become only the dimmest of childhood memories. When those feelings did return, I held back from sharing them; I was letting everyone—myself, most especially—know that I was too strong to be hurt that way again. It was not until the night on Pico, when I spoke freely to people who loved me, that I could fully mourn all I had lost.

15

The lake appeared suddenly, a near-perfect circle of pure blue just below the golden trail of fallen pine needles we had followed through the forest. A high sun was reflected at its center, and I adjusted the brim of my hat to get my bearings. To one side was the near-vertical face of Ponta do Pico; to the other, pale green pastures and dark forests led to an endless sky. A narrow peninsula, packed with bristly evergreens, projected into the middle of the lake, deepening the shadows at the edge of the water. The fresh mountain air was scented with the tang of pine, rather than the more familiar brine of the ocean.

Others were already there. Men, naked to the waist, stretched out on the grass and napped. Women wore modest bathing suits or shorts. Toddlers babbled contently while playing with balls of yarn, and older children hovered near the shore, testing the water with their toes.

Clara and I spread quilts on the grass and laid out two cold ducks, fresh bread, and half a plum pudding from the large covered basket Francisco had placed near us.

"Anna, come rest," Rita said. "Remember, you are still recovering, and you worked a lot yesterday."

"This is not work, and yesterday I had some very good help."

"It will make you tired."

"I'm not ..." I stopped. I had learned not to expend any energy protesting when Rita looked me directly in the face. In any case, I was actually longing to sit down after my first real hike since my fall. Calendars had little meaning in my new life, but it must have been less than four weeks since I hit the bottom of the hill behind Casinha Goulart. Still, it felt like the people around me had been with me for years, and I knew I didn't want to live the rest of my life without them.

We sat comfortably in an open field of purple, pink, and white lupines. Everyone seemed content with the silence in our little group. Umbelina wove a small basket from dry flower stalks. Francisco whittled scraps of olive wood into beads for a rosary. Rita lay back, closed her eyes, and covered her face with her hat. Clara and I looked out at the scenery and the children splashing at the edge of the lake.

"Mama, can I go into the water?" Umbelina stood over her mother and peeked under Rita's hat.

"Baby, the water is too cold." She took off her hat and raised herself up on her elbows.

"Please, Mama, please." She looked down to the water, where her cousins and nieces were splashing.

Rita pursed her lips, looking back and forth between her daughter and the other children. Umbelina's little body was twitching with anticipation. "Isabella! Maria Clara!" she motioned to her two oldest granddaughters. The twelve-year-olds came immediately, arms covered with goose bumps and bare feet still wet. Rita told them to watch Umbelina and each other, and to stay in the water for only a few minutes at a time.

"I love you, Mama!" Umbelina bent over, kissed the top of her mother's head, and ran toward the shore.

Under the cloudless sky, the glare of the sun was blinding. I stood, screened my eyes, and scanned the lake, a habit from my days as a lifeguard. A woman, whose relation to the family I was unsure of, carried over a large kettle that had been heating over a fire on the beach and filled our cups with hot, fruity tea. I sipped as I watched the children hopping in and out of the water.

One of Rita's sisters brought over her newborn grandchild and settled herself on the quilt. I marveled that I looked at them without anger or jealousy or grief. I accepted that having a child was behind me; it was a biological function I could no longer fulfill, like being blind or deaf. I was letting go of the pains of my past and releasing myself from chasing the future.

I asked if I could hold the child and settled myself cross-legged on the quilt. She was nestled into my lap. Perfect, dimpled hands peeked out from the sleeves of her loose, cotton dress. Without conscious thought I placed a forefinger near her palm and felt her fingers grasp mine. I rocked back and forth, watching her peaceful breathing, and remembering Laurel.

If I could smile when I imagined all the discoveries that were ahead of that newborn, I could smile for myself. Many of the joys in store for her were also there for me to experience again: rolling down grassy slopes and floating in warm water, white clouds streaming across the sky, black clouds gathering, raindrops and mist, the songs of birds and of people, curiosity, fluffiness and oiliness and stickiness, warm sweaters, warm dog bellies, arrays of colors and scents, the taste of blackberries and of cocoa, dancing leaves, blossoming trees, climbing trees, expressions of love, expressions of creativity, knowledge, grins and giggles and laughter, anticipation, aspirations, triumphs— and failures—born of struggle, memories.

Rita's eyes kept darting to the water to locate the children, who were happily splashing near the shore. My mind was empty, my skin taking pleasure in the heat of the sun, when I realized

Rita's expression had changed. She stood and pointed to where her child was flailing in deeper water. "Umbelina!" The little girl stopped thrashing and started to paddle her arms calmly. Rita shook her head slowly and looked down at me: "Sometimes, they worry you for nothing."

I ignored her, walking, then racing, to the water, a Red Cross instructor's voice in my head. *When a person is about to drown, panic movements stop. Involuntary arm flapping keeps them afloat for another twenty seconds or so, but they cannot call out for help. They look calm.* They look like Umbelina.

I unbuttoned my skirt, let it slip off, and dove in. I cut through the water fast, but she had already gone under. I tried to remember where I had seen her last and plunged to the bottom. The water was clear but sunlight didn't penetrate to the deepest parts. I headed for a dark form in the twilight of a ledge. A rock. I looked up and scissored quickly to the surface. Where was she? Eyes burning, I drove below again. Another black shape. Another rock. *Where were the others?* I needed help. I needed air. I surfaced with a gasp and whirled around, hills spinning around the shore. I went under, trying an area closer to the center. Again nothing.

Others had joined me, but they were churning the water and making it even more difficult to see. I tried to cover the lake methodically but kept getting turned around. I was losing focus in the icy water. I rose to the surface and, treading water, called her name—not realizing that she was past hearing me. I took a deep breath and dove again. Water rushed in through my nose, and I started to lose consciousness. Something swept past my ankles, and I grabbed at it, pulling her up and toward me. I hooked my arm around her lifeless body, floated up, and made my way to the shore.

Francisco appeared and swam alongside me until the water was shallow enough to stand. He took his sister's body from my arms. My teeth began to chatter as soon as the air hit my wet skin. Someone wrapped a blanket around me. I slowly stumbled toward the knot of people standing at the water's edge. I wanted to see how Umbelina was doing, but she was surrounded by a ring of her relatives, all looking down to the grass. It was then that I heard Rita's voice, murmuring, and then giving way to an anguished cry. "Não! Não! Não!" Francisco looked back at me, and I saw tears in his eyes.

I raced the remaining few steps, yanking apart children and adults to see Umbelina's still body. Rita was on her knees, cradling her beloved child's head in her lap, moaning.

I took a deep breath to compose myself. "Francisco. Take your parents over there. Everyone else, move away." My voice must have carried authority, because a moment later I was alone with Umbelina. I laid her out on the warm grass. Her skin was cold and bluish-white. I put my ear to her chest. There was no heartbeat.

It may be possible to rescue a drowning victim even after a long time under the water, especially if it is a young child and the water is very cold.

I tilted her head back, wiped some algae from her mouth, and lowered my head to her cold lips. I blew my breath into her mouth. Once. Twice. Nothing. *Come on child. Please. For your mother. Breathe.* Once. Twice. Her chest rose and fell with my breaths but was dead without them. Far away, I could hear Rita crying.

"You can't have her!" I screamed at an evil God. "Please don't take her," I pleaded with a benevolent one.

I turned her onto her belly and pressed on her back, trying to squeeze the water out, but she didn't respond. Her skin was a dusky blue. I lifted her gently and laid her face-up again. Her hair splayed out around her like a crown, a feather of seaweed decorating one ear, the way she loved decorating herself with the wildflowers she gathered.

It had been so many years since I had renewed my CPR certification, I couldn't remember how many compressions to apply. I put my hands over Umbelina's chest and pressed wildly again and again. Umbelina's small body jumped with every compression. I heard voices saying it was too late. I counted without knowing what number I wanted to reach. *One-two-*

three ... One-two-three ... My arms trembled. Someone cried out, "Stop her!"

Then there was a brief spasm of her chest muscles, and she coughed. She coughed and coughed. Water spurted from her mouth and nose, and she started shaking with cold. I quickly stripped off her clothes, reached for a quilt, and wrapped her in it. Francisco carried her to the fire and placed her in Rita's arms.

I was dry before I realized that the lakeside meadow had been cleared of everyone but Francisco, who was sitting beside me.

I joined one of the rivulets of people streaming into the center of town. It was the most important day of the season for Porto Velho. Houses had been freshened with white, the color that symbolized the Holy Spirit, who was central to the beliefs of the community. Flowers cascaded from window boxes and market stalls. They twirled around the railings of the church steps, and framed doorways. The morning air carried aromas of rich meat and fresh mint from the web of lanes that surrounded the village square.

Festivities had started early, and would continue with a special Mass at which Carlos would be crowned Emperor, a parade, the community banquet, and evening prayers at Rita's house. I was looking forward to being part of the observances. I no longer thought the crown and other relics reflected ignorance; in their society, they were symbols of generosity, equality, and hope for a better future. And their society had become mine. Although still the American woman who lived alone, a label that might very well apply to me for the rest of my life, I was greeted with nods, smiles, and a pat on the back that let me know I was not an outsider.

I stepped into Rita's house, and she looked up from the chair Francisco had made her. Our eyes met. She took a breath and her lips parted, but she couldn't find the words she wanted to give me. She put a palm on Umbelina's head and, still looking at me, smiled. We understood each other.

Umbelina and her nieces were sewing white roses onto wide bands of white ribbon. She ran over, squeezed her arms around my hips, and buried her face in my belly.

"Anna!" came her muffled voice.

"So many flowers!" I said brightly.

"They are a symbol of sacrifice," Rita explained. "When you pick them, you are sacrificing the fruit that would come from them." She was passing her culture to the next generation, and to me. Her daughter looked at her with solemn eyes, and Clara and Josefa, who were stacking loaves of freshly baked bread on the windowsill, nodded.

"The day is to honor Santa Isabella. Some say she sold her crown to buy seeds for us to grow food. Others say she sacrificed it to the Holy Spirit to ask for rain."

Without asking, I picked up a ribbon and followed what Rita and the girls were doing.

"For over five hundred years, we have remembered her love for the people, and in her honor we feed everyone today," Rita continued.

"Mama's *carne e sopas*, is the best soup you will ever eat!" Francisco had come in. He turned to me and explained, "We say sopas feeds more than the stomach; it feeds the soul." He dipped a cup into the broth and drank. "It is indeed a day to celebrate."

"Today is to remind us of our responsibilities, Francisco, and the privilege of sharing what we have with others," his mother scolded gently.

"Today Umbelina has the privilege of wearing a crown!" Francisco lifted his sister high in the air, showering the table with roses. "She will walk in the procession and stand on the altar."

"And I will wear a white dress and have flowers in my hair," she said as Francisco returned her to her chair. Her face slowly collapsed. "Bárbara was going to be one of the attendants," she said, looking to her mother.

"Now Bárbara is attending Santa Isabella in heaven, my love," her mother said.

Umbelina nodded. "How long until we have the crown, Mama?" I followed her gaze to the altar set against the far wall. "I want to pray to Santa Isabella to take care of Bárbara, since her Mama is not in heaven yet."

And Laurel?

"We will have the crown before the sun goes down," Rita answered, "but you can pray anytime." She wrapped an arm around her daughter and held tight.

Umbelina left early, accompanied by Carlos and his two granddaughters. They would be at the center of attention in the solemn procession to the church and the joyous one that would follow Mass. The rest of us set off at the sound of the church bell, falling into smaller groups: Cajo and Josefa with their sons, Manuel and Clara with theirs, Rita next to Joca. Francisco walked with me. We didn't say anything until the church was in sight, and then he spoke only once. "You ...," his voice quavered. "You are a good friend to our family."

They were meant as kind words, but they brought me down. Since the night of the party, I had told myself not to make too much of those brief moments when he put his arm around me. I had been the one who caressed him; I had been the one who laid my head on his chest. His words seemed to relegate me to a certain role in his life, and to confirm what had become an irrational infatuation with a man who could not be mine to love.

I said, "Thank you. Umbelina is dear to all of us."

People lined the streets and the square, and stood in front of the church, all waiting. It was almost certainly the entire population of Porto Velho, with those who lived high on the neighboring hills and visitors from others parishes adding to the number. With no signal that I was aware of, quiet descended and all heads turned east. A few people pointed. Others blessed themselves. Father da Serra appeared at the head of a procession, followed by a plaster statue of Santa Isabella balanced on a platform carried by four brothers of the Irmadade, all wearing bright red jackets. Behind them, Umbelina slowly led four young girls dressed as she was, completely in white. A powerfully-built older man—who I recognized as the one who had made the boat model at Rita's party—followed, holding up another smaller platform. On it was a silver crown with four arches that met at the top to hold a gold dove, the symbol of the Holy Spirit. Carlos walked ceremonially behind it. The rear was brought up by more men in red jackets, some carrying flags embellished with white doves, one holding a silver scepter, and another with a stack of thin silver diadems. The townspeople fell in line behind them as they passed, and the procession made its way through the narrow streets.

The heavy statue was maneuvered around sharp corners, and up and down steep lanes, listing and tottering from side to side, until it reached the church doors, where everyone stopped. People quietly moved around the statue and went inside, some packing the pews and others standing in the aisles. As hymns were sung to the Holy Spirit, the statue was positioned at the center of the church altar.

The Mass was a tribute to Santa Isabella; accordingly, Father da Serra began with a passage from the Bible, "And now abideth faith, hope, charity, these three; but the greatest of these is charity."

I started to think about the people I had met on Pico, those whose lives I had passed through briefly and those who had embraced me as one of their own. I had experienced their charity, and in more ways than Francisco carrying me down the hill or Rita caring for me so tenderly. From the day I first stepped on Pico, when Jack had proudly shown me his island and Manda had held me as my world spun around, I had been shown kindness.

My neighbors had welcomed me in so many ways I had not appreciated at the time. Remembering Umberto and Celina brought a smile to my face; I could picture him raising his hat to greet me and the gift of hydrangea stems she had left by my door. Jacinta had brought me to Two Trees to share the bounty of the *big olive year*, and Maria Cecilia had generously offered me what little she had. I had been cared for by the people of Big Meadow.

The villagers who knew me only in passing had shown their goodwill, too. The candlemaker had given me honeyed melindres from her beloved birthplace. In the café, Isabel had shown me her father's scrimshaw and told me stories of whaling. And all around me, people smiled and greeted me when I walked through the town.

I focused again on the priest's words. "By mercy, we will be reborn." Through the mercy of the people of Pico, I *had* been reborn to a new life.

The priest motioned first to Umbelina, and then to Rita's granddaughters, Isabella and Maria Clara, and to the two other young girls dressed in white. They lined up in front of him, and he placed a small silver crown on each of their heads. Every eye was fixed on him when he held his arms high and opened one hand to show a spool of white satin ribbon. Umbelina was given one end of the ribbon, which she carried slowly around the pews before returning it to the altar.

The entire congregation was encircled. Father da Serra spoke, "We are all connected. When one among us stumbles, we are all in danger. When one among us needs help, we are all here to help. We are comforted on our paths through this dark forest by knowing we are tied to each other." The priest took it the two ends of the ribbon and made a knot.

Father da Serra nodded to Carlos, who knelt under the statue of Santa Isabella. "Carlos José Maria de Simas, do you make a promise to accept the responsibilities of Emperor by doing good in our community?" The priest held a silver crown over his head. Rita swelled with pride.

"Yes."

The priest lowered the crown, saying, "In the name of the Holy Spirit, I bless you."

Carlos rose and turned to face the congregation. "I give my promise to the Holy Spirit in the name of Santa Isabella." He nodded and each of the five girls held up a candle. He lit the first, held by Umbelina.

"Hope," he announced loudly, "We have hope that people will enter a time of spiritual growth."

He moved on to the second candle, held by Isabella. "Faith. We have faith in the Divine," he again raised his voiced and looked up at the congregation.

"Equality. All brothers are equal; all are to be respected."

"Charity. The Holy Spirit forgives your offenses when you show charity."

"Autonomy from the Church." The last pronouncement was received with some discomfort on the part of those at the altar and by fervent nods from others. It did seem an unusual declaration in the devoutly Catholic village. "We show our devotion to the Holy Spirit through the good works we do, not through the Mother Church. But," Carlos raised a finger in admonition and proclaimed fiercely, "we voluntarily bring our faith to the Holy Church and to Father da Serra for guidance."

Leaving the church, the procession re-formed, this time festive. Cheerful greetings were exchanged with onlookers as it meandered through the town again and became more a parade, with people breaking into song and children chasing each other up and down its length. Some sat on steps and atop walls, holding out flowers or cups of wine to everyone who passed. I stayed close to the family, content to breathe the salty air and stroll in the warmth of the sun. I looked at Francisco, and we both smiled at the same instant. Romance might have been beyond what was in store for us, but I was still glad to have him in my life.

The diadems of the honorees and the gold letters that emblazoned pennants glinted in the bright sun, blinding me for a moment. After blinking away the afterimages, I found myself separated from the family and next to two fragile elderly women, their suncreased skin dark against snow-white hair. They went to either side of me, and each hooked an arm around my waist. One squeezed me tight and asked, "You are enjoying yourself, American woman?"

For the first time, I realized that being known as *the American woman who lives alone* did not marginalize me; it included me in a place where many shared the same name and descriptive nicknames were common and affectionately meant. "Yes. I am very happy to be here."

They led me to the small Irmadade, where everyone was gathering for the Holy Spirit banquet. I saw Rita outside with other women, all tending enormous pots of Holy Spirit soup. Beef broth was ladled over buttered bread, mint leaves, boiled beef, potatoes, and cabbage. Carlos and the male members of the family carried out their responsibility to feed the hungry by bringing heavy bowls of the ritualized meal to the waiting people. I sat on a curb with others, listening to the conversations around me. It was an occasion to catch up on news from relatives and friends who had moved away, to share memories of past festas, and to enjoy time away from the routine days of hard work.

The family walked back to the village square together, where we listened to the music of two groups competing for attention from the people. Sitting on the seawall, five men— their almost identical Roman noses and wide mouths identifying them as family—played small guitars that rested on their knees. In addition to the bright music of drums, cymbals, and tambourines, a second group entertained us with dancers, the men sporting straw hats and cotton kerchiefs around their necks and the women swishing long full skirts and embroidered aprons. To the accompaniment of small whoops, spectators joined in informal versions of the dances, and between sets cups of wine were shared.

Rita, happy but too tired to dance, sat on the retaining wall with me. Carlos stood in the middle of the square, still the center of attention. He reminded me of politicians in my former life, laughing loudly with his followers and scrubbing the heads of passing children. His voice was strong and he spoke with passion, whether it was to call out compliments to the women who had prepared the meal or to set a date for the next fishing expedition. Rita smiled as she listened to him. Theirs was a comfortable partnership. There was no doubt they loved and respected one another.

When the crowd began to thin, Rita tilted her head in the direction of the house, and our little group gathered and quickly headed for home. The music followed me out of the square, the rhythmic clapping and wood shoes of the dancers emphasizing the tempo. *One-two-three-four. One-two-three-four.* My feet picked up the beat, and I heard the pulsing in my ears. *Stay on Pico. Stay on Pico.*

After a restless night sharing a bed with Rita and Umbelina, alternately cocooning myself in quilts and throwing them off, I fell into a deep sleep around dawn. When I awoke again, it was late morning and the house was empty. Santa Isabella's crown was on the flower-festooned altar where everyone had worshiped the Holy Spirit together the night before. The water in the kettle was still hot, and I made myself a cup of tea with some dried mint I found in a jar, and I wandered around the small house.

I looked into the room shared by Francisco and Joca and smiled when I saw the bed, whittled on every surface with an assortment of flowers, seashells, birds, and insects, the record of a skilled artisan perfecting his craft. On a shelf was a small olive wood box inlaid with slivers of pearly shells, and as beautifully carved as the chair Francisco had made for his mother. When I picked it up by its lid, it opened. Inside were my earrings.

I found Rita and Umbelina in the garden, each looping and braiding fine threads to make a piece of needle lace as delicate as a cobweb, artistry Pico was known for. Umbelina was worried about losing her place with the threads. She barely moved when she greeted me with a hushed, "You slept a lot, a senhora."

I walked over and gently kissed the top of her head. "I guess I sleep well when I am close to you."

My back was pressed against the rough stone side of the house, and I was trying to enjoy the last minutes outside before the sun set and the clouds that were moving in brought rain. It was hard to recall my other world, and that other society with its greater triumphs and greater flaws. I let my senses fill with the beauty around me and my thoughts to wander to the life in Porto Velho that I didn't want to part with. I pictured sipping tea with Rita. I thought about Umbelina growing up and marrying. I imagined being with the family for the births of the new generation and the passing of the old generation. I remembered the sense of community I found when people welcomed me at church and greeted me in the town square. And I relived how I felt when I was close to Francisco.

Mist turned to sprinkles. One last ray of sun filtered through a slit in the gray clouds and lit the top of the eira wall, where the tile that Bárbara and Umbelina had painted still rested. The water refracted light, and the colors glowed.

Raindrops made concentric circles in puddles and melted into the surface of the cup of tea I had made from the last of the leaves in the green flowered tin. I quickly gathered my things and headed inside. Before closing the door, I looked at the tile again and smiled at the memory of the day the girls had given it to me.

After I turned away, the tile's afterimage made me think of a Renoir with pastels dissolving into one another. It took me a moment to process what was happening. I dashed out, reaching the wall just in time to see pale blue hydrangea petals disappear into the white sky, and cows spread into amorphous purple dots, their borders blending into a meadow that had lost its blades of grass and become a mottled sheet of green. The tile had been painted with watercolors.

I carefully picked it up, holding it flat and shielding it against the rain with my body, and ran back into the house. When I turned to close the door behind me, it slipped from my wet fingers and crashed to the floor. Some fragments skittered away and were lost between the boards, never to be recovered. Others were dashed to powder. I picked up the largest fragment. It cut my hand and clattered back to the floor.

Early the next morning, I shuffled out of the bedroom to light a fire. I had put aside the memory of breaking the tile, so the painted shards took me by surprise. I gathered them up and placed them on the wide sill beneath the window. Looking at them with fresh eyes, they took on a different beauty. I fit the pieces together, some in new ways. Tiny flowers stood against a blue sky, born of the hydrangea petals that had bled onto unpainted places. Bubbles of watery cows had splashed outward when they hit the ground, making lavish starbursts of dusty lavender flowers in a rolling meadow. My blood had dried to leave rich brown soil.

Rita put down her cup and looked up at me. "What is it, my daughter?"

"Could we talk?" I asked.

She pulled a chair close to hers and patted the seat.

"I have to decide whether or not I should stay in Porto Velho."

"Even if he is not aware of it yet, Francisco loves you."

I took a deep breath but said nothing. I had no way of knowing his feelings or his intentions.

"He would be a good husband."

"I know he would be," I said, remembering how much he had done for me and the long-gone feelings he had awakened, "but this place may not be my home."

"Every person belongs somewhere."

That was my problem. I didn't know where I belonged. "I love my life here, but it is very different from the one I intended to have." The previous night I had been filled with thoughts of the life I had fled, and I had fallen asleep remembering happy times there.

"Life is not like that, Anna. It can be very different despite your plans. Sometimes that is good, sometimes not. She looked into my eyes and said gently, "And sometimes you think it is not good when it is."

"I know there is good in both places. I don't want to lose what I have here with you and ..." I couldn't bring myself to say Francisco's name. "It's something I've always wanted." I was trying to sort through my thoughts, but I had no way of explaining much of what I had left behind: the joy of discovery, the importance of my research, art and technology that were there for the taking, people who shared the same history and values.

Rita stood and put a hand on the back of the chair Francisco had made for her. The afternoon light burnished the wood, and the perfectly rendered grape leaves seemed to flutter with life. "This is beautiful?"

I nodded.

"And this?" Rita stroked the small flowers that embellished the armrests.

"Yes," I said quietly. I thought she was calling attention to her son's craftsmanship.

"Francisco has also carved birds and roses and even designs that look like nothing we know." I remembered the bed I had seen in his room and smiled. "He could not put everything beautiful into any one piece, so each piece has its own different beauty—just as each life has its own beauty.

Letting go of all the good you might have in one life means you cherish the good you have in the other one even more."

I took off my grandmother's onyx ring. In the sunlight, the round stone gleamed like an eye. "You have been a mother to me. I would like you to have something that is special to me." I placed it on her finger. It fit perfectly.

Would this be the last time I felt her skin? The last time I saw her face or heard her voice?

Rita looked at the ring and smiled. "This is not needed, Anna. What I did is part of being family."

"So is this," I said, enclosing her hand in both of mine. "Wherever I live, we will always be family."

Ever since the night he had wrapped the shawl around my shoulders, Francisco's blend of pine and lavender and salt had swirled around me at night. Thoughts of us kissing had invaded my waking hours. Recollections of his voice had distracted me. I felt his arms around me when the sun warmed my back, and his hands on my face when I was touched by a gentle breeze.

I saw the top of his head first, as he breasted the hill. I rose from my seat on the eira wall, and our eyes locked. Before we closed the distance between us, at the bottom of the steps because his pace had quickened and mine slowed, we exchanged thoughts in subtle signals, messages with a distant evolutionary origin, perhaps born in an era when spoken language was not known. The meaning was clear.

I've been waiting for you.

I've come to tell you I love you.

I love you, too.

I want you.

Come quickly.

I reached up and crushed his curls in my hands, he circled my waist with his arms, and we rested against each other. I lifted my mouth to his, and we kissed.

Just before stepping into the house, he stopped and took a deep breath. "Anna Pavka, daughter of Vilem Pavka and Clara, will you stay on Pico," he stopped, swallowed, and continued less certainly, "and be my wife?"

For a decade, I had lived in the past with people who were gone, and I had chased a future that moved away more quickly than I could reach it. It had left me with ghosts and dreams. *Saudade.*

The present was good.

I looked up and whispered, "Yes."

16

I watched as she took my treasures out of the olive wood box and arranged them on the new shelf. At only five years of age, my daughter's face was already so much like my grandmother's.

"Who is the pretty lady, Mama?"

"That is a picture of my Nana, and I named you Amelia after her."

"Can I have it, Mama?"

"It is yours to keep, and to give to your child."

Made in the USA
Middletown, DE
16 October 2023